W9-BQK-020

A GATHERING OF SPIES

A GATHERING OF SPIES

John Altman

G. P. Putnam's Sons
New York

G. P. Putnam's Sons
Publishers Since 1838
a member of
Penguin Putnam Inc.
375 Hudson Street
New York, NY 10014

Library of Congress Cataloging-in-Publication Data

Altman, John.
A gathering of spies / John Altman.
p. cm.
ISBN 0-399-14641-5
1. World War, 1939–1945—Secret Service—Fiction. I: Title.
PS3551.L7938 G38 2000
813'.6—dc21 99-462174

Printed in the United States of America

1 2 3 4 5 6 7 8 9 10

This book is printed on acid-free paper. ♾

BOOK DESIGN BY AMANDA DEWEY

The author would like to thank the following
for their invaluable help on this book:

Anicée Gaddis, Megan Newman, Richard Curtis, Jen Hackworth, Laura Taylor, Neil Nyren, Rachel A. F. Edelson, Joyce Glazer, Jennifer Altman, Michael Strauss, Sarah Jane Cohen, and Ronald Kessler, and William L. Shirer for his books.

For my parents

I have often felt a bitter sorrow at the thought of the German people, which is so estimable in the individual and so wretched in the generality . . .

—GOETHE

PROLOGUE

NEW YORK CITY
DECEMBER 1933

A light dusting of snow had fallen; the city looked almost pretty.

They walked toward the waterfront. Catherine could hear the whisper of a halfhearted Christmas carol from somewhere, the mystical hoot of a foghorn, the soft diffuse sound of music drifting over the river.

Her coat had lost all but one of its buttons; she was forced to hold the neck closed with one hand. How did Katarina manage to keep her coat looking so new? she wondered. How did Katarina always manage to traipse around a half foot above the realities of life, *floating* around, really, so untouchable and stylish and happy?

Katarina was talking about a movie she had seen: *The Eagle and the Hawk*, starring Cary Grant and Carole Lombard. Her green eyes sparkled; her blond hair bounced around her shoulders in time with her steps. She chattered on gaily, without a hint of self-consciousness. Katarina's English, Catherine found herself thinking, was better than the English of people who had lived here twice as long. Why, she even spoke with less of an accent than Catherine, who had been born in the Bronx. How on earth did Katarina do it? How was it that everything came to her so naturally?

Farther uptown, a ship was coming in; the water of the Hudson was alive with a thousand dancing lights. Catherine could see the bustle of activity on the quay, but she couldn't make out any detail—just a shapeless, undulating mass of humanity. A band was playing on the cruiser's deck, something brassy and celebratory but small with distance.

She shivered. She was cold. She shouldn't have come out in the first place. It was time to go home.

She turned to tell Katarina, but Katarina was gone.

After another moment she spotted her friend—moving off down a deserted dock, out over the black water.

"Katarina!" she called.

"Come on!" Katarina called back.

Then she vanished into the darkness somewhere beyond a stack of crates on the dock.

Catherine stared after her. *I won't follow her,* she thought. *It's late and it's cold and my coat only has one button, and besides, I'm not like Katarina. I don't enjoy adventures on dark, deserted docks late at night.*

Besides, she was starting a new job the next day. She wanted to make a good impression on her new employer—be in passable shape, at least, when he first saw her coming off the train. Not that she was hoping for anything to develop in that direction, of course. He was a widower, true enough, but she had no illusions about her own attractiveness. No, she didn't harbor even a tiny little hope. Still, a solid night's sleep seemed like a good idea. She wanted to be as presentable as possible when he first laid eyes on her.

She stepped onto the dock, hesitated for a moment, then took another step forward. God only knew who was lurking around out there at this time of night. She held her beaded purse more tightly to her body. A freezing sea spray leapt up from nowhere, turning her coat damp. She shivered again. Where had Katarina gone?

"Katarina," she said, "I've got to get home."

"Just come look at this, Cat, and I'll walk back with you."

"Look at what?"

No answer.

Catherine stayed where she was for another moment, still holding the coat together with one hand. A flicker of some odd, foreign emotion was moving through her. After an instant, she recognized it as anger. Why was Katarina dragging her out onto this deserted dock the night before she started a new job? Katarina was jealous, that was why. Katarina had to keep working at Owen and Dunn, getting pawed by old George Gardner every time she turned around, while Catherine got to go off to the country and live in a nice house with a respectable man. Katarina wanted to ruin it for her. . . .

That's ridiculous, she thought. *She came to see you off. She's your friend.*

She took another few steps forward, moving around the crate.

"Katarina?" she said.

It had been two years since the last time.

But it went perfectly. Her body took the responsibility itself, without waiting for instructions from her mind. She watched from a polite distance as her hand dug into her purse and removed the switchblade. She watched as her thumb depressed the catch and the blade *snick*ed out into the night. She watched as she put her back against the crate, waiting for Catherine to step into range; and then as her left arm came up and snaked around Catherine's throat, expertly, the fingers slipping inside Catherine's mouth. She watched as her right hand moved the blade up, finding the correct angle perfectly, elegantly, as if she had done this just yesterday.

She slid the blade between the fourth and fifth ribs, directly into Catherine Danielson's heart.

Catherine began to shake. Katarina, embracing her from behind, held on tightly. For a few seconds, Catherine shivered almost sensuously; then she let out a papery sigh. Not dead yet—but her chest cavity already would be filling with blood. Her punctured heart would drown itself.

Katarina removed the switchblade before she lowered Catherine to the dock. She wiped the blade clean on Catherine's raggedy coat, then flung the knife into the water.

After that she worked quickly, without looking at the body lying on the dock by her feet. She found the box she had put there earlier in the night, a small cardboard parcel tucked between two crates. From the box she withdrew two heavy, misshapen pieces of scrap steel, already entwined with ropes. She tied the loose ends of the ropes to Catherine's ankles. The wind was bitter and cold; she ignored it. From farther up the dock she could hear intermittent cheers as the cruiser discharged its passengers and the band played on.

Once she had the weights fastened to Catherine's ankles, she stood up and surveyed her handiwork. She took a long, critical look; a small furrow of concentration appeared on her brow. Then, abruptly, she rolled the body off the dock with one foot. The splash sounded very loud. Following the splash came a few moments of hissing as the ocean closed back up over the intruding object.

Then silence.

The band struck up a fresh tune—"Don't Blame Me."

Katarina picked up Catherine Danielson's purse, dug through it, and found a cigarette. She slung the purse over her shoulder, lit the cigarette, and moved back down the dock.

PART ONE

CHAPTER ONE

SALISBURY, WILTSHIRE
DECEMBER 1942

They had been driving in silence for twenty minutes. Winterbotham's eyes were beginning to drift shut, despite his best efforts to keep them open, when Colonel Fredricks suddenly said, "You know, Professor, you're not at all what I expected."

For a few moments, Winterbotham considered letting it pass. He knew what the colonel meant, and he wasn't in the mood for a fight. He was too goddamned tired. But then his pride—his old bedraggled pride, never knowing when to stay down—forced him to respond.

"How do you mean, Colonel?" he asked.

The colonel let out a small chuckle. "I had been led to expect a sort of wildcat, I suppose."

Winterbotham looked out his window for another moment before answering. The countryside drifted past in absolute darkness; he couldn't make out even the top of the tree line. For the previous two years, all of England had been shutting itself down every night when dusk fell. He supposed they served their purpose, these voluntary blackouts; they made it difficult for the *Luftwaffe* to find their targets. But they also took a toll, one that was purely psychological but very real. Hitler hadn't won the war, not yet—but he had forced them to live in darkness, like animals in caves.

Then Winterbotham turned his head slowly to look at the man sitting beside him in the gloom. Colonel Fredricks was a tall, pallid man who resembled a cadaver. In the darkness, Winterbotham could see only a pale smudge, which would have been his face.

"A wildcat," he mused.

"So I had been warned."

"I'm sorry to disappoint you."

"Oh, don't apologize, Professor. It is my great pleasure to find you . . ." He trailed off.

"Manageable?" Winterbotham said.

"Yes," Fredricks said, relieved. "That's exactly right."

"You thought I would demand to know where we're going," Winterbotham said, "and I would make the trip as unpleasant for you as possible."

"It had occurred to me. Yes."

"So it must have been Taylor who sent you."

Fredricks didn't answer.

"Taylor has always overestimated me," Winterbotham said, and allowed himself a thin smile at the man's silence.

"I'm afraid I can't—"

"I haven't demanded to know our destination," Winterbotham said, "because I already *know* our destination, Colonel Fredricks. We're going to a small nondescript house somewhere in the countryside, correct? I can't see that it much matters if I know the precise location or not. Once we've arrived, we'll meet with my old friend Professor Andrew Taylor, correct? And he will explain the reason for this rather bizarre invitation you have extended me, correct?"

Again, no answer.

"I haven't asked you what the matter is," Winterbotham said, "for the simple reason that you don't *know* what the matter is. Isn't that right, Colonel? You're his retriever, but you don't know what you're retrieving, let alone why, correct?"

Fredricks cleared his throat. "We're nearly there," he said stiffly.

Winterbotham turned and looked out his window again, feeling vaguely satisfied.

He knew they were near Salisbury because he spotted the extraordinary, unmistakable spire of the gothic cathedral—a stab of darkness just slightly darker than the sky behind it—shortly before they stopped. The car pulled up outside a small Tudor house that stood among a row of similar houses, modest dwellings all, with crossed slats of honey-colored wood on the peaked roofs.

Winterbotham waited for Colonel Fredricks to open his door for him, then stepped out into the night, trying to keep his teeth from chattering. A bitter wind immediately took his chestnut hair and increased its disarray. He pulled his tweed jacket more tightly around himself, crinkling his eyes against motes of flying dust.

The room they entered had a claustrophobically low ceiling; it smelled of cabbage and fish. The only light came from a crackling fire in a stone hearth. Blackout shades had been drawn over the windows nonetheless. A wireless radio somewhere, turned low, was playing softly "She's Funny That Way."

Winterbotham had guessed right: Andrew Taylor was sitting in one of two easy chairs by the fireplace. He rose as they came into the room, and offered his hand. He was a man of a certain age, like Winterbotham himself, and, like Winterbotham, he was a man of a certain weight, even in the midst of wartime rationing.

Winterbotham had not seen Taylor for several years, not since they'd been teaching together at the university. His first impression was that the man looked older, more haggard, more harried. His second was that he also looked healthier, in a strange way: His eyes were sparkling, and his handshake was firm. The war was doing him good, Winterbotham realized. Sometimes you found people like that; these dark days brought out the best in them. They were the Churchills of the world, the ones who thrived on conflict.

"Evening, old chap," Taylor said. "They found you."

"That they did. In my bath."

"Sorry about that, Harry. Come in, have a seat. Thank you, Colonel. That will be all."

Colonel Fredricks executed a courtly half bow, then stepped back out through the front door and closed it behind himself.

"You've got him well trained," Winterbotham remarked.

"Not I. It's the Royal Artillery who trained him so well. Tea?"

"Something stronger, if you've got it."

Winterbotham settled down in one of the easy chairs beside the fire. A marble chessboard had been set up on a table between the chairs. He inspected it with a small smile. Perhaps Taylor had dragged him all the way out here simply because he was hungry for a good game of chess . . . although he rather doubted it.

Taylor handed him a chipped mug and sat opposite the chessboard, holding one of his own. Winterbotham raised the mug and sniffed suspiciously. Whiskey. He took a sip into his mouth and rolled it around. Not just whiskey, but good whiskey. How long had it been since he'd had good whiskey?

"You're looking well," Taylor said.

Winterbotham glanced at him with a raised eyebrow—he knew

how he was looking, and well had nothing to do with it—and drank some more of the good whiskey without comment.

Taylor seemed content to let the quiet linger. The fire crackled and the wireless hummed and a whistle of wind rustled through the eaves of the house. Presently, Winterbotham turned his attention to the chessboard. The ranks were arranged in starting position. He reached out, took the king's pawn between thumb and forefinger, and moved it forward two spaces. The king's pawn opening, so simple, so *workable*, had always driven Taylor mad with frustration. Taylor felt that every move in a chess game, as in life, should be a feat of brilliance. He had no appreciation for the simple pleasures of a job well done if there was not some element of spectacle.

Taylor leaned forward, rubbing his chin, and then countered with the knight's pawn—nothing ever could be simple with him.

He said, "I didn't bring you here to play chess."

"I didn't think so," Winterbotham said, bringing a bishop out.

"I heard about Ruth," Taylor said. "I'm sorry, Harry."

Winterbotham nodded without looking up.

"Any word on her?" Taylor pressed. "Any hope?"

Winterbotham shrugged. "There's always hope," he allowed.

In Ruth's case, however, there wasn't much. She had gone to Warsaw, despite Winterbotham's warnings, in the summer of 1939. She had family there—two brothers, assorted cousins—and she had been determined to convince them to come out before it was too late. But by the time she arrived, it already was too late. Hitler and his SS squads marched in a week later. Now she was either dead or imprisoned; Winterbotham had no way of knowing. But her chances, as he long ago had admitted to himself, were not good.

He remembered that Taylor had a wife of his own. He couldn't quite recall her name. Alice, he thought, or possibly Alicia—or possibly Helen, probably Helen. He took a chance.

"How's Helen?"

Taylor was staring at the chessboard. "She's passed on," he said. "Nearly two years now."

"The bombs?"

"Tuberculosis."

"I'm sorry, Andrew."

"Mm," Taylor said.

For ten minutes, then, they played without speaking. Taylor tripped himself up, as was his habit, with his own ambition. He played dramatically, unwilling to take the time to build simple defenses, always looking for an unexpected cross-board coup.

Winterbotham whittled him down pawn by pawn, then split his king and his rook, nabbed the rook, and began to press his opponent's flank. He finished his mug of whiskey and waited to be offered another. Finally, Taylor tipped his king over and laid it down in resignation.

"The more things change . . ." he said with a sour smile. "Care for another drink?"

"I won't refuse."

"I didn't think you would. So, old chap, still teaching?"

"You must know that I'm not."

"I do know that, as a matter of fact. But I've been unable to discover exactly what it is that you *are* doing."

"Very little," Winterbotham said. "Locking myself in the library with my books, for the most part. Except when I'm being mysteriously interrupted during my bath and dragged out into the countryside."

"That's a shame," Taylor said. "A bloody shame."

He had fetched the bottle; now he refilled the mugs and then sat again, looking at Winterbotham contemplatively.

"It's a waste of talent, is what it is," he said. "England could use you. Now more than ever."

"The way she uses you?"

"Mm," Taylor said.

"It does seem to agree with you—whatever it is that you're doing."

"Mm."

"Bringing your extensive knowledge of the classics to bear on the Nazis," Winterbotham said. "What scares them the most, Andrew? Chaucer? Or is it Shakespeare?"

"You're digging," Taylor said, smiling.

"I'm curious. I don't understand exactly how elderly professors like ourselves are of service to His Majesty in wartime, I'll admit."

"How curious are you?"

"Mildly."

"Curious enough to want to know more?"

"I wouldn't have asked otherwise."

"Honestly, old chap, I wish I could tell you everything I'm doing. But I'm afraid that's not possible."

"Yet you didn't bring me out here just for a game of chess."

"No."

"Then why?"

Taylor chewed on his lip for a moment. "There was a time," he said slowly, "when you were not eager about this war."

Winterbotham said nothing.

"You were rather vocal with your opinions," Taylor said. "*Extremely* vocal, as I recall. What was it you called Churchill?"

"You know very well," Winterbotham said crisply.

"Of course I do. You called him a warmonger. You don't have many friends in my sphere, old chap, I'll tell you that. Do you know what they call you?"

"I could hazard a guess."

"Go ahead."

"Something along the lines of an appeaser."

"Right again," Taylor said. "You'd have been happy to sit back and watch Hitler take all of Europe, they say, just as long as we were left out of it. Let Germany and Russia take care of each other."

Winterbotham looked at the chessboard, at Taylor's king resting on its side. He took a long drink from the mug in his hand. A dark shadow crossed his face.

"We all make mistakes," he murmured.

"That we do."

"Perhaps that was one of mine."

"Perhaps it was."

"Are you telling me, Andrew, that you can't tell me what you do because of my politics?"

"I'm telling you that I need to be very careful with what I tell you, old chap, because of your politics. In fact, I'm taking quite a risk just by meeting with you."

"So I should be flattered."

"You should be."

"Then I am. I'm sincerely flattered. Now, tell me: What can I do for you?"

"Same old Winterbotham," Taylor said. "Too impatient for his own good."

"Same old Taylor," Winterbotham answered. "Too fond of games for the sake of games."

"We're living in a new age now, Harry. We're fighting a new kind of war. Games are what we do."

Winterbotham waited for elaboration.

"We're always looking for qualified men," Taylor said, "to help us win the games we play."

"What sort of games, exactly?"

"Ah!" Taylor smacked his hands together. "That's the rub, isn't it? The nature of the game *is* the game. I can't tell you anything without telling you everything. And I can't tell you everything, old chap, until I'm satisfied that you're on our side—completely."

Winterbotham drained the mug in his hand. "My time may be

worthless these days," he said, "but it's all the time I have. You know whose side I'm on, Andrew. Get to the point."

"You don't understand, Harry. If I tell you what we're up to, here, then there's no turning back. Either you're with us or you're not. And if you're not . . ." He hesitated, looking at the fire.

"If I'm not?"

"If I choose to bring you into this and it doesn't work out, you could not be allowed to . . . remain at liberty."

"I see."

"And I've no wish to deny you your liberty, old chap."

"Of course not."

"So I would need to be absolutely certain, before I could tell you any more, that you are the right man for the job—that you will do whatever is required of you."

"I suppose," Winterbotham said, "that I couldn't promise that until I knew what would be required of me, could I?"

Taylor shook his head. "That won't do."

"It's the best I can offer."

"Then I've wasted your time. I'm sorry to have brought you out here. Although I did enjoy the game."

He stood up suddenly and began to move toward the front door, leaving his drink by the chessboard.

"I'll have Fredricks take you back. And I'd appreciate it if you didn't mention—"

"This is hardly fair, Andrew."

"What?"

"You can't expect me to offer my services if I don't know what I'm volunteering for."

"Perhaps not. Well, then, I'm sorry to have—"

"Surely you can give me a clue."

"I'm afraid not."

He opened the front door, paused, and then turned to look at Winterbotham.

"Have a think on it, Harry," he suggested. "Colonel Fredricks will give you my card. Ring me if you change your mind."

Winterbotham looked back at him for a moment, without moving. Then he stood, formally, and buttoned his tweed jacket. He stepped out past Taylor without saying a word, and made for the car by the side of the road.

Taylor closed the door behind him.

The man who had been listening from the next room stepped in.

"I told you," the man said, "he doesn't want to have anything to do with it. He just wants to sit it out."

Taylor shook his head. "Bloody hell," he said.

PRINCETON, NEW JERSEY
JANUARY 1943

Richard Carter paused before climbing the steps to his front porch, and cocked his head to one side, listening. He was a tall, gangly man wearing an oversized, ragged winter coat; his hair was thin and gray. With his head cocked, he bore an uncanny resemblance to a scarecrow.

He couldn't hear any sounds coming from inside the house. Perhaps Catherine was taking a nap, or perhaps she had gone out into town to do some shopping. He hoped it was the former. He didn't think his news could wait.

He trotted up the steps and burst through the front door, making as much noise as possible. If he could stir up enough racket, he thought, maybe he would be spared the responsibility of waking her.

"Cat!" he bellowed. "Hello! Anybody home?"

He walked a quick circuit through the living room, through the tiny dining room, into the kitchen, peeking out into the backyard. By the time he had returned to the foyer she was coming down the stairs, rubbing at her eyes blearily.

"Darling," he said, "come into the living room. I've got news. Wonderful news."

As she came off the lowest riser, he steered her, by the crook of her arm, into the living room. Bright winter sunshine, thick with dust, gushed in through a window. There was a lot of dust in the house; Catherine was not much of a housekeeper.

She sat heavily on the couch. Richard looked down at her, trying to contain himself. He should really give her time to wake up. She could be moody, as he well knew, if she wasn't given enough time to wake up. But he had just come from a meeting with the most brilliant men in the world—*me,* he thought, *they chose me!*—and proximity to such brilliance had set him on fire. He couldn't help himself. He blurted it out.

"Darling," Richard said, "it's a job. A phenomenal job."

She blinked up at him sleepily.

"Government work," he said, sitting down beside her. "It's a great honor, Catherine, just phenomenal."

She yawned.

"Out of all the people in the department, they chose—"

"Richard," she said.

"Me. They chose *me.*"

"I need tea," she said.

She stood up and brushed past him into the kitchen.

Richard sat and listened as Catherine made herself a pot of tea. So far, he was thinking, so good. He had told her only half of it, of course. The easy half. He hadn't gotten to the part about needing to leave Princeton. But that could wait until she'd had her tea. Her mood after waking improved greatly, as a rule, with the consumption of caffeine.

After a few minutes she came back into the living room, cup in hand, her blond hair bouncing, and sat beside him on the couch again. She looked more alert now. Her eyes, green flecked with gray, were sharp. The beginnings of crow's-feet were imprinted around those eyes, but in Richard's opinion they only made her look more lovely. Catherine possessed a rare kind of beauty, a *true* beauty, which would only grow deeper and more profound as she got older.

She had brought her pack of cigarettes from the kitchen. She lit one and exhaled a thin stream of smoke. Her eyes found his.

"A job," she said.

He nodded eagerly. "Not just any job. A phenomenal job. A phenomenal oppor—"

"What does it pay?"

"Pay?" he said.

The truth was, he hadn't even thought to ask what it paid. He didn't even know, as a matter of fact, if he *would* get paid. And he didn't especially care. This was a chance to work alongside the most brilliant men in the world. Elbow to elbow; cranium to cranium. Hell, *he* would pay for this opportunity, if that was what it took.

But Catherine's eyes, over the rim of her cup, were not only sharp—they were arch.

"I don't know exactly what it pays," he said cautiously. "But I'm sure the money's good."

"How good?"

"Good."

"How good?" she asked, taking a drag from her cigarette, chasing it with a sip of tea.

"I don't know exactly. But that's not the point, Catherine. The point is that I'll be working with the greatest thinkers in the world. *The greatest thinkers in the world.*"

"The greatest thinkers in Princeton, you mean."

"No, no, no. They'll be coming from all over. Chicago, Berkeley, maybe even—"

"Coming to Princeton?"

He blinked.

"Not coming to Princeton?" she said.

He shook his head.

"Coming where?" she asked.

"Well . . . Albuquerque."

"Albuquerque?"

"New Mexico."

"We're going to New Mexico?"

"That depends," he said. "Some of the boys are bringing their wives. But some of them . . ." He left the thought unfinished.

A ridge of concentration appeared between her eyes.

That ridge, even after nearly eight years of marriage, mystified Richard Carter.

The things Catherine said, after getting that ridge between her eyes, invariably came as a surprise to him.

When Catherine had first arrived in Princeton nine years before, she had been far less prone to scowls. She had not smiled often, even then; she had kept mostly to herself as she went about her housekeeping duties. But she had possessed, at least, a pleasant air.

For the first few weeks, Carter had barely noticed that she was in the house. By the fifth week, he had become aware of her presence in an abstracted, affectionate sort of way. By the seventh, he'd found himself looking forward to their brief encounters—a polite passing in the halls, the occasional meal together.

By the time Catherine had been in the house for three months, he had fallen hopelessly in love with her.

At first he had refused to accept it. The girl was half his age, his own dear wife had been gone for only four years, and he was making progress in his work—the separation of uranium isotopes—which a love affair could serve only to slow down.

But the heart was not logical. Once set upon a course, no amount of rational argument could dissuade it.

Finally he had decided to bring the matter to a resolution. He had gathered his courage and proposed.

Catherine, in accepting, had made him the happiest man on earth.

But soon after had come the ridge.

He first saw the ridge appear between her eyes when he had suggested that they find another cleaning woman to hire. She had been about to become his wife; it had never occurred to him that she would want to continue in her capacity as housekeeper. But the ridge had shown up and she had thought hard for five silent minutes. Then she had announced that she didn't know what she would do with herself if he hired someone else to take her job, and she'd really rather he didn't. He had capitulated without argument—he could never argue with her—and had then watched, baffled but silent, as she did less housework with every passing month.

Who knew how her mind worked? Not he. But the ridge meant trouble; he knew that much.

The ridge was also there when she had told him out of the blue, the previous year, that she wanted to go to work for the Federal Shipbuilding Company in Kearny, New Jersey. She felt guilty for doing nothing, she said, lazing around the house all day while the country slogged off to war. She wanted to manufacture ball bearings like the other women, tossing in her own two cents. This from a woman who couldn't manage to keep a modest little university house dust-free, although she had fourteen waking hours a day in which to do it.

But he hadn't argued.

The Kearney adventure, of course, had lasted less than a month. Cat hadn't expected to work fifty-hour weeks driving rivets; nor had she expected to be required to wear slacks.

Finally, she stirred. The ash on her cigarette had grown long. She tapped it into a ceramic ashtray on an end table, then said, "How long will it last—this job?"

"A few months. Maybe longer."

"In Albuquerque."

"Yes."

"Who else is going?"

"A bunch of boys from the university. But I'm the only one from my department. That's why it's such a phenomenal—"

"Yes, it's a phenomenal honor, you've made that clear," she said. "What would I do, Richard, if I stayed here while you went away?"

He shrugged. "Whatever you want, I suppose."

"What would I do if I came with you?"

"There wouldn't be much. It's in the middle of the desert."

"What does the government want with an old mathematician, anyway?"

"Darling, I don't really think you'd—"

The ridge began to appear again.

"It's a bit technical," he said quickly. "Besides, it's a secret."

"But I'm your wife."

"Yes, of course you are. But . . ."

"Oh, forget it. I'm sure you're right. I wouldn't understand."

She stabbed out her cigarette, barely smoked.

"I'll come with you," she decided, and then watched him closely.

"I would be the luckiest man in the world," Richard said, "if my gorgeous wife was really willing to follow me out into the middle of nowhere."

She looked at him for another moment, clinically. He wondered if he had said something wrong. It was so hard to know how she would react these days. He never would have guessed that she would have any interest in following him to Los Alamos. She had become a stranger to him at some point. . . .

Then she dropped into his lap and gave him a kiss. A real kiss, full on the lips. It was rare, lately, to get a real kiss from Catherine. He kissed back. God, but she was beautiful.

In the last instant before his eyes drifted closed, he took a look at her forehead.

The ridge was nowhere to be seen.

They had chosen *him*—and his beautiful young wife was willing to accompany him to the middle of nowhere.

There was no doubt in Richard Carter's mind at that moment that he was the most fortunate man on the face of the earth.

HOLLAND PARK, LONDON

Three weeks had passed since Winterbotham's cryptic meeting with his old friend Andrew Taylor. During that time he had not gotten a single good night's sleep—but there was nothing unusual about that.

At some point in the nether hours of each morning, he would give up and seek refuge in his library. He would sit wearing his favorite faded bathrobe, poring over some dusty old tome or other, smoking pipe after pipe of orange-flavored tobacco, sometimes drinking a bit of the mediocre whiskey he had squirreled away. None of it helped put him back to sleep or even put his mind at ease. It was the worst insomnia he had suffered since the early days of the war, when Ruth first had been lost. He had slept better during the worst of the *Luftwaffe*'s bombing raids than he was sleeping now.

We all make mistakes.

That we do, Taylor had agreed.

Perhaps that was one of mine.

Perhaps it was.

Of course it had been. Winterbotham knew it now. For the first few months following the outbreak of war, he had refused to admit that he had been mistaken. He had stuck tenaciously to his old line: Germany was not their enemy; Germany had been given a poor deal by Versailles, and England had nobody to blame but herself; peace in their time was the ultimate goal. But then there had come a time—had it been with the first bombing raids?—when he was no longer able to delude himself. As a matter of fact, he saw, Germany *was* the enemy. Nazi Germany was the worst enemy they had ever faced, and rather than appeasing Hitler, they should have done just the opposite. They should have done it from the very beginning.

None of which meant that he liked Churchill any more than he ever had. The man was a warmonger, and that was the plain truth. It just so happened that Hitler was even more of a warmonger, and fire had to be fought with fire. But in peaceful times he never would have supported Churchill. When a man needed combat to thrive, in Winterbotham's opinion, there was something wrong with him.

Still, Churchill was what England needed now.

And I, he thought, *am I what England needs now?*

Of course he wasn't. He was an old man, for one thing, not the wildcat he once had been. But even when he *had* been a wildcat, he had been a devoutly pacifistic one. His wildness had been reserved for academic discussions and lively barroom debates. What England needed now was fighters, and he would never be a fighter.

It's a waste of talent, is what it is, Taylor had said.

What talent? The talent to discuss literature? He had that in spades, but Taylor wouldn't want to hear any of what he would have to say. Winterbotham would be liable to quote Oscar Wilde: *Truth is rarely pure and never simple.* No, Taylor would want rhetoric, blood-stirring rhetoric, the better to rally the boys so they could cross the Channel, go back to Dunkirk, and start laying claim to Europe. *We shall fight on beaches, we shall fight on landing grounds, we shall fight in fields and in streets, we shall never surrender . . .*

What other talent did he have? What else about him could have interested Taylor enough to account for the meeting?

Chess?

It was true, he had roundly trounced Taylor for years. But chess was just a game. And there were far better chess players than he in England.

We're fighting a new kind of war. Playing games is what we do.

What was that supposed to mean? It was a new kind of war, all right, but as far as Winterbotham could see, the newness was a result of technology. Hitler's armies had rolled over France in short order thanks to the force of their tanks; the Japanese had devastated Pearl Harbor with their air power from half a world away; but nowhere along the line were games being played that bore the slightest resemblance to chess. Brute force was the rule of the day.

What else? What else could he have that Taylor would think made him valuable?

His pipe was empty. He repacked it, tamped it down, and lit it. The library was heavy with the stillness of early morning. There wasn't so much as an air-raid siren to distract him . . . and he still couldn't figure it out.

I'm taking quite a risk just by meeting with you.

That was understandable. Winterbotham had become the enemy when he hadn't been paying attention. His arguments for peace had made him a villain in his own country. So why would Taylor risk his peers' disapproval by making contact? Why *him*?

Because of Ruth, he thought suddenly.

He's hoping I'll feel guilty enough about Ruth to want to throw myself into harm's way.

The thought enraged him, not least because it smacked of truth. It wasn't his fault that Ruth had demanded to go to Poland, of course; he had tried to dissuade her. But perhaps he hadn't tried hard enough. Perhaps . . .

"Nonsense," he said aloud.

Perhaps, perhaps not. In any case, it still didn't explain things. There were better chess players than Winterbotham; there were men with better politics than Winterbotham; and there was no shortage of men who had lost loved ones in the war and would be hungry for revenge.

He sighed. He couldn't sleep, but he was tired . . . so tired.

It was 1943, and the war raged on. The war would keep raging on, regardless of his participation, for the foreseeable future. Things didn't look as bleak as they had looked a few months before, that was true, but the outcome of the conflict was still far from certain. Hitler's *Wehrmacht* had overreached in Russia, caught unawares by the devastating winter, and had suffered losses. There was no way to know how bad these losses had been, but Winterbotham thought they might have been very bad, very bad indeed, for the little Austrian corporal. At roughly the same time, Rommel had foundered in Africa. But these German setbacks were by no means enough to finish the war. At some point, before the end, the Allies would have to cross the pond and set foot in France. . . .

It has nothing to do with me, Winterbotham thought.

He sat and smoked pipe after pipe, and he kept thinking, *It has nothing to do with me, nothing to do with me.*

When the sun came up, he found Taylor's card and made a call.

CHAPTER TWO

HAM COMMON, SURREY
JANUARY 1943

The road meandered past St. Andrew's Church, wandering through gently rolling hills, over a landscape glitter-bright with pinpricks of frost. Winterbotham, gazing out his window, found himself appreciating the view. The trees were skeletal but lovely in a rather bleak way that appealed to him. One forgot the small pleasures of nature, he reflected, when one spent all one's time in the city. She was bleak and she was harsh, but she was also beautiful. And she would outlast them all—the war, the generals, the games, the bombs, the madmen, the soldiers, all of it.

Taylor, sitting beside him, noticed the appreciative look on his face. "It's pretty," he said, "isn't it?"

Winterbotham nodded. "The war seems very far away," he murmured.

"It does indeed. But that's deceptive, old chap. The real war is being fought—and won—not very far from here. Not very far at all."

"The real war?" Winterbotham said.

"Well, some might take exception with that. The ones doing the fighting, for instance." Taylor was watching him with bright, eager eyes. "But it's true nonetheless. Our boys in the field would be doing a lot worse if we weren't doing what we're doing here. Take my word for it."

Now the car was moving alongside a low stone wall, approaching a gate festooned with barbed wire. Winterbotham could see two guards, machine guns in hand, coming forward to meet them.

"What, exactly, *are* we doing here?" he asked.

Taylor smiled. "That's what you're about to find out, old chap. And if you're having second thoughts, now's the time. Once we go through that gate, there's no turning back."

They pulled up to the gate.

Winterbotham held his tongue.

"Good afternoon," Taylor said politely, handing his papers to the stone-faced guard outside his window.

Latchmere House, behind the low walls, behind the curls of barbed wire, between the spill of hastily constructed barracks, was a pale-green monstrosity.

The building, three rambling stories of damp and mildew, had been built as a mental hospital after the Great War. The army had found euphemisms to disguise Latchmere's true purpose; they had called it a "home"—so much nicer than "hospital"—for "victims of shell-shock"—so much nicer than "mental patients." But the architecture screamed "lunatic asylum," and there was no mistaking it. The windows were narrow slits, far too small for a man to slip through. The rooms were bare, dark, drafty, and draconian.

Taylor ushered him into a small chamber furnished with one small table and two rickety chairs. Grayish sunshine filtered in. The air smelled sour and earthy, like the air in a fruit cellar.

"Have a seat," Taylor said grandly, "and I'll tell you the greatest secret of the war."

More dramatics, Winterbotham thought. But he sat, settling his bulk carefully into an unsteady chair, and took out his pipe.

A small suitcase was resting on the table. Winterbotham looked it over curiously as he packed his orange-flavored tobacco. The case was tarnished metal, compact and nondescript. It was slightly too squat for a chessboard. He considered asking about it, and then decided that Taylor would explain in due time. This was Taylor's show, after all, and he had to let Taylor go ahead as he liked—unnecessary drama and all.

Taylor sat in the other chair, produced a cigarette, and waited until Winterbotham had his pipe going before lighting it. Then he leaned back, crossed his pudgy legs at the ankles, and said, "It's rather a lot to digest, what I'm about to tell you. Stop me if I go too fast."

"Never fear," Winterbotham said.

"You remember what I said the last time we met—about playing games?"

Winterbotham nodded. "Playing games is what you do."

"Not just us. Hitler, too. He and his friend Canaris."

Winterbotham nodded again. Admiral Wilhelm Canaris was one of Hitler's more infamous cronies—the head of the Nazi intelligence service, the *Abwehr.*

"Would you care to guess, Harry, how many spies the *Abwehr* has sent to England since the early thirties?"

"I wouldn't have any idea."

"Well, we would, thank God. About a hundred. And that doesn't include the Brits who sold us out to the Nazis—there are a few of those, too."

He waited to see what impact this revelation would have on Winterbotham. Winterbotham waited to see how long Taylor would wait. Finally, Taylor cleared his throat, disappointed, and continued.

"Now, here's the good part," he said. "Of those hundred-odd agents, Harry, we've captured . . . How many would you guess?"

"I wouldn't have any idea."

"All of them," Taylor said, and grinned.

This time Winterbotham couldn't help himself. He blinked with surprise. "*All* of them?"

"Every last one."

"How can you be sure?"

"We weren't, at first. But as time went on . . . Suffice it to say that if we had missed even one, Harry, we would know about it by now—for reasons that will become clear in a moment. We got most of them right at the start of the war. In September of thirty-nine, we rounded up all the enemy aliens in the country. We went over each case individually. If there was any doubt, we interned them. They're not made of terribly stern stuff, these *Abwehr* agents, and few of them have any training worth mentioning. They cracked quickly. And then . . . What do you think we did then?"

"You hanged them, no doubt."

"Some of them, yes. But some of them, we realized, could be of more value to us alive . . . and so we started Double Cross."

"Double Cross?"

"That's what this place is," Taylor said. He made an expansive gesture with the hand holding the cigarette. "The headquarters of Operation Double Cross. The greatest misinformation campaign ever conducted in war or in peace. We have dozens of *Abwehr* agents here, Harry, and they're all working for us. They use these"—he tapped the suitcase on the table—"these radios to send intelligence back to

Hamburg. But in reality, everything they say is coming from us. Do you see?"

Winterbotham nodded slowly. "You're feeding them worthless information."

"Not . . ." Taylor trailed off.

Winterbotham read his face in an instant. Taylor may have had his talents in this world, but concealing his thoughts was not among them.

"Andrew," Winterbotham said mildly, "if we're going to be working together, it goes without saying that I'll require your full confidence."

Taylor frowned. "Of course," he said, but he didn't look pleased. He cleared his throat. "Not exactly worthless," he said. "And that's where it gets tricky. We can't simply feed them worthless information, or they'd realize that their spies have been compromised. No, Harry, the intelligence has to be true, at least for the most part. If Canaris loses faith in his spies, the jig is up, as they say—and we'll need the operation to be in good working order as the war goes on. Whenever we send troops back to the mainland, next year or the year after, we'll use Double Cross as our ace in the hole. We'll make sure Hitler expects the landing to be exactly where it won't be."

"So you're sending true information?"

Again, he could see Taylor hesitate.

"It's extremely delicate," Taylor said then. "Yes, the bulk of the information is true. But of course, we don't want to help our friend Canaris too much, or he might just win the war. We walk a very fine line here, Harry. Sometimes we provide intelligence of some value—it's a sacrifice that has to be made. Sometimes we put a bit of a spin on the truth. If there's an accident at an airfield, we'll let one of their spies take credit for it, claiming sabotage. Sometimes we'll manufacture something out of whole cloth that will seem, to reconnaissance planes, to be real. We have all sorts of people working for Double Cross. All sorts. Chess champions. Musicians. Crossword puzzle enthusiasts. Illusionists—magicians.

Once we used mirrors to make one tank look like thirty. And they believed it."

Winterbotham whistled.

Taylor nodded, finally satisfied with the effect he had created.

"But you must appreciate the fragility of our situation," he went on. "We have all sorts of fictions, mixed in with the truth, going out over these little suitcase radios. All it would take to raise suspicion is one *Abwehr* agent that we missed—just one—sending a report that goes against everything else. If *one single agent* slips through our trap, Harry, the whole operation could be compromised."

"It sounds dicey."

"It is. So you can see why I needed a total commitment from you. As I said, this is the best-kept secret of the war, and, if I may allow myself the conceit, the most important."

"Yes, I can see."

"So, you'll forgive me my theatrics?"

Winterbotham made a loose gesture.

Taylor frowned. He took a long drag from his cigarette. The paper crackled. He exhaled a rafter of smoke toward the ceiling, then said, "Those are only the basics of Operation Double Cross. There's more to it, of course. In fact, it's phenomenally complicated. We need our intelligence to seem *real*, Harry, and we go to great lengths to create that impression. We try to keep our pet agents here at Latchmere for as little time as possible. Once we're convinced they can be trusted, we put them back out into England, doing whatever it is Canaris thinks they're doing. They live with their case officer, who conducts the surveillance that they are supposed to be conducting. Then, together, they go over what intelligence will be sent, what will be held back, what will be spun."

"What if they don't prove as trustworthy as you think?"

"Then they hang," Taylor said.

He looked at Winterbotham levelly.

"Hm," Winterbotham said.

"I won't keep anything from you, Harry. It's a bloody business. Sometimes they go bad, and sometimes they need some extra convincing to turn in the first place. We try to keep everything friendly, for obvious reasons. We want them to be satisfied in their work for us. In fact, we damn near pamper them, trying to keep them happy. But it doesn't always work out."

Winterbotham said nothing.

"Our hands are far from clean," Taylor said. "In our effort to keep Canaris in the dark about Double Cross, we've had to make sacrifices. We've had to pretend not to know about enemy operations that we did know about. There have been difficult decisions, and there have been casualties. Civilian casualties. Casualties that could have been avoided . . . but at the cost of the entire operation."

Winterbotham nodded shortly.

"It's not pleasant," Taylor said.

"No."

"But it must be done."

"I suppose."

"Don't suppose. It's a fact."

"Mm."

Taylor looked at him for a moment. He bit his lower lip. Then he nodded in agreement with some secret thought. "Somebody has to take the responsibility," he said softly. "It's not easy, Harry. But it must be done."

Winterbotham set his pipe down on the table. "What do you want from me?" he asked.

"Three weeks ago—when I first got in touch with you—we received a new crop. Four agents, straight from Hamburg. Two of them parachuted in. One came on a U-boat and then paddled ashore in a dinghy. One came in under a false passport—Swiss. We got all of them, of course. As soon as they arrived, they got in touch with their contacts here. And their contacts work for us."

"They're here now, at Latchmere?"

"Three of them are, yes."

"Where's the fourth?"

"She chose not to cooperate," Taylor said, and left it at that.

Winterbotham picked up his pipe again. It had gone out. He held it without relighting it.

"Of the remaining three," Taylor continued after a moment, "there is one of particular interest to us here at Double Cross. His name is Rudolf Schroeder, although his papers call him Russell Webb. His assignment is to find work in a pub in the vicinity of the War Office. He's to listen to the conversation, get a feeling for the atmosphere, and keep his eyes open for a possible convert. You understand what I'm saying?"

"He's looking for someone to turn."

"Precisely. Men come into the pub after a hard day of work and have a few pints, and their tongues loosen. Perhaps they talk about what they're working on, or perhaps they complain about their bosses. If anybody complains too much, Schroeder moves in. He makes an offer. Straightforward—quid for service. And of course, a place of honor in their magnificent thousand-year Reich when this is all over."

"Hm."

"As far as the *Abwehr* knows," Taylor said, "Schroeder is doing remarkably well. He's already found work in a pub, and he's settled into a boardinghouse that doesn't suspect him. He's sent back his first few reports. Nothing very earthshaking: weather data, a few words about British morale, some demands for more spending money. But sometime soon, within the next few weeks, Schroeder is going to accomplish something far more impressive. He's going to find the perfect candidate for turning. He's going to make contact, and he's going to have spectacular success."

"I see."

"All fabricated, you understand. But the appearance of truth is vital."

"Yes."

"To create the appearance of truth, Harry, we need to cleave very close to the *actual* truth."

"Yes."

"That's why you're our man."

Winterbotham lit his pipe again, and puffed on it thoughtfully.

"Harris Winterbotham," Taylor said. "Professor of classics, war widower, and known dissembler. You don't like Churchill, Harry. You don't like his way of doing things, and you've made no secret of it. If Canaris checks on you, he won't have to dig very deep to find out about your past."

"But I don't work for the War Office."

"Ah! That's where you're wrong. For the past five months you've been working in the code-breaking division of Military Intelligence. Very hush-hush. Your expertise at chess, not to mention your all-around acumen"—the slightest edge of sarcasm crept into his voice—"makes you a valued member of our team. Of course, we're aware of the . . . sensitive . . . nature of your politics, and so you don't know as much as you might. We've kept you fairly isolated. But you know enough. You'll be irresistible to Canaris."

"I see."

"Schroeder will mention in tonight's report that he's found a valuable lead. But for the time being, we'll leave it at that. We want the *Abwehr* to be hungry for you, Harry. We'll take our time on this. In two weeks, or four, or six, Schroeder will feel comfortable enough to approach you with an offer. He'll find you willing. And at some point after that—"

"At some point after that, I'll begin spying for the Nazis."

"You'll likely begin by telling them what you already know. And for that, Harry, God willing, they'll want to meet with you face-to-face.

They'll want their own code-breakers working on you. They'll want their information direct, not coming through Schroeder."

Winterbotham sent a ring of smoke floating toward the ceiling.

"How will I meet them?" he asked.

"We're hoping they'll arrange a *treff*—a clandestine meeting between *Abwehr* agents. It may be in a neutral place, like Portugal, or they may wish to bring you directly to the center of their operations: the headquarters of the *Abwehr*, in Berlin; their training facilities in Hamburg; or possibly, if Canaris thinks you're important enough, all the way to the top—to Hitler himself. Into the *Wolfsschanze*. The Wolf's Lair."

"At which point—"

"At which point you'll tell them exactly what we've told you to tell them. A bit of truth, a bit of lies, and a lot in between. And in the meantime you'll keep your eyes open, Harry. You'll see how the *Abwehr* works—from the inside. With luck, you'll discover how much they know, or how much they suspect, about Double Cross. You'll learn whatever you can about their plans, both past and future. You'll remember every question they ask you, and the tone of voice when they ask it. Then you'll come back and you'll tell us everything. Everything."

Taylor leaned forward, elbows on table. "I don't have to tell you how sensitive this is," he said. "If they guess what you're there for, Harry, they'll kill you. But there's more to it than that. If they manage to get you talking—"

"The whole operation is compromised," Winterbotham finished.

"Exactly."

"That's a risk you're willing to take?"

"Risk is an essential element of our game. For the chance to see the inner workings of an enemy intelligence organization, while they're actually at war with us . . . for that, old chap, we're willing to risk a lot."

"Everything."

"Yes. Everything."

"Hm," Winterbotham said.

"Problems may arise. Schroeder may prove less cooperative than we hope. Or Canaris more suspicious."

"Yes."

"But if it works, old chap . . . if we dangle you as the bait, and they bite . . ." He trailed off again, and arched an eyebrow inquisitively.

"Do I have a choice?" Winterbotham asked.

"Of course. This is dangerous, Harry. I think I've made that clear. And if you choose not to take part in it, nobody will blame you. We would invite you to remain here, at Latchmere, as our guest, for the duration of the war. But we wouldn't blame you for an instant."

"Hm," Winterbotham said.

"So?"

Winterbotham took a moment before answering. He made two more smoke rings, a large one and a small one, and sent the small one floating through the large one. Then he looked up at Taylor. Later, when he thought back on it, Taylor would remember Winterbotham's eyes at that moment. They were small and sharp and hot, like twin smoldering coals. They were the eyes of the young Winterbotham—the wildcat.

Looking back, Taylor realized that those eyes should have warned him. He should have known, at that instant, that Winterbotham had ideas of his own about working for MI-5.

Winterbotham smiled, a rather morbid smile.

"Where do I sign?" he said.

LOS ALAMOS, NEW MEXICO
APRIL 1943

Catherine Danielson Carter couldn't believe her eyes.

She read the letter again, certain that she would find some indication that it was not what it seemed to be—it was a prank, a mistake, a gag. When she reached the end, her eyes skipped immediately back up to the first line. She was extremely conscious of the fact that she should really get the hell out of there, get away before somebody noticed she was missing from the party and came looking for her. But the letter in her hand was so incredible, so *impossible*, that she felt compelled to read it again, and then again, and then still again, although she had memorized it the first time through.

Finally, after finishing it for the fifth time, she tore her eyes from the page. She felt loose and shaky inside; she steadied herself against the desk with one hand. She had known that something was going on, of course. You didn't bring a hundred scientists and engineers and military personnel into the middle of the desert if something wasn't going on. You didn't build a hospital and a dormitory and a laboratory and an entire town if something wasn't going on. But she had never suspected . . .

She realized that she was going to throw up.

She couldn't do that, not there. She began to modulate her breathing the way Hagen had shown her so many years before, during her training. *Panic is your worst enemy*, Hagen had said. *It comes from inside. You cannot kill it, and that makes it dangerous. The secret is not to let the panic control you. You control the panic.*

She focused on her breathing. Shallow, rhythmic. Soon enough, the nausea was slipping away. It left her feeling hollow. What had she stumbled onto? The thought brought the panic back all over again. Her breathing accelerated; her heart thudded violently in her chest. She would throw up, she thought, any second now, vomiting all over the makeshift office of General Leslie Groves. And then she would be lost. They would know she had been there—and they would find . . .

No.

She controlled the panic again.

Steady breathing, shallow, in and out.

Better.

After a moment, she began to move. She returned the letter to the file, put the file back into the desk, closed the drawer, and jiggled the handle until she heard the tumblers fall home. The lock was a standard double wafer—more secure than a conventional wafer tumbler lock, but just barely.

Catherine straightened. She looked around to make sure she hadn't left any evidence of her visit. The office was faintly illuminated by a slab of light coming through a pane in the door. The room looked much as it had fifteen minutes before, when she had allowed herself entrance by picking the lock with a bobby pin. Security at Los Alamos, to somebody with her training, was a joke. Each Friday night for the past two months, she had slipped away and explored the camp, secret documents and all, almost at her leisure.

She crossed the room and listened at the door. She knew from experience that two guards patrolled the hallway outside Groves's office. But they were responsible for the entire building, which meant that one passed by only every ten minutes. She waited until she heard footsteps rapping down the corridor. She kept waiting until they had passed. Then she slipped out, closed the door behind herself, checked to make sure the lock had taken, and walked quickly and quietly toward the rear exit.

When she came out into the night, the cold air was bracing. She moved back toward the canteen, where the party sounded as if it was gaining momentum. She could hear music, conversation, and much drunken laughter. It was always the same. There was a lot of steam to be blown off at Los Alamos. Before tonight, she had wondered why. Now she understood.

My God, she thought again, *what have I stumbled onto?*

Before going back inside the canteen, she took a moment to check herself. Her hair was fine; her clothes were fine, or as fine as they got, considering the shortage of good material; but her face, surely, would show something. Her face would reveal that she had discovered the secret. Her face would betray her.

No.

Her body was an instrument, and she was its master.

She smiled—quite convincingly—then climbed the wooden steps and went to rejoin the party.

That night she woke with a scream rising in her throat.

She bolted up in bed. Richard was sleeping beside her, his chest rising and falling almost imperceptibly. Catherine sat with one hand clamped over her mouth, not looking at him, trembling. From not far away came the sounds of generators humming and, below that, the eerie whistle of desert wind.

After a few minutes, the shakes began to subside. She let out her breath slowly, wiping a hand across her brow. The hand came away clammy.

It had been a variation of the nightmare she had dreamed on and off for more than ten years, now. But this had been the worst in a long while—perhaps the worst ever. They all were gathered around her, everybody she knew from this life and the last, pointing and laughing. Hagen was there, barking orders in hoarse German, and Richard, her husband, looking at her with his imploring and somehow pathetic eyes. And Fritz was there, naked, as he had been the last time she had seen him, standing at the rail of a balcony in a hotel in Hamburg, tall and lean and fair. And behind them all was the gallows, swinging back and forth, creaking in a cold wind. . . .

Just a dream, she thought.

She got out of bed and padded into the bathroom. They shared the bathroom with another couple, who lived in the next apartment in the dormitory. She checked cursorily to make sure their door was closed. The bathroom had no running water at night, but a bucket by the sink was filled with an already drawn supply. She splashed two handfuls onto her face—freezing, no surprise—and then went back to bed.

The letter. The goddamn letter.

Why did she have to find the letter?

It meant, of course, the end of Catherine Danielson Carter. And in one way that was a terrific relief. She hadn't let Richard touch her in an intimate way for years, now, and yet the fact of being his wife was trying enough. He was old, and he *smelled* old—his smell was probably what bothered her most about him. But there was more to it than that. There was the hurt look that lurked eternally in his eyes, and the eager-to-please way he carried himself around her. Pandering. It made her feel guilty and disgusted all at once.

But there was more to it, even, than that. The fact was, she was still a young woman, or at least fairly young. She still had hopes of falling in love during her lifetime. And her relationship with Richard—even if it had not been founded on a lie—would never really give her any satisfaction. Every day she spent with him was another day she wasn't spending falling in love with somebody else.

That was the worst of it.

Perhaps, she sometimes thought, perhaps it was even possible that Fritz would still think of her in that way. Ten years had passed, a third of their lives, and yet . . .

She settled her head down on the pillow, gently. But she couldn't fool herself into thinking that sleep would come again that night.

The end of Catherine Danielson Carter, she thought again.

It would be a relief in other ways as well. Catherine Danielson Carter was an immensely boring person who lived an immensely boring life. The reason she had gotten into this game in the first place, so many years before, was that she was precisely the *opposite* of an immensely boring person. She required adventure, risk, intrigue. She would relish the opportunity to stop playing the role of mousy little Catherine Carter . . .

Except . . .

Except that her chances of living long enough to play any other role were not very good.

There. She had thought it.

It was the end of Catherine Danielson Carter, but it was probably also the end of Katarina Heinrich.

She didn't want to die. But when she thought about the task that lay before her, now that she had found the letter, she realized that her chances were poor.

The letter, in a way, was her death sentence.

The night dragged on, and she thought about what had to happen next.

She would have to report the contents of the letter to Germany. Not just the letter, of course, but the blueprints and the technical data and everything else she had found during her months snooping around Los Alamos—she had learned it all, using the photographic memory techniques Hagen had taught her. But the letter was the most important part, the part that proved the significance of the rest. She had perused the blueprints over and over again during the previous few months, absorbing every detail without ever understanding just what they meant; but there was no mistaking the letter.

How would she get to Germany?

She didn't have her AFU—not that the AFU had the kind of range she would need to make contact with Hamburg from Los Alamos. Nor did she have a weapon. She had left it all behind when she had assumed the role of Catherine Danielson.

She did not even have a network to help her, not one worth mentioning. Most German agents in America had been rounded up, condemned in the trial of 1941, and summarily executed. No, she would have to get the information to Germany herself, somehow, without depending on any help from anyone . . .

Except, perhaps, from Fritz.

She thought about Fritz. He was stationed in England; she knew his address there. She had wrangled it from Hagen shortly after arriving in New York. Hagen, she knew, had bent his own rules by giving her the information; but then, Hagen had always been fond of her. He had sent the address along with an admonishment: not to contact Fritz unless she could contrive no other method of reaching her spymasters.

When she had started spying again, after taking work at the Kearny plant, she had sent her intelligence directly to Fritz so he could wire it on to Berlin. She trusted Fritz. They had trained together under Hagen, in Hamburg, so long before. They also had been lovers, but at this point that was incidental. They both were Hagen's agents, and so both had nothing to do with the incompetent *Abwehr*—that was what mattered now.

If she could get to Fritz, he could get in touch with Hamburg.

But getting to Fritz would not be easy.

Still, the thought made her feel a bit more at peace. The odds were against her, but she was not completely alone. She would find Fritz, and then they would be in this together.

She decided, eventually, that it was a great blessing, finding the letter. Yes, it might get her killed. But it would also force her to find courage. It would allow her to break the pattern she had fallen into, the safe but dull pattern of domestic life.

There had been some black days spent as Catherine Danielson Carter. Days filled with monotony, self-doubt, and—until she had put her foot down—unwanted attentions.

She had gone so deeply undercover, so suddenly, that she had not even informed her own spymasters of her plans. Hagen, she realized, would have no way of knowing about the opportunity onto which she had stumbled; and she, ironically, could not risk losing the opportunity by informing him of it—she never knew for certain that the American censors had not discovered her.

Or perhaps that was only a rationalization.

Who was to say, she'd begun to wonder with the passage of years, that she hadn't simply lost her nerve?

She'd watched the unfolding drama in Europe playing out from a safe distance, after all, in banner newspaper headlines. The coup of the Rhineland; the *Anschluss* of Austria; the invasion of Poland, and war; then Pearl Harbor and America's entrance into the conflict. When the *Abwehr* agents in New York had been rounded up and executed in 1941, Katarina had felt equal measures of regret and relief—for she, and precious few others, had been spared.

She had tried to gather her courage, to reenter the fray. She had taken the job at Kearny. But the blueprints she'd found there were of limited value, and she was no ordinary agent, no collector of trivia. She would not jeopardize herself for mere trifles.

Now she had found something worthy of her skills. The letter made the point irrefutable.

Catherine Danielson Carter was dead. But in her death, Katarina Heinrich would find life.

For a few days, anyway.

She began to think about routes; a crease of concentration appeared between her eyes. There was a fantastic distance to be covered, and they would, of course, be looking for her the moment she left. A train to New York; a boat to England. Or perhaps a boat to Lisbon, or Madrid . . . from there to England . . . to Fritz . . . comforting, really, to fall back into the old ways of thinking, like coming home . . .

When Richard Carter woke up with the sun, he was pleased to find his wife sleeping soundly.

BENDLERSTRASSE, BERLIN

Hagen was nervous.

He climbed the steps of 72-76 Tirpitz Ufer, a drab five-story building made of colorless granite situated by the similarly drab waters of the *Landwehrkanal*. He told himself, as he climbed, that there was no reason to be nervous. Canaris had nothing on him. He, on the other hand, had plenty on Canaris. Much of it was speculative, but if push came to shove he would have ammunition readily at hand.

There was no doubt in Hagen's mind that Canaris was part of the sloppy conspiracy against *der Führer*, a conspiracy made up of military men left over from the toppled Weimar Republic. These men were crippled by their loyalty to the old ways, the Christian ways, the weak ways. Their conspiracy was doomed to failure. But so far the conspirators had not made any serious mistakes. They had covered their tracks well; and since Canaris had not made any serious mistakes, few in Germany today were willing to speak out against him.

But in the coming months, Hagen knew, more and more people from all through the Reich would be willing to levy accusations against Canaris. The war was going badly. The Russians were pushing back German forces every day, recapturing cities with terrible speed; and when the war went badly, people looked for somebody to blame. If one had given reason to be singled out for this blame, one was in trouble. Canaris was living on borrowed time—and if Hagen knew it, then Canaris knew it, too.

So there was no reason to be nervous. Whatever questions Canaris had called him there to ask, Hagen could answer or not answer as he saw fit. The man would not dare push too hard, not at this precarious moment in his career.

And yet he *was* nervous. Canaris, all appearances to the contrary, was a devious man. He was also a capable one. He had escaped from a prison camp in Genoa, during the first war, by killing the prison chaplain, putting on his clothes, and walking out past the guards. And this, they said, had been the *second* prison Canaris had escaped from. The first had come two years earlier, in Argentina; Canaris had escaped by rowboat and horseback. He was a resourceful man, and it would not pay to underestimate him.

Hagen, who had killed his fair share of men himself, reached the top step of 72-76 Tirpitz Ufer. He took a moment to reassure himself again that there was no need to be nervous, then stepped into the shadowed foyer and received a security check from the guard in the booth on his left. The elevator was out of order. He was forced to clamber up the five flights of stairs. By the time he reached the high-ceilinged top floor, he was out of breath. He paused for a moment before proceeding through the great double doors at the end of the corridor. To be out of breath would reveal weakness.

After a few moments, he felt ready to proceed. He stood up straight, tugged the wrinkles out of his dark suit, and went to his meeting with Canaris.

Canaris, like Hagen, did not like to wear military regalia. Like Hagen, he wore an ordinary dark business suit. These men operated in a strata both above and to the side of standard military business. Like most spies, they tried to avoid calling attention to themselves.

As Hagen entered the office, Canaris stood behind his desk and offered his hand. He was a slight, short, unimpressive man who looked considerably older than his fifty-six years. His hair was thinning and gray, his shoulders narrow, his skin pasty and sagging. The only feature that betrayed his capability was his eyes. They were an incisive blue, and as Hagen reached out to shake the proffered hand, he could feel those eyes boring into him.

"*Herr* Hagen," Canaris said. His voice was soft, almost womanly, and weak. "My thanks for coming on such short notice."

Hagen grunted. He sat on one side of the desk while Canaris retook his seat on the other. The office around them was clean and unremarkable. One wall was covered with a map of the world. Underneath the map sat a black leather sofa, where Canaris was known to steal quick naps during his long workdays. On the wall opposite the map hung two framed pictures, one a Japanese-style portrait of the devil, the other a photograph of Canaris's favorite dog, a dachshund called Seppl. On the desk itself was the symbol of the *Abwehr*: a small statue of three monkeys covering their eyes, ears, and mouth.

See no evil, hear no evil, speak no evil.

"I won't waste your time," Canaris said briskly. "The *Führer* feels that with the continuing problems in Russia, it is time we begin to anticipate the possibility of an Allied landing on the continent. To do this effectively, I feel that we need to synchronize the efforts of our agents in the field. *All* of our agents in the field."

He paused for a moment to let the words sink in. Benign as they had sounded, Hagen realized immediately that there were at least two startling pieces of information contained in those three sentences. First was the admission that the campaign in Russia was truly troubled. Although this had been the overriding impression during the past few months, Hagen had not yet been told it so starkly by anybody in a position to know. Goebbels and his propaganda machine went to great lengths to make the troubles on the eastern front seem like only a temporary setback.

Second, and of more personal interest to Hagen, was the part about synchronizing agents in the field—*all* the agents in the field. The implication was that Hagen and his organization—what once had been known as the *Reichssicherheitshauptamt*, the RSHA, and was now known as the SS—had agents operating about whom Canaris was not aware.

It was, of course, true. Since the early 1930s there had been an ongoing feud between Canaris's *Abwehr* and Himmler's SS. Both had seen themselves as the primary security agents of the Nazi Reich, after the blood purge of June 1934 had smashed the SA, and both had engaged in a game of cat-and-mouse with each other as well as with the enemy. As time had passed, the two organizations had found ways to live with each other, however reluctantly. But Himmler had never given up hope that his organization would become the one true security organ of the Third Reich, the primary force responsible for "safeguarding the embodiment of the National Socialist ideal." Recently, in fact, Himmler had begun to keep even more secrets from Canaris. How else, except by maintaining his own cadre of loyal snoopers, could he prove that Canaris was involved with the conspiracy and remove him from his seat at the head of the *Abwehr*?

Hagen leaned back in his chair, keeping his face neutral.

"*Herr* Admiral," he said blandly, "I do not believe that I have any knowledge of agents in the field which you do not possess yourself."

Canaris smiled thinly. He nodded. Then he reached into his desk drawer, removed a file, and slid it across to Hagen. Hagen leaned forward and lifted the file open just enough to see the heading on the first page.

"I believe you trained this woman personally," Canaris said, "many years ago."

Hagen let the file fall closed again, frowning. The agent, who went by the code number V.1353, represented something of a sore spot for him. She had been one of the best he had ever trained, if not the very best, and he'd had high hopes for her. But then something had gone terribly wrong.

It had been back in the halcyon days of the Nazi party, when Hitler's star was rising faster than anybody would have thought possible and the future was filled with promise—the promise of acquiring unlimited *lebensraum* for future German generations; the promise of racial purity and the rightful return of Austria and the Sudetenland to Germany; the promise of not only shaking off the shackles of Versailles but of avenging them. Caught up by the optimism, and already conscious of the need to produce greater results than such competing agencies as the *Abwehr* and the SA, Himmler had sanctioned the training of several special agents. The agents would infiltrate Britain, America, Poland, Czechoslovakia, Denmark, and Holland. They were symbolic of how far the Third Reich would eventually reach, and they had been the best young Germans Himmler could find. They would not be dependent on anything except themselves. They would be able to operate with any weapon, to memorize intelligence at a glance, to improvise their way out of any situation.

And to train these agents, the best of the best, he had chosen Hagen personally.

Agent V.1353 had distinguished herself even among this impressive company. She excelled at the physical side of the game, learning how to kill with any blade, how to change identities when it was required, how to improvise complex strategies with little notice. Improvisation was her greatest strength; in her hands no natural opportunity, no matter how small, was wasted. She was also possessed of a great natural beauty and a way with people. In addition, she was very young—so young, to Hagen's way of thinking, that she was above suspicion.

They had planted her in America under her real name, but with a false background: the daughter of German Jews who would want nothing to do with Hitler's rising National Socialist party. She had found work with a naval architecture firm, and for eight months had sent back solid, if unremarkable, intelligence.

Then, abruptly, she had vanished.

It was easy to figure out what had happened. She had become scared. She had felt too much affinity for her adopted country. Perhaps she had fallen in love. She was only human, after all.

Hagen had sometimes allowed himself, over the years, to speculate that perhaps the appearance of this case was misleading. It was always possible that Katarina had stumbled onto some opportunity too tempting to resist that had required her to go deep undercover. If that was the case, she might not have dared to inform her own spymasters of her plans. If that was the case, it was always possible that she might someday reappear. . . .

More likely, however, she had simply lost her nerve.

Since Katarina's disappearance, the FBI had cracked down—visibly—on *Abwehr* agents in America. In 1941 they had rounded up every agent Canaris had placed there, tried them publicly, and hanged them. For the few RSHA agents who had remained at liberty, the message was clear enough. They scrambled home at the first opportunity. Since then Germany had enjoyed little success in penetrating America. They had agents in Mexico, but their effectiveness was limited by their distance. Canaris had sent a few more stragglers into New York, but they were frightened, unorganized, and clumsy, like everybody trained by the *Abwehr.* The only *truly* valuable agent still in America—agent V.1353—was no longer on the job.

"You remember?" Canaris pressed. "You trained this woman?"

Hagen nodded. "Of course I remember. She was my star pupil."

"According to the file," Canaris said, "she vanished in 1933. According to the file, she has not made contact since."

"That is true."

"You understand, *Herr* Hagen, how valuable she would be to us now if she were truly as skilled as the file claims. She has been in America for over ten years; she is thoroughly integrated. We would have many questions for her, if we could find her."

"I understand, Admiral."

"*Herr* Hagen, let me speak frankly."

Canaris leaned forward. His eyes, already pointed, became razor-sharp.

"I am aware that differences exist between our agencies," he said. "I do not wish to level any accusations. But I would not be surprised if certain facts available to the Gestapo were not immediately made available to me. Be that as it may, my only concern now is finding this agent. I have heard that you and she enjoyed a close professional relationship. And so I ask you—without requiring an explanation for why I haven't already been told, understand—I ask you now: Has this agent made contact with you during the past decade?"

"No, *Herr* Admiral, she has not."

Hagen was no longer feeling nervous. Now he was feeling irritated. Katarina Heinrich was a subject that reminded him of an error in judgment he had made more than a decade before. And Canaris's words contained many implied insults, no matter how judiciously he phrased them.

Along with the irritation, he felt disdain. Canaris made it sound as if he had a great personal stake in infiltrating America and discovering valuable information before the Allies attempted their invasion. But in truth he was against Hitler, as Hagen knew and would someday prove; he was a traitor. He was asking, Hagen was certain, only on the *Führer*'s personal orders.

"Do you think she could have made contact with anybody else during this time, without your knowledge?"

"No, *Herr* Admiral. I do not believe so."

"Do you know of any other agents in America, *Herr* Hagen, of whom I might not be aware?"

"No, *Herr* Admiral."

Canaris thinned his lips. He reached out and pulled the file back across the desk, then deposited it in his drawer.

"*Herr* Hagen," he said, "if you do come into possession of any information which may be valuable in this matter, I request that you submit it to me immediately."

"Of course, *Herr* Admiral."

"Or if you happen to recall some contact which you cannot, for whatever reason, recall at this moment—"

"There was no such contact, Admiral. To my regret."

"I see," Canaris said. He looked dismayed, but this, Hagen thought, was also an act. Beneath the dismay, he was pleased. Another thing gone wrong for the *Führer*. Another chance that the Allies would take care of Hitler without Canaris and his cowardly conspirators ever having to extend themselves.

The disdain washed over him again. He could hardly keep it off his face. "That is all, *Herr* Admiral?" he said.

"That is all."

Hagen rose, rapped his heels together smartly, and extended his right arm, held straight, with the palm facing Canaris. "*Heil* Hitler!" he said.

"*Heil* Hitler," Canaris answered, somewhat lackadaisically.

Hagen turned and moved toward the door. Before stepping out, he looked over his shoulder at Canaris. The man was bent over his desk, making a note.

Traitor, Hagen thought darkly.

What he would have given for agent V.1353 to be alive and operating in America, just so he could withhold that information from Canaris. What he would have given for agent V.1353 to resurface, priceless intelligence in hand, proving to one and all that his judgment had been flawless . . . proving that she really was the best of the best.

But he had given up hope long before.

Hagen faced front again and let himself out of Canaris's office.

CHAPTER THREE

HAM COMMON, SURREY
APRIL 1943

Rudolf Schroeder, alias Russell Webb, was a charming psychopath.

He sat in one of the rickety chairs in the damp, gray room, looking damnably comfortable. Except for the brief walks between his barracks and this chamber, he had not spent any time under the sun since his capture four months before, but his skin possessed the ruddy color that comes with natural good health. He had a handsome face, narrow in the cheeks and broad across the forehead, with a sharp hooked nose. His blond hair fell over the broad forehead in a curly lock. He smiled easily. His turquoise eyes sparkled. One would never guess, upon first acquaintance, that he was a psychopath; one would know only that he was charming.

Winterbotham sat in the chair across the table. Taylor was standing by the slit window, running the antenna of the suitcase radio out through the aperture. It was half past midnight, and they were preparing to make Schroeder's latest transmission to the *Abwehr* center in Hamburg.

Schroeder kept smiling at Winterbotham. The smile was making Winterbotham feel antsy. That, he guessed, was the point. He tried not to fidget, and, for the most part, succeeded.

On the table between them sat the AFU set with which *Abwehr* agents communicated with their home base. Beside the suitcase radio sat a variety of small parcels. Taylor had brought these gifts for Schroeder; he brought similar ones every time they met. To Winterbotham, it seemed as if Schroeder was a woman and Taylor his suitor. The parcels included chocolates, a carton of cigarettes, two paperback novels, several books of matches, and a bottle of adequate Scotch.

Schroeder popped one of the chocolates into his mouth and kept smiling at Winterbotham.

"Delicious," he said in his heavily accented English. "Andrew, you've outdone yourself."

"Only the best for you," Taylor said from the window.

Schroeder kept staring at Winterbotham as he chewed, and smiled. "Next time I'd like a plant," he said. "Some nice, hearty plant that could stay alive in my cell. I hunger for life. Could you do that for me, Andrew? A plant?"

"Perhaps I could manage it."

"A spider plant," Schroeder said. "Or—how do you call it?—a Wandering Jew." He grinned even wider.

Winterbotham felt an urge to lean across the table and put his fist through that grin. He restrained himself.

This was his third time meeting Schroeder, and he liked the man less with repetition. Schroeder was the worst kind of spy, one with no real allegiances whatsoever. He had been an aristocrat in Germany, the son of a wealthy hotelier, and had spent much of his life working in his father's business. He had been invited to join the *Abwehr* only half a year before, when things in Russia had been going well and Hitler had been turning his thoughts back to an invasion of England. He had joined up happily, promising to infiltrate the enemy—nobody, including Schroeder, seemed to have realized how quickly his accent would give him away—and then send back intelligence that would pave the way for an invasion.

As soon as he was caught, however, he had turned into a double agent without putting up so much as a token resistance. It really made no difference to Schroeder, Winterbotham knew, which side he was fighting on. To him the war was just another distraction from his pampered life. He seemed to enjoy his new role as a double agent even more than he had enjoyed his initial role as a spy: It was juicier. Right now he was dressed in prisoner's overalls, gray, and soft shoes with no laces. He wore the outfit with pride, as if it were a costume and he were an actor in a play.

Winterbotham hoped that Schroeder felt more kindly disposed toward him than he did toward Schroeder. There would come a time, after all, when he would have to trust his life to this man—in fact, they had reached it already. It was always possible that Schroeder and his masters had worked out a system of signals that was still unknown to MI-5. A certain letter inserted into a Morse code message might indicate that everything that followed was false information. Or a tiny hesitation during the transmission, a missed beat or half beat at a certain time. All it would take was one clue that Taylor and his friends had overlooked . . .

Schroeder kept grinning at him.

Taylor finished with the antenna, came back to the table, and switched on the transmitter. He spun the dial, finding the arranged frequency. Schroeder himself would key the message back to Hamburg, with Taylor watching closely to make sure he didn't play any tricks. Having Schroeder key the message himself was a necessary risk. A man's

Morse code style is as unique and distinctive as his fingerprints: If somebody besides Schroeder were to send the message, the Nazis would know immediately.

Finally, Taylor pulled up a third chair, reached into his briefcase, and produced a file. He passed it to Schroeder, who opened and read it, still chewing his sweets and looking bored.

"I've been busy," he remarked.

"You have," Taylor agreed.

Winterbotham had already read the file. It contained details of Schroeder's supposed discoveries over the previous two weeks. While working at his pub near the War Office, he had overheard two officers talking about a new anodizing process being experimented with by the navy. He had noticed increased numbers of servicemen on a train line that terminated in the vicinity of Portsmouth. And, most striking of all, he had approached for the second time a hoary old professor who had been spending a lot of time at the pub lately. Said professor seemed extremely disenchanted with his work for Military Intelligence. With permission from the *Abwehr*, Schroeder would now proceed to the next step—broaching, with this professor, the subject of spying for the Germans.

"I must say," Schroeder said, "that I'm rather pleased with my success. I must be something of a hero in Berlin these days."

Taylor lit a cigarette and offered a dry smile.

"If only it were true," Schroeder said. "Imagine the reception when I returned home. Imagine the women!"

He launched into a dissertation on the women in Germany, who were, he felt, the most beautiful in the world. This segued into a story about one of his last nights in Hamburg, spent at the Valhalla Klub in the red-light district. The Valhalla Klub was famous for its system of telephones connecting the tables. When one saw a young woman of whom one felt enamored, one simply picked up the phone and placed a call. In Schroeder's case, however, the women had been taking the initiative and calling *him*. He had always fared well with women. One time, he and three friends had spent a weekend in Venice . . .

Winterbotham listened with half an ear. He was waiting for the correct moment to spring his surprise on Taylor. Ten minutes remained before they made contact with Hamburg. He decided that the time was right. He cleared his throat.

"Andrew," he said.

"Hm?" Taylor said absently.

"A figure like you've never seen," Schroeder said. "*Mein Gott*, this one . . ."

"Perhaps I should be mentioned by name in this report," Winterbotham said. "Perhaps he should ask for information on the whereabouts of my wife. If he were to find that she were still alive, that could be a strong motivating factor for my treason."

Schroeder paused in mid-boast. He and Taylor both turned to look at Winterbotham. For several seconds, nobody moved; then the German took another chocolate and popped it into his mouth, chewing slowly.

"Harry," Taylor said. "May I have a word with you outside, please?"

They moved a dozen feet down the concrete hallway. Taylor stopped. He looked at Winterbotham with icy eyes, then said: "What the hell was that?"

"It makes perfect sense," Winterbotham said. "I go into the pub every night and drink a few pints and talk about my wife. Schroeder gets an idea. If he were to find that she is alive, somewhere, that would provide a strong incentive for my—"

"For Christ's sake, Harry, what do you think you're doing?"

"Only trying to be helpful."

"If you're trying to be *helpful*," Taylor hissed, "do me a favor, old chap. Take it up with me in my office in Whitehall. Not in the presence of an enemy agent. Not ten minutes before we broadcast!"

"It just occurred to me."

"Like hell it did," Taylor said.

"You must admit—"

"You've had this idea in your head the whole bloody time, haven't you?"

Winterbotham said nothing.

"You've had this idea in your head the whole bloody time," Taylor said again. He had become incensed to the point of repeating himself.

"Andrew—"

"I'll tell you something, Harry. I'll tell you something right now. This is the greatest secret of the war. The greatest goddamn secret of the war. And we're not going to jeopardize it for one man, no matter how much he might miss his wife. And you've no goddamn business pulling this on me, either. Not here, not now. No goddamn business."

"Andrew—"

"Oh, now I see. Now I see. How could I not have seen it before?"

"You make it sound as if I planned this."

"Next, no doubt, you'll threaten to withdraw your cooperation if we don't play along."

Again, Winterbotham said nothing. That was precisely what he planned to threaten next. That was why he had waited to make the suggestion—so that the months already spent arranging the ploy, training him, developing him in the eyes of Hamburg, would be on his side. They *could* cut him loose now, he knew, and start developing some other story involving some other disenchanted Military Intelligence agent, but it would set them back.

"Good bloody Jesus Christ," Taylor said, disgusted.

"If you'll just take a minute to think about it, you'll see that it makes perfect sense."

"What makes perfect sense is the story that six of Military Intelligence's top strategists have spent the past three months putting together. The one—"

"The one that has me betraying my country for a few shillings? I don't think so," Winterbotham said. "If the Nazis check on me at all, they'll find that I'm not especially wanting for funds. They'll smell a rat. And since I'm the one who's going to be putting myself in danger, I'd like a story that stands up. Now, if Schroeder were to tell them that I'm worried about my wife, and they were able to find her alive, and he were able to dangle that in front of me as bait, *that* would be a motivation for treason."

"Harry—"

"Yes?"

"We both know that Ruth is dead."

"I know no such thing."

"The chances—"

"If they check and find that she's dead," Winterbotham said, "then Schroeder simply offers me money. But he starts by looking for his strongest move. You've got to admit, Andrew, it makes sense."

Taylor opened his mouth, then closed it again. He shook his head. His mouth opened and closed several more times, impotently. His face was beginning to return to its usual shade of red.

"Goddamn it," he said, "you're right. It does make sense. Why didn't you suggest this sooner?"

Winterbotham shrugged.

"Never mind, I know why. Because now we're stuck with you."

"You think the worst of me, Andrew."

"Christ, but you put me in a bind, Harry."

"I don't mean to."

"You sure as bloody hell do. Now, come on. We've got ten minutes for me to clear this before Schroeder goes on the air."

Ten minutes later, they were sitting in the dank room again, Schroeder and Taylor wearing matching headphones. Schroeder, who had set aside half of his box of chocolates and was smoking a cigarette, had just sent a burst of Morse identifying himself to Hamburg. Now they were waiting for acknowledgment and the order to proceed.

Taylor had hastily rewritten the message Schroeder would send, after receiving a reluctant OK from his highers-up at the War Office. Now the message identified Harry Winterbotham by name. It mentioned that his wife, called Ruth, had vanished in Warsaw in 1939. It suggested that if she were alive, she could be dangled as very effective bait in front of this man. It requested an update on her circumstances, if at all possible.

Schroeder had read the new message without comment. Then he had given Winterbotham a tight, knowing smile, followed by a small nod. Winterbotham hadn't liked that. It was a bit too familiar.

Taylor was pacing endlessly around the small table. "I hope you know what you're doing," he muttered. "Good Christ, I hope you know what you're doing."

Winterbotham, sitting calmly at the table, smoked his pipe and held his tongue and looked for all the world like a man at peace.

LOS ALAMOS

"You're not dressed," Richard Carter said.

His wife lay sprawled across their bed, one hand draped over her forehead. She inclined her head a few degrees, looked at him, and said: "I'm not feeling very well, Richard."

Concern immediately creased his face. He moved toward the bed, crouched beside her, and placed his palm on her temple. The skin was warm and dry. He frowned, turned his hand over, and left it there for a few moments.

"I don't think you've got a fever," he said then.

"I'll be fine. Go on and have a good time. I just want to lay here."

"Maybe we should bring you to the infirmary. Just to make sure."

"I'm fine," she said. "I must have had too much to drink last night, that's all. Just go on. I'll see you when you get back."

"I'll stay here with you, if you like."

"No, go. Go."

"I wouldn't mind—"

"I just want to sleep, Richard. Please go."

The frown was replaced by a look of hurt. He stood up; his suit flapped with the movement. The suit was two sizes too big for him. It looked ridiculous. He stood by the side of the bed, undecided, in his ridiculous suit. She had to resist an urge to scream at him: *Go! Just go!*

"Really, truly," she said, mustering a weak smile, "I just want to sleep."

"Well . . ."

"Go, Richard."

He hesitated for another moment, then nodded. "I'll stop by the infirmary and ask them to bring over some aspirin, if you like."

"You know I can't stand it when you push, Richard. I just want to sleep."

He bristled. "All right," he said. "If that's what you want. Sleep. I'll see you when I get back."

"Have a good time," she said.

"Feel better," Richard said, and turned to the door. Before stepping out, he looked back at her one more time. She had rolled over to face the wall, showing him her back.

It was the last time Richard Carter ever saw his wife.

He stepped out of the room, closing the door softly behind himself.

Catherine gave him ten minutes. She would have liked to have given him more, but time was of the essence—they would be gone for only a few hours, and the hunt would begin as soon as he got back and found her missing. By then she needed to have changed trains.

She counted the ten minutes without moving. Then she sat up, threw her legs over the edge of the bed, and dressed quickly.

It was a Saturday, and while work at Los Alamos did not stop on a Saturday, there was a certain laissez-faire attitude around the camp that weekend. Several of Los Alamos's residents, Richard included, were going into Albuquerque that night to have dinner at the new ten-story Hilton hotel. Rumors had been flying that Conrad Hilton himself was staying at the hotel, along with his glamorous wife. The residents of Los Alamos were not immune to the lure of celebrity. Even Oppenheimer, something of a celebrity himself, had spoken avidly at the previous night's party of the chance to meet the beautiful Gabor woman.

Catherine found her purse and then ran through a mental inventory one last time, to make sure she had everything she needed. The conclusion she reached was that while she had everything she could reasonably get, she was very far from having everything she needed.

Her chances were not good.

But she felt excited, even happy, nonetheless. As of this moment, Catherine Danielson Carter had ceased to exist.

But Katarina Heinrich had been reborn.

She found Tom Bradley sitting alone in the canteen, eating a sandwich and drinking a cup of coffee. Tom, one of the theoretical physicists at Los Alamos, was smitten with her; Catherine had seen it clearly in his myopic eyes. He was a mousy little man with thick glasses, barely twenty-four, and would never dare to approach her. But that was fine. She could approach him.

She had expected to find Tom Bradley left behind—socializing was not one of his strong suits. She had, moreover, depended on it. Tom was one of the lucky few at Los Alamos who enjoyed the unsupervised use of his own car. It was a military staff car, a Studebaker, deep black with flared fenders. Tom made frequent trips to Oak Ridge, Tennessee, where some other part of this project was going on—Catherine wasn't exactly sure what—for which he served as some sort of liaison.

She moved to the table, smiled disarmingly, flipped her hair, and took a seat.

"Tom," she said, "what are you doing here, eating all alone? Didn't you want to see the new Hilton?"

Tom blushed. He put down his sandwich awkwardly and tried to return the smile. The thing his face made was closer to a grimace.

"I had an idea," he mumbled. "I wanted to check it out in the lab."

He was unable to meet her eyes as he spoke. He leaned slightly away from her, as if she were exuding some terrible heat. She felt touched, and a bit heartened. If Tom was so overwhelmed by her beauty, then maybe Fritz would react the same way. Ten years had passed, but she still had an effect on men. One tended to forget, living with an ancient husband like hers, that one could still have an effect on men.

"That's a shame," she said lightly. "I was hoping you could give me a ride somewhere."

A tendril of desiccated lettuce clung to his mouth; he wiped it off self-consciously. "A ride?"

"Just down to the station at Santa Fe. I wanted to run and catch up with my husband. I wasn't feeling well, you see, so I told him to go on ahead, but now I'm feeling better. And I'm just dying to see that hotel. It sounds marvelous."

Tom licked his lips. "I'd be happy to give you a ride," he said.

"No, no, not if you're working. I was just hoping—"

"I'd be happy to, Catherine." His blush had deepened.

"Really?" she said. "It wouldn't be too much trouble?"

"I'll take you all the way to Albuquerque, if you like. My idea isn't so important that it can't wait."

"No, don't be ridiculous. If you could get me to Santa Fe, I'll just hop on the train."

"You might have to wait awhile, this time of day."

"Well," she said, "it's a chance I'll have to take. I do want to see that hotel."

"I couldn't leave you stranded in Santa Fe, Catherine. Let me take you to Albuquerque."

"No, that's ridiculous."

"Please," he said, blushing furiously now. "I'd really like to. I'd like to see that hotel myself, now that I think of it. I could use a break."

"What about your idea?"

"It can wait. It'll probably work out better if I give it some time to settle."

"You're sure?"

"Sure," he said, grimacing wider than ever. "Sure I'm sure. You ready now?"

"Anytime," she said. She reached out and put a hand on his knee and squeezed softly.

As the sun went down, they were just leaving Santa Fe.

Tom drove slowly and carefully, both hands on the wheel, staring straight ahead. Between the poor quality of the road and the poor quality of the tires—rubber was scarce these days—driving required most of his attention. Above them, stars were starting to glimmer through the gloaming like precious stones scattered carelessly on dark velvet.

Catherine sat in the passenger seat, one hand inside her purse, touching the scissors there and trying to prepare herself to commit murder. She had not intended to use these scissors as a murder weapon. She had brought them along only so she could cut her hair, at some point. But now . . .

It was a stroke of luck, Tom insisting on driving her all the way to Albuquerque. It meant she would have a car. Not just any car, but a military staff car. That improved her chances dramatically.

For Tom, on the other hand, it was not a stroke of luck. Quite the opposite. But Katarina Heinrich, trained by Hagen himself, would never have allowed herself to think of that; that was a product of living as Catherine Danielson Carter for so many years. She shut it off.

Tom Bradley had to die—because in her mind was the secret that could win the war.

The letter she had memorized read:

Albert Einstein
Old Grove Rd.
Nassau Point
Peconic, Long Island

August 2nd, 1939

F.D. Roosevelt,
President of the United States,
White House
Washington, D.C.

Sir:

Some resent work by E. Fermi and L. Szilard, which has been communicated to me in manuscript, leads me to expect that the element uranium may be turned into a new and important source of energy in the immediate future. Certain aspects of the situation which has arisen seem to call for watchfulness and, if necessary, quick action on the part of the Administration. I believe therefore that it is my duty to bring to your attention the following facts and recommendations:

In the course of the last four months it has been made probable—through the work of Joilot in France as well as Fermi and Szilard in America—that it may become possible to set up a nuclear chain reaction in a large mass of uranium, by which vast amounts of power and large quantities of new radium-like elements would be generated. Now it appears almost certain that this could be achieved in the immediate future.

This new phenomenon would also lead to the construction of bombs, and it is conceivable—though much less certain—that extremely powerful bombs of a new type may thus be constructed. A single bomb of this type, carried by boat and exploded in a port, might very well destroy the whole port together with some of the surrounding territory. However, such bombs might very well prove to be too heavy for transportation by air.

The United States has only very poor ores of uranium in moderate quantities. There is some good ore in Canada and the former Czechoslovakia, while the most important source of uranium is Belgian Congo.

In view of this situation you may think it desirable to have some permanent contact maintained between the Administration and the group of physicists working on chain reactions in America. One possible way of achieving this might be for you to entrust with this task a person who has your confidence and who could perhaps serve in an inofficial capacity. His task might comprise the following:

a) to approach Government Departments, keep them informed of the further development, and put forward recommendations for Government action, giving particular attention to the problem of securing a supply of uranium ore for the United States;

b) to speed up the experimental work, which is at present being carried on within the limits of the budgets of University laboratories, by providing funds, if such funds be required, through his contacts with private persons who are willing to make contributions for this cause, and perhaps also by obtaining the co-operation of industrial laboratories which have the necessary equipment.

I understand that Germany has actually stopped the sale of uranium from the Czechoslovakian mines which she has taken over. That she should have taken such early action might perhaps be understood on the ground that the son of the German Under-Secretary of State, von Weizsäcker, is attached to the Kaiser-Wilhelm-Institut in Berlin, where some of the American work on uranium is now being repeated.

Yours very truly,
A. Einstein
(Albert Einstein)

Catherine had also memorized the response, which was short, to the point, and utterly chilling. It read:

October 19, 1939

My dear Professor:

I want to thank you for your recent letter and and the most interesting and important enclosure.

I found this data of such import that I have convened a Board consisting of the head of the Bureau of Standards and a chosen representative of the Army and Navy to thoroughly investigate the possibilities of your suggestion regarding the element of uranium.

I am glad to say that Dr. Sachs will cooperate and work with this Committee and I feel this is the most practical and effective method of dealing with the subject.

Please accept my sincere thanks.

Very sincerely yours,
(signed) Franklin D. Roosevelt

It was the tone of the letter that she found most chilling. *Please accept my sincere thanks.* Polite, businesslike, and efficient—as they discussed building a bomb that could ravage Germany beyond her worst nightmares. If one of these bombs, exploded in a port, could destroy the entire port (and some surrounding territory), then what about a dozen? Or a hundred? Or a thousand? The Americans were working on something that could erase her people from the face of the earth. And she harbored no illusions that they would hesitate to use it.

Please accept my sincere thanks.

It could not be allowed to happen.

"Look at the stars," she said dreamily. Her hand, in the purse, was still touching the cool metal of the scissors. "I bet you know some things about constellations, right, Tom?"

He smiled without looking over at her. "I know a few," he admitted.

"Pull over, will you? Just for a second?"

He dutifully pulled the Studebaker over to the side of the road. Catherine quickly opened her door and stepped out, holding her purse. She walked a few paces off into the desert, scowling up at the sky.

"Catherine," he called. "You don't want to—"

"Come on, silly! Show me the constellations."

She didn't look back to see if he was following. After a moment, she heard his door open and close. He had left the engine running. She could feel him come up beside her. Around them, the desert stretched cold and bleak in every direction.

"Show me," she said, moving closer to him.

Tom seemed paralyzed by her proximity. He mumbled something, but his voice didn't catch. He cleared his throat and tried again. "There's Orion," he croaked, pointing.

She moved even closer so she could look down the line of his arm. She could feel a feverish heat coming off him. For a moment she felt pity—this poor, love-struck boy didn't know what he had gotten himself into. But she pushed the pity down. She slipped her fingers through the loops of the scissors and prepared to use them.

"It's beautiful," she said.

"And there's the Little Dipper. See?"

"Where?"

"There," he said. "Follow the—"

She slid the scissors between his fourth and fifth ribs, into his heart.

Tom stiffened beside her. He let out a small sound, more confused than hurt. She let go of the scissors and put her arm around his waist. She lowered him gently to the ground as he made a series of low noises.

He was still alive. His eyes, locked on her face, were baffled.

He doesn't know what happened, she thought. For some reason, the thought gratified her.

"Shh," she said.

It took nearly five minutes for Tom Bradley to die. Finally he sighed—a sigh of relief, she thought—and then he was gone, although his eyes remained open, his lips parted.

Catherine pulled the scissors from his torso and wiped them clean on his pants. As she was doing it a wave of nausea took her by surprise. She tried to ignore it. But it came again, and she was forced to spin around, away from the corpse, to vomit a stream of bile into the sand.

Afterward, she spat, disgusted with herself. The ten years spent as Catherine Danielson had left her soft. Fritz would never love her, not if she had really become so weak.

When she had finished spitting, she returned her attention to the body. She checked it professionally and found forty dollars in a wallet in the hip pocket, which she took for herself. Then she put her hands under the armpits and dragged Tom Bradley a few dozen yards into the desert. She deposited him in a shallow gully. They wouldn't find him until daylight, at least.

She returned to the car, breathing hard. The scissors went back in the purse, along with the money. She still had the taste of vomit in her mouth. She spat again, and then again, but couldn't get rid of it.

She slipped behind the wheel and lit a cigarette with shaky hands.

They wouldn't begin looking for her until midnight at the earliest. With luck, they wouldn't begin until the next morning. Richard would try to get immediate help, of course, but it was possible that he wouldn't be able to convince anybody of the seriousness of the situation right away. They would know that she and Tom Bradley had left the camp shortly before twilight, heading to Albuquerque. Perhaps they would assume that an illicit affair was involved. They both were young, she and Tom, while Richard was old. It seemed a natural assumption. But she couldn't count on it. Considering what was going on at Los Alamos, she had to be prepared for the worst.

She had a military staff car, with a gas tank almost three-quarters full. If she drove through the night, she could make good distance. The cover of night was appealing; driving for pleasure had been banned by the Office of Price Administration months before, and while the staff car might put off some questions, the fact that she was a lone woman would invite scrutiny. She could drive through the night, hide and sleep during the day, siphon some gasoline—it was strictly rationed, so buying more was not an option—and then drive again. At some point she would get rid of the car and change her appearance. She would prefer to avoid the trains, but she couldn't afford to dismiss the alternative completely. Before reaching New York and boarding a ship, she would need to change her identity and raise some money . . . but first things first. First she needed to get out of New Mexico, to put as much distance as possible between herself and Tom Bradley.

By the time she finished the cigarette, her hands were steady. She pitched the butt, then rolled the car back onto the road. As she did, she caught a glimpse of her eyes in the rearview mirror. They were wide and horror-stricken.

She stopped the car. She breathed, shallowly, in and out until she felt more in control. Then she checked her eyes in the mirror again.

They were sanguine.

She drove north. At Lamy she turned east. Ahead of her was the Texas Panhandle and, beyond that, Kansas, Iowa, Illinois . . . and, eventually, New York City. Then England, and Fritz.

CHAPTER FOUR

THE WAR OFFICE, WHITEHALL
MAY 1943

Taylor was on the phone when Winterbotham was shown into his office. He waved a hand, indicating that Winterbotham should sit and wait. Winterbotham did so. He forsook the deep red couch against one wall, settling instead into an armchair facing the desk. His stomach was a nest of writhing snakes; his eyes ached. He had slept even less than usual the night before, which meant not at all.

As soon as Taylor was off the phone, Winterbotham would find out whether his wife was still alive.

He had not been able to make himself go to Ham Common the previous night, when Schroeder and Taylor had gotten their answers over the wireless from Hamburg. He could not sit in that dank little room with those men—one an enemy, the other a strange kind of friend—while he heard this particular piece of news. What if he burst into tears? There would go the last tattered remnants of his credibility. Instead he had paced his flat, trying to read but ending up drinking. He had drunk every drop of whiskey he could find, to little effect. Then he had smoked his pipe until his throat burned and the sun came up.

All morning he had been moving about in a strange, surreal sort of fog. He had taken a bus to Trafalgar Square and then walked to Whitehall, relishing the fresh air. En route he had noticed that the flowers were in bloom, even in the midst of the wreckage from the bombs. This had transfixed him. There were more flowers in London than there had been for the past hundred years, he knew, and the bombs—irony of ironies!—the bombs were responsible. Nitrates from the burning shells had enriched the soil. There were purple crocuses everywhere he looked, and even *Sisymbrium irio*, the London rocket—more irony—which had not been seen in England since the great fire of 1666. In the aftermath of destruction, Mother Nature had once again proved her resourcefulness.

He had arrived at the War Office a few minutes early for his eleven o'clock appointment, and had been forced to wait with a dour secretary who refused to meet his eyes. But now the moment was imminent. As soon as Taylor hung up the phone, he would find out one way or the other. He felt on the verge of a nervous fit. Christ, but he was tired. . . . How long would Taylor remain on the phone? He was talking about sabotage of some kind, and it sounded as if it might go on for a while. Part of him hoped it did. As long as Taylor was on the phone, Winterbotham would still have a shred of hope. As long as Taylor was on the phone, he wouldn't know for certain that Ruth, his beloved Ruth, was dead . . .

Still more irony. That he should be sitting here, today, with his entire being focused on the question of whether Ruth was alive—Ruth, who, in the beginning, had not been to his taste whatsoever.

Her family, for one thing, had a long history on the music-hall circuit. Winterbotham had seen the vaudevillian strain in Ruth's blood on their very first meeting. He had stopped by her brother's flat—her brother, something of a rogue, had been a mate of Winterbotham's from the first war. Ruth had greeted him at the door with an unladylike hail of off-color quips at the expense of his impeccable posture, his tightly clutched umbrella, and his stiff upper lip.

She could be a maddening woman. But somehow it was her most maddening qualities that had, over the years, come to captivate him so completely. The way she played the piano, for instance—speeding up and slowing down as it suited her, improvising entire passages in the midst of a piece. Reckless. The way she read the most shameless rags—*The People* was her favorite—and made no effort whatsoever to conceal it.

Taylor hung up the phone.

"She's at Dachau," he said.

Winterbotham felt his eyes prickling with tears. He reached up to wipe them away. Taylor pretended not to notice.

"The *Abwehr* is not exactly eager to trade her for your services, Harry, but they sounded open to the possibility. They instructed Schroeder to let you know that she's alive, and to demand some information immediately in exchange. If the information checks out, they'll move on to the next step—arranging a *treff* and giving you their own once-over."

Winterbotham nodded. He was digging through his pockets, looking for a handkerchief.

"Here," Taylor said.

He looked up. Taylor was offering him a sky-blue hanky. He took it and dabbed at his eyes.

"You all right, old chap?"

Winterbotham nodded again, handed the handkerchief back, and sat up straight in the chair. "Very well, thank you," he said.

"It's good news, Harry. But you know that it doesn't necessarily mean anything. The chances that they'll really exchange her—"

"I understand."

"Nevertheless, I'm glad for you, Harry."

"Yes," Winterbotham said. Then, very suddenly, he began to weep. Taylor fidgeted in his chair, embarrassed. He held the handkerchief ready, but Winterbotham was beyond that; his face was glistening with tears. There was nothing for Taylor to do but wait, eventually trying to seem busy with a stack of memos sitting on the desk.

Finally Winterbotham dried up a bit. He sniffled, wiped his hand across his nose like a schoolboy, and smiled. "I'm sorry," he said.

"No need to apologize."

"Not very curmudgeonly of me."

Taylor laughed, a genuine laugh. "That's the good news," he said after a moment. "There's also bad."

"Go ahead."

"It doesn't involve your case directly. But indirectly, it may have some bearing."

"I'm listening."

"Something of an emergency has come up," Taylor said. "We've been told to assign it top priority. Chances are it will shake out before Schroeder sends his next message, two weeks hence, and so it won't interfere with the rendezvous. But if by chance it's not taken care of by then, we'll have to continue to give it top priority. In that case, your assignment may be put on the back burner."

"Can I help?"

"I hope so," Taylor said. "For this one, old chap, we can use all the help we can get."

"Thirteen days ago," Taylor said—he was standing, now, looking out the tall window behind his desk and smoking a cigarette—"our American friends seem to have lost something of some value. They want us to get it back for them."

Winterbotham, still seated in front of the desk, was filling his pipe. It was taking him longer than usual, as his vision was still somewhat blurred.

"By the way, Harry, I hardly need mention that what I'm about to tell you is classified."

"I think from now on I can assume it."

"Very good," Taylor said. "Are you familiar with the phrase *chain reaction*?"

Winterbotham shook his head.

"I wasn't myself. It's a scientific term. I can't honestly say that I understand it very well. It has something to do with molecules, elements and such. Seems these elements are capable of giving off bits of energy when they smash together. Each tiny piece of element has a tiny bit of energy to give off. A chain reaction is a phenomenon in which one tiny piece of an element gives off its energy, thereby forcing the other tiny pieces nearby to give off their energy, thereby forcing others nearby to do the same, et cetera. The point is that it all happens nearly instantaneously, so a very large amount of energy ends up being created. That's the theory, anyway."

"I suppose I'm following."

"When I say a very large amount of energy," Taylor said, "I'm referring to an *extremely* large amount of energy. Enough to wipe London off the map, or at least to put a good solid dent in the East End."

Winterbotham got his pipe going and puffed out two smoke rings, both imperfect—he was still distracted. "A bomb," he said.

"Just so. A bomb. The Germans are working on it, and so are we. Or, I should say, so are the Americans. They've got all their best scientists squirreled off in the desert somewhere over there, slaving away. From what we know, we're well ahead of the Nazis. Hitler, as you may be aware, has his own ideas about science. He thinks Einstein's theories are a lot of nonsense. He insists that relativity is a Jewish idea designed to befuddle the Aryan mind. Such thinking has interfered with their work on the bomb . . . although they're getting past that, now, as reality sets in. In fact, we believe they're on the right track. They're just not terribly far along."

"Thank God."

"Yes. But there's a problem, Harry."

"There always is, isn't there?"

"Hm," said Taylor. "Yes, I suppose there is. But this one is greater than most. It seems the Yanks have suffered something of a security breach. A young woman, the wife of one of their scientists, has disappeared from their laboratory. They believe she may have had access to some vital blueprints and technical data regarding their research on the bomb. What she may have is not enough to let the Germans make their own; the Yanks don't even have theirs working yet. But if she were to deliver her information to the Nazis, the race could become neck-in-neck. And that, obviously, is something we'd like very much to avoid."

"Who is she?"

Taylor turned away from the window and faced him.

"We know exactly who she is. Her name is Catherine Danielson Carter—Carter because she married Professor Richard Carter, one of the scientists who is working on the bomb. She came to work for Carter in 1933, in Princeton, as his maid. Her mother, who died in 1925, had known Carter at school. After two years he proposed. They were married. Except we have reason to believe that Catherine Danielson was not really Catherine Danielson at all."

"I'm afraid you've lost me," Winterbotham said.

"Let me explain. Before coming to work for Carter, Catherine Danielson worked at a naval architecture firm in New York City, a place called Owen and Dunn. It just so happens that at the same time Catherine left to pursue her new job, another employee of the firm vanished. Her name was Katarina Heinrich. A German immigrant who arrived in New York in 1932."

"Vanished?"

"Without a trace. She had no family in the States, nobody who cared enough to try and track her down. But now we know that it wasn't really she who vanished; it was Catherine Danielson. Katarina Heinrich murdered her and took her place. Carter wouldn't have known the difference. He hadn't seen Catherine since she was a child."

Winterbotham took a long drag from his pipe. His head was spinning. Whether this was from the tobacco, the lack of sleep, the news about Ruth, or what Taylor was saying, he wasn't sure. "Murdered," he repeated.

"Absolutely. Two days ago, the FBI matched some fingerprints of Catherine Danielson's, taken from Los Alamos, with records of Katarina Heinrich's prints from her days at the naval architecture firm. They're the same person, beyond any doubt. The only thing we don't know for certain is whether Heinrich was trying to get out of the game when she replaced Danielson or if she was just looking to go deep undercover. Whichever—the secrets she found at this laboratory were evidently too tempting to resist. She took them, and she ran."

"Can't the FBI locate her?"

"They're trying. But if Katarina Heinrich is who we think she is, she's been very well trained. Which brings me to the next part—the reason we think that we're in a position to catch her for them."

"Go on."

"One of the spies we've been using at Double Cross is a man named Fritz Meissner. He entered England before any of Canaris's spies—in 1932."

"The same year Katarina Heinrich arrived in America."

"Precisely. Both entered foreign countries under their real names, and both were placed before the *Abwehr* was in the business of exporting spies. Meissner, who has been fairly cooperative over the past decade, insists that he was one of a kind. He's told us that he was working for Himmler and was trained by a man named Hagen. A real horror, this Hagen—an ex-Brownshirt—the kind of glorified thug who does so well in Hitler's Germany. He's Himmler's right-hand man now in the Gestapo. In any event, until now we've believed Meissner that he was a unique case. But now, with what's happened in America, we're thinking that perhaps he has been less than honest with us. Perhaps there were several spies trained by Hagen under Himmler's guidance, shipped out to various countries around the world. Perhaps Katarina Heinrich was one of them. That would explain the naval architecture job in the first place, and would also shed some light on why she chose to vanish in 1933. She saw that the *Abwehr* agents beginning to arrive in America were clumsy, and had no desire to go down with them. So she removed herself."

"But you've no hard evidence to link the two of them?"

"No hard evidence. But one tantalizing clue. Meissner began to receive letters last year—three letters, all arriving within the space of two months. Of course, they came directly to us. They were from New Jersey. They were signed with the name Anna Wagner. Meissner told us that Anna Wagner was a woman he had met in Germany in 1928, a married woman who had moved to America with her husband. He swore that the letters meant nothing. They seemed to bear him out; they were filled with affectionate drivel and, as far as we could see, no intelligence or anything of that sort. Nothing to raise suspicion."

"Perhaps they were in code."

"We gave them a good looking-over, Harry. If they were in code, it was a masterful job. They seem to be just what Meissner claims—love letters from an old flame. But now, with Catherine Danielson's disappearance, we're thinking that perhaps we dismissed them too hastily."

"You think she'll come to him with her secrets about the bomb."

"It seems like a fine chance. Assuming she has managed to board a boat without the FBI knowing about it, her choices are limited. She may try for Lisbon or Madrid, but there's a rule in the spy game, Harry:

The more valuable a piece of intelligence is, the more perishable it is. If Heinrich knows what she's got, we don't think she's likely to take the chance of getting hung up in some neutral country. We think she'll come straight to England. She does seem to be an American, after all, to all appearances. And once she's here, she'll try to contact Meissner, whom she believes is still operating independently and is still in contact with Hamburg."

"And then she'll walk into your trap."

"Assuming, of course, that we're right about Meissner being her link to Hamburg, yes."

"Have you spoken with Meissner about this?"

"I'm heading over there this afternoon. I was hoping you'd come along."

"What about the letters he received?"

"They're trying to find them in records even as we speak."

"Where is Meissner?"

"He's in a safe house not so far away. Come along, and I'll show you."

The route from Whitehall led up, always up, to the Highgate section of north London. They passed through Waterlow Park, where antiaircraft guns, surrounded by sandbags, lay quiet under the sun; then through Highgate Cemetery, where such distinguished persons as George Eliot and Karl Marx slumber away for eternity, mindless of the Nazi bombs.

"We choose the highest possible points for our safe houses," Taylor explained. "Those are the points that the spies themselves would seek out; wireless contact is much easier with height. There's no real way, of course, for the Nazis to know exactly where the signal is coming from, but we go to great lengths to achieve—"

"I know," Winterbotham said. "The appearance of truth is vital."

"It helps keep us sharp, anyway. Every time I go to visit Meissner, I see what he would see if he were actually at liberty. It keeps me on track when I draft the reports he sends back to Hamburg every week."

"You're his case officer, then."

"Yes."

"But you told me he's been in England for ten years. And you, Andrew, only began to work for Military Intelligence fairly recently, right?"

Taylor gave him an odd, slanted half smile. "As a matter of fact, Harry, I was MI-Five long before I ever took the job at the university."

"What?"

"Thought you knew me inside and out, eh? I may still have a few surprises left for you, old chap."

"Next you'll tell me you threw all those chess games in order to keep a low profile."

Taylor smiled wider. "Here we are," he said.

The house was a three-story Victorian of red brick, perched on the very top of a hill in one corner of Pond Square. They were met just inside the front door by a squat, thickset young Briton who looked to Winterbotham as if he had seen too many flicks about Scotland Yard. Taylor introduced him as Dickens, and they shook. The young man had a crushing handshake. Winterbotham could see the bulge of a gun in a breast holster beneath his tweed jacket.

"How's our guest today?" Taylor asked.

"Same as ever," Dickens said. "No lack of complaints with that one."

"What is it now?"

"Same as ever. Boredom. Claustrophobia."

"Let's see if we can't liven up his day," Taylor said.

They climbed a narrow, musty staircase, leaving Dickens standing guard by the front door. Winterbotham found himself not quite believing where he was or what he had just found out about Taylor. Games within games they were playing, here; and him without any sleep; and

Ruth alive—alive!—in Dachau, and he with a chance to get her back, if he played his cards right; and a spy in the room above them, keeping secrets; and another spy crossing the ocean at that very moment, secrets in tow. Secrets within secrets, games within games—it boggled the mind.

Another heavy-set young man was sitting by a closed door on the second story. He was holding a thin novel—Conan Doyle, Winterbotham saw. The man stood as Taylor came off the top step, and looked as if he were about to salute.

"At ease." Taylor smiled. "Harry, this is Alf. Alf, Harry Winterbotham."

Alf nodded and grunted. Winterbotham nodded back.

"Who's that I hear?" said a voice from behind the door. The English was crisp and perfect. *Ten years,* Winterbotham thought. *Ten years spent living in this country. A spy who is now spying on his spymasters. Games within games. Secrets within secrets.*

"Come on," Taylor said in a low voice. "I'll introduce you to the feather in Double Cross's cap. We'll see if we can't shake the truth out of him yet."

Fritz Meissner was extremely tall and thin, pale, with receding blond hair and prominent blue veins in his temple. He lounged on a bed by an open window, enjoying the fresh spring air, smoking a cigarette. When Taylor and Winterbotham entered the room, he turned his eyes to face them—no other part of his body moved. There was something insolent in the man's demeanor, something that Winterbotham found extremely distasteful.

"Fritz!" Taylor said brightly. "I hope we're not interrupting."

"Interrupting?" Meissner said. He smiled. "God forbid. But it's not your usual day, Andrew. To what do I owe the pleasure?"

"I wanted you to meet a friend of mine. Fritz Meissner, Harry Winterbotham."

Meissner brought his cigarette to his mouth and took a laconic drag. "Pleased to meet you," he said.

"The pleasure's mine," Winterbotham said stiffly.

"I've brought you some things," Taylor said, and handed Meissner a package he had carried from the car.

Meissner immediately dug through it, lining up his treasures on the bed: a carton of cigarettes, matches, chocolates, a bottle of vodka, and a copy of *Esquire* magazine. He held the last up and examined the cover, where a leggy, hippy Varga girl was posed seductively. He looked pained.

"Andrew," he moaned, "what are you trying to do to me?"

"All the way from America, Fritz. Take good care of it—soon enough the American censors will put a stop to it."

"You'll make me crazy," Meissner said. But he took the magazine and added it carefully to the pile on the bed.

There was one chair in the room; Winterbotham took it while Taylor remained standing. For several moments they went through the rituals of lighting their various tobaccos. Meissner ignited a new cigarette from the butt of his last. Winterbotham puffed out a cloud of orange-flavored smoke.

Taylor said, "Perhaps it is a bit cruel of me. But you must admit, she is attractive."

"Hm?"

"The girl," Taylor said, nodding at the magazine on the bed.

"Ah," Fritz said. He looked at the Varga girl again, then nodded. "She's not bad."

"Just not bad?"

"I've seen better."

"Like Anna Wagner?" Taylor said.

Something flickered in Meissner's eyes. "As a matter of fact," he said, "yes. Anna Wagner, among others."

"Tell me about Anna."

"I've told you before, Andrew. Are things that lonely at home?"

Taylor smiled. "Tell me again, Fritz, if you don't mind."

"Anna," Meissner said. "Anna, Anna. So long ago, but I think I remember. A true beauty, Anna was. She worked in her husband's shop in Berlin—"

"What kind of shop?"

"A pastry shop."

"Go on."

"And she took a liking to me," Meissner said, "and I to her. We were friends, for a time. Then she and her husband moved to America. And that was the end of it."

"And suddenly, after ten years, she wrote to you."

"Mm," Meissner said.

"Why do you think she waited ten years, Fritz?"

Meissner shrugged. "Perhaps that's how long it takes for a wife to become bored enough of her husband to start thinking of old love affairs."

"She wrote to you three times in two months. Then she stopped again."

"Yes," Meissner said.

"Why is that, do you think?"

"Andrew, you ask too much of me. Who could understand the mysteries of women?" He looked at Winterbotham and grinned a sly grin that spoke of male camaraderie.

"I suppose so," Taylor said. "But I should warn you, Fritz, that we are in the process of reexamining the letters you received from Anna Wagner. I sincerely hope that we will not find anything, of course. Because if we were to find something, that would mean that you've been lying to me. And we've known each other far too long to be lying to each other."

Meissner exhaled a cloud of smoke, seemingly unperturbed. "You won't find anything," he said, "except the sad words of a sad woman who wishes she had never let me go."

"Very good. That's all I wanted to know. Harry, do you have anything to add?"

Winterbotham shook his head.

"Then I suppose we'll be off."

Winterbotham stood, pipe clamped between his teeth, and followed Taylor to the door.

"Ah! One more thing," Taylor said, turning back with his hand on the knob. "Do you know the name Katarina Heinrich?"

"Katarina Heinrich?" Meissner said.

"Katarina Heinrich, yes."

"No, I don't think so."

"Right! Well, then, take care. I'll see you later in the week."

"Pleasure," Winterbotham said.

They left Fritz Meissner sitting on his bed, looking after them with a slight frown tugging at the corners of his mouth.

"What do you think?" Taylor asked.

"He's lying."

"With any luck we'll find the proof in those letters. Then we can go back and confront him with that." Taylor pinched out his cigarette and tucked it carefully into his breast pocket. "I almost hope we're wrong. If she's got the same training that Fritz had, she'll be a handful."

"When do you expect she'll try to make contact?"

"It's been thirteen days since she went on the run. I would say she could reach England as early as next week."

Winterbotham nodded. "I assume you're watching the ports."

"As best we can. But there's an awful lot of cargo coming in from America these days, human and otherwise."

Winterbotham frowned. Even in his sleep-deprived state, he had begun to get a clear picture of the tasks before him. Getting Ruth back to England was the priority. But to do that, he would need to move farther ahead with his masquerade for the *Abwehr,* convincing them he had information of use to them. To do that, he would need Schroeder to continue brokering the deal. To do that, he would need the full support of MI-5. And to get that, he would need to help them clear their plate of *their* top priority: finding the Heinrich woman before she got her information back to Germany.

Besides, he reminded himself, *if she does get the contents of those blueprints to Berlin, and they do manage to build the chain-reaction bomb before the Americans, rescuing Ruth won't make any difference. We'll all be dead and Hitler's armies will be goose-stepping right down Downing Street.*

"Let's go have a look at those letters," he said.

"Very good," Taylor said. "Care to stop for a bite first? I've got a friend at the Savoy—"

"Now," Winterbotham said.

CHAPTER FIVE

NEWFOUNDLAND BASIN, THE ATLANTIC OCEAN
MAY 1943

The *RMS Queen Mary* sailed through the night.

Her cargo holds were stocked with timber, meat, sugar, fuel oil, explosives, powdered milk, diesel, steel, tobacco, and lead. Her cabins and decks were filled with people: merchant seamen, American servicemen, Catholic missionaries, women from the Red Cross, and a handful of brave civilians who were willing, for reasons of their own, to risk the roving U-boat patrols scattered throughout the Atlantic.

Sister Abigail Harbert believed that she had just met one of the nicer people on board the *Queen Mary*, a young woman named Eleanor Lewis. *Young woman* was not the fairest way to think of her, perhaps, since she was actually very close to Sister Abigail's age, but Sister Abigail considered herself to have been made wise and ancient by her devotion to Jesus. Eleanor Lewis, on the other hand, had not yet accepted Christ as her savior. But she was a brave and kind young woman nonetheless, and Sister Abigail believed that she might very well be able to convert Eleanor Lewis before they pulled into port six days hence, if she kept at it.

Eleanor was a pretty young woman with dark-brown hair cut short, a conservative style of dress, and a wet look in her green-gray eyes. That wet look, to Sister Abigail, encouraged sympathy. Eleanor always seemed on the verge of tears, even when she was telling a story as inspiring as the one she had just finished telling.

"My darling Al," Eleanor said, when Sister Abigail asked her why she was willing to risk the wolf packs roaming these black waters. "He was wounded in an accident last month—blinded when some G.I. threw his cigarette into a munitions dump. I got the letter two weeks ago and booked passage on the very next ship headed to England. Al needs me now. But I'm not sure he knows it. Do you know what he did? He said in his letter that we should break off our engagement. He doesn't want to burden me, he said, now that he's blind."

Sister Abigail clucked sympathetically. "He sounds like a fine young man," she said. "Has he accepted Christ as his savior?"

"Oh, I don't think he gives it much thought," Eleanor said breezily. "Although being blind, now, he may change his ways. I wish this boat could go faster, I'll tell you that. He sounded hopeless in his letter. Just hopeless. But blind people can live very productive lives. Why, I just read about a blind man who's doing his part for the war. I read about him in *Time* magazine. He joined the Signal Corps and taught them how to make emergency repairs in the dark."

"That's fascinating," Sister Abigail said. "He's very lucky to have a young woman like you as his fiancée."

"Oh, no, I'm very lucky to have *him*. He's wonderful."

It was this selfless devotion that had impressed Sister Abigail so deeply. In this day and age, it was rare to find women who were willing to devote themselves so completely to their husbands. Women these days played baseball and worked in factories and dressed in two-piece bathing suits. They cared little for the old values, the Christian values. The war was taking its toll in countless ways, ways that wouldn't even reveal themselves until the war was long finished.

But with a few more young women like Eleanor Lewis around, Sister Abigail thought, they all might get through this with their priorities intact.

The story Katarina had told was half true.

Eleanor Lewis did indeed have a fiancé named Al, and he had indeed been blinded in the war. But the incident had occurred at Guadalcanal, the result of a Japanese bullet. Al *had* sent a letter to Eleanor telling her that he wished to break their engagement because he didn't wish to be a burden; but he had done this from the San Diego Naval Hospital, where he had been recovering. Then he had gone home to Dennison, Ohio, where Eleanor had informed him that she would stick by him through thick and thin. Their engagement had been resuscitated, with a date set in June. Then had come a piece of good news from the doctor: Al had some hope, although slim, of regaining partial sight in one eye.

Katarina had learned all of this from Eleanor Lewis shortly before killing her.

Now Eleanor Lewis and Al Burke were rotting in the basement of Eleanor's small frame house in Ohio. Katarina had met Eleanor Lewis at the Palace Movie Theater in Dennison, to which she had gained admission with her last fifty cents. By then she had been desperate, and Eleanor Lewis had provided her with a way out. The fact that her fiancé was blind only made things easier. Had he been left alive, an alarm would have been raised and her new identity would have been compromised. But Eleanor had been only too happy to invite her to dinner that night to show off her wonderful, worldly, heroic, half-blind fiancé.

She killed Eleanor first. Eleanor was the one more likely to cause trouble, after all. Al was easy. He had tried to come to his fiancée's rescue and had tripped over her corpse.

Katarina wanted to be proud of what she had done. It had been resourceful; it had been effective; and it had been for the Fatherland. But thinking back on it, she felt nothing but disgust and shame.

She had killed a blind man as he lay sobbing over his fiancée's corpse.

The act had enabled her, at least, to book passage on the *Queen Mary*. She had discovered nearly three thousand dollars in an El Duelo cigar box underneath Eleanor's bed. Before boarding she had colored her hair, cut it into a bob, changed her wardrobe. She felt fairly certain that the FBI had no idea where Catherine Danielson Carter had gone. She believed that her chances of reaching Fritz in London were better than they had ever been.

And yet she was unable to take much pleasure from it.

She had gone soft, at some point.

It was distressing.

WOHLDORF, NORTH HAMBURG

A sleek staff Mercedes carried Hagen up a long wandering drive to a gabled mansion. As he stepped out of the car he saw a flicker of movement to his right—a man standing off to the edge of the porch, among the trees. The man glistened in black. After a moment, Hagen realized that the man was beckoning to him.

After another moment, he realized that the man was Himmler.

He smiled, as he always did when he saw Himmler.

"*Herr Reichsleiter,*" Hagen said. "*Heil* Hitler!"

"*Heil* Hitler!" Himmler said back.

He was an officious little man, Heinrich Himmler, who looked more like a banker or an accountant than like the head of the SS. Today he was wearing the black uniform of the Gestapo, with the death's-head insignia prominently displayed—he had wanted to frighten somebody, Hagen thought, or at least to intimidate—but on Himmler himself the outfit looked ill-fitting, several sizes too large. If one did not know what this man was capable of . . .

Hagen knew what this man was capable of.

Himmler, in Hagen's opinion, was both the primary architect and the greatest creation of the Third Reich. Hitler was fine as a figurehead, and priceless as an orator, but with his penchant for grandiosity and his lack of ability to make concrete decisions, he needed harder men to handle the day-to-day business of Nazi Germany.

Himmler, an ex-chicken farmer, was a hard man. Even better, his hardness was balanced, in Hagen's view, by a great natural sympathy and sensitivity. Hagen had seen this firsthand not so long ago, when Himmler had come back from a tour of the front lines in Russia. The *Reichsleiter* had witnessed the execution of a hundred Russian Jews there, including women and children. The sight had put him into a state of extreme nervous agitation—and Himmler was a man who prided himself on his lack of nerves. But he had demonstrated his immense capability as well as his boundless sensitivity by his reaction to the executions. He had instructed his SS to create more humane methods of execution, even going so far as to personally tender the suggestion of gas chambers.

They began to walk around the outskirts of the grounds without speaking. The mansion behind them was the epicenter of Germany's wireless receiving operation; two vast underground bunkers housed dozens of booths containing radio sets and trained signal receivers. It was an *Abwehr* headquarters, and Hagen wondered why Himmler had requested to meet him there, of all places. Now, as they strolled through the sparse forest on the mansion's eastern side, he realized that Himmler was waiting to gain distance from the house before speaking. Walls had ears, and Nazi walls had more ears than most.

The day was splendid, warm and dry, with a soft wind. Hagen found himself enjoying the walk. They moved for five full minutes without speaking, past a susurrous duck pond, into the fringe of the forest. Then Himmler stopped and looked back over his shoulder to make sure they had not been followed.

"From this place they can hear the whisper of men a thousand miles away," Himmler said quietly, "and yet, with all their equipment, they cannot hear us, here, within a stone's throw."

At forty-two, the *Reichsleiter* usually appeared his age, but today he seemed older. The skin under his bespectacled eyes was tight and shiny. His hair was unkempt. He had been awake all night, Hagen guessed.

"But they have their tricks," Himmler said. "Face away from the house when you speak. They have their tricks."

"Herr Reichsleiter," Hagen said, "you look tired."

Himmler waved a hand dismissively. "No time for sleep," he said. "Our enemies are all around us. They are within that mansion even as we speak, *Herr* Hagen. Do you doubt it?"

Hagen shook his head. "No, *Herr Reichsleiter*," he said. "I do not."

"They supply me with fresh evidence on a constant basis," Himmler said with a derisive curl of his lip. "Last night I received word that Canaris has a new trick up his sleeve. A British code-breaker who is willing to trade his services for the return of his wife. But had I not received word, would Canaris himself have told me? No. Never."

"He is not loyal," Hagen said.

"Fortunately, I was able to arrive before the message was transmitted," Himmler said. "I stood and watched myself as they received the man's terms. Canaris, I am sure, has his own plans for this man. No doubt they involve treason. He hopes to forge a direct link with the British, I suspect, so that he can negotiate a separate peace."

Hagen shook his head with disgust. Himmler glanced at him. A slight smile touched his eyes, but not his lips. "You have no fear of Canaris," he said.

"None at all, *Herr Reichsleiter.*"

"That is why you will be my agent in this matter. You will make yourself available to Canaris as the representative of the Gestapo in dealing with this man. You will make it clear that they have no choice but to accept your help. You will watch. And you will report back to me."

"I understand."

"It is possible," Himmler said, "that this is some trick of Churchill's. The man may only be posing as a traitor. If you find evidence to support this theory, you will not report anything to Canaris. You will report directly to me. I will decide how to best make use of the information."

"Yes, *Herr Reichsleiter.*"

Himmler looked satisfied. He pursed his lips, then looked at Hagen as if seeing him for the first time. "I forget my manners," he said. "How are you, my old friend?"

"I am as well as can be expected, *Herr* Himmler. And yourself?"

Himmler shrugged. "Weary," he said. "If only all our enemies were outside of Germany, I would be less so. I can appreciate fighting the enemy. But fighting our own . . ."

"Patience," Hagen said. "They will betray themselves."

Himmler, unconvinced, frowned into the sun. "Sometimes I think that we're already finished," he said slowly. "We did not move fast enough—or perhaps we moved too fast. Sometimes, old friend, I give up hope."

"You need rest, *Herr Reichsleiter.* That is all."

"Perhaps you're right," Himmler said. "But perhaps what I really need is to see Canaris dangling at the end of a meat hook."

"If you like, we could content ourselves with one of his dogs in the meantime."

Himmler brightened. "If only we could," he said, and laughed. "If only we could."

THE WAR OFFICE, WHITEHALL

Three men stood in Andrew Taylor's office, all leaning over a small stack of letters on the desk. One of the men was Taylor himself, smoking the remains of the cigarette he had pinched out after leaving Highgate; another was Winterbotham, who, for a change, had left his pipe unkindled. The third was David Smith, an expert from the Bletchley outpost of Military Intelligence, which was concerned with breaking enemy codes.

Smith, Winterbotham reflected, was what *he* was supposed to be—according to the fictions of Operation Double Cross. He was a chess master of considerably more talent than Winterbotham who had been drafted into MI, along with all sorts of other civilian geniuses at the start of the war. He had broken two important German codes so far, one a naval code, one a standby of the *Luftwaffe*. But he (and the rest of the geniuses at Bletchley) had been unable to find any codes in the short, simple letters that Fritz Meissner had received from Anna Wagner.

The letter that all three men were examining now, written in English, was typical of the lot:

Dearest Fritz,

I know I shouldn't be writing to you but I can't help myself. I dreamed of you last night. Why I should be dreaming of you after ten years I can't say, but it's happening. I spoke your name aloud and my husband asked me about it this morning. I told him you were a character in a radio show! I think he believed me.

Is there any chance that you think of me as much as I think of you? I'm sure you never think of me. I'm sure you're married by now to some nice English woman, and you probably have a family.

Deep inside, however, I haven't given up on you. I want you to know that. Even if you do have a family now, it doesn't mean that we could not give each other things that family does not give. I never expect to see you again, but please know that I'm thinking of you always.

With love,
Anna

"Hm," Taylor said, and took a long drag from his cigarette. "Rather purple," he decided.

"For a time I was intrigued by all the *I*s," Smith said. He was a slender, dark man with a perpetually knitted brow; he smelled, rather peculiarly, of brine. "See, here, how many sentences begin with the letter *I*? All but three. But if there's a pattern beyond that, I can't pick it out."

"Perhaps a hidden message that's not in code," Winterbotham said. "A secret ink?"

Smith shook his head. "The Nazis use three kinds of secret inks. All three use a ferrous-chloride solution in water for the decryption compound. We've tried it. The other possibility is a microdot: The message is reduced to the size of a postage stamp, then photographed through a reverse microscope. The negative is covered with collodion, and a hypodermic needle is used to transfer the information—now infinitesimal—to the paper. Another application of collodion smoothes down the fibers of the paper. But it is still visible to the naked eye—the size of the dot on a dotted *i*. Unfortunately, all of these letters have been examined and reexamined. There are no microdots."

"The messages must be here somewhere," Taylor said.

"Why must they be?" Smith asked.

"Because if they're not, it means that the woman we're seeking hasn't been in contact with Meissner. If that's true, we have no reason to think she'll go to him with what she has now. And if *that's* true, we're in trouble."

"Perhaps a message hiding in plain sight," Winterbotham said. "Perhaps the mention of a 'radio show,' or a 'nice English woman.' "

"We need more than guesses, old chap."

"I'm afraid you may not get more," Smith said. "Needing something doesn't make it any easier to find."

"A new ink?" Taylor suggested. "Something we haven't seen before?"

Winterbotham frowned. "You said that this woman severed communication years before sending these letters—if she was the one who sent them. Besides, she was never *Abwehr* in the first place. Why would she be the first one to use some new sort of ink? How would she get it?"

"If—"

"Quiet," Smith snapped.

They both looked at him, surprised. His brow was furrowed deeper than ever. He was holding one hand up to silence them, flaring his nostrils rhythmically, staring at the page.

"You've got it," he said then, and grinned, showing many carious, yellowed teeth. "You've got it. I'll be damned."

"Got what?" Taylor said.

"*It,* he's got *it*, that's what he's got," Smith said. "Not a new ink, but an *old* ink. An older ink than we would ever think to look for."

Winterbotham saw what he was saying; he grinned himself. "She's been out of contact for years," he said. "She wouldn't have the means to get *any* of their secret inks, let alone a new one."

"Especially not if she had really tried to remove herself from the game at some point," Smith said. He seemed genuinely thrilled—more at the pleasure of figuring out a difficult puzzle, Winterbotham thought, than at the service he had just rendered for England. "She must have gotten rid of whatever equipment she'd originally had long ago. She was forced to improvise."

"Improvisation is one of Hagen's emphases during training," Taylor put in.

"I'll be damned," Smith said again. "That's it. That's got to be it. Iodine!"

"What?"

"Iodine, God damn it, iodine!"

The ink used by Katarina Heinrich dated from the Great War. It was made from a solution of a common headache powder, Pyramidon, which could be purchased without raising suspicion at any pharmacy. The ink responded to household iodine, and as soon as Smith applied it to the backs of the letters, the men found themselves regarding the evidence they had been seeking.

The first letter contained information on the weather, including barometric pressure, temperature, ceiling and visibility, precipitation, and wind direction.

"She sent this one when the Nazi U-boats were busy off the coasts of New Jersey and Virginia," Taylor said. "They sunk a handful of Allied ships, all within two months; caused quite a stir. She must have been expecting a full-scale invasion at any time. Of course, the information would be of limited value, considering the time it would take to reach Meissner. Let's see if she came up with anything better."

She had. The second and third letters contained intelligence regarding an American ship-building plant in Kearny, New Jersey. Katarina Heinrich had included specifications on two destroyers under construction, along with brief descriptions of their blueprints. She had signed the letters with her code number: V.1353.

"She must have found work in the plant to get such details," Taylor said. "Rosie the Riveter indeed."

"Well, we've got her now," Winterbotham said. His mind was already turning ahead to the next challenge—arranging and keeping a *treff* with the *Abwehr.* If Ruth could hold on in the hell of Dachau for just another few weeks . . .

"We don't have her yet," Taylor said. "Don't underestimate her, old chap. Meissner may appear harmless these days, but he's one of the best I've ever come across, and she's of the same breed."

"We know where she's going, and roughly when. It's just a matter of laying a trap."

"And springing it," Taylor said. "Don't forget springing it."

He lit a fresh cigarette from the butt of his last.

PART TWO

CHAPTER SIX

LONDON
JUNE 1943

The air-raid sirens were blaring again.

Clive Everett could hear them from his spot in the Piccadilly Circus Underground station, even above the murmur of people all around him. He could also hear the regular thud of antiaircraft guns, the hoarse shouts of emergency workers, and the high-pitched insectile drone of the *Luftwaffe* planes themselves—although the latter may have been only his imagination.

The bombs had started up in force again, Clive knew, because the Allies had been bombing the hell out of Germany lately in order to soften up the Nazis before the inevitable landing of troops. These German retaliatory blitzes, he thought, were just sour grapes. Still, he was not unthankful. He had met more women crouched in Underground tube stations over the past two years than he had met for the ten years preceding. All the young men in England had been sent off to foreign lands, leaving the slightly older men (like himself) in what Clive considered a rather enviable position.

Right now he had his eye on a young woman who was crouched only a few feet away from him. He could see, in the flickering light of somebody's torch, that she seemed on the verge of tears. He could also see the swell of her breasts beneath her dress. She was about thirty, he guessed, relatively full-figured, really quite beautiful. Best of all, she looked utterly terrified.

He inched a bit closer. Somebody to his left was crying; he ignored it. He reached the young woman, put a hand on her thigh, and said, "It'll be okay, love. Sour grapes, that's all it is."

The woman sniffled and looked up at him. "Sour grapes?" she said.

"That's the way I see it. Uncle Adolf's upset because it's finally come around to him. So he sends it right back around to us."

"Bloody right," somebody behind him said.

"Sour grapes," somebody else said. "That's just about right, isn't it? Sour grapes. That's all it is."

The phrase moved through the huddled masses—*sour grapes, sour grapes, that's all it is.* This was the way it always was when the bombs started falling. Everybody was scared, and everybody was forced to huddle together and wallow in their terror, and so everybody looked for courage wherever they could find it. Sometimes it was a group singalong; sometimes it was a communal turn of phrase. Clive felt a quick flash of pride at having provided this particular turn of phrase and having it picked up so quickly, but he pushed that aside. He wanted to concentrate on the young woman in front of him, who was, he could see now, not just beautiful, but exquisite. Her hair was short and dark, her face high-cheeked and lovely, her eyes a spectacular greenish gray.

"I'm frightened," she said.

"Hush, love, it's okay. Come here, let Clive give you a squeeze. There you go."

She huddled up against him; he could feel her quaking through a thin layer of cotton. He squeezed tightly.

"My home," the woman said, and sniffled again.

"What's that, love?"

"It's gone," she said. "My home is gone. I was at the market—I heard the sirens—I was nearly home and I saw the bomb—I saw the bomb that—one more minute and I would have been inside—"

"Shush, love," Clive said. "It's all right."

"My h-h-h-h-*home*—"

"It's all right," he said. "Everything will look better in the morning. Believe old Clive."

"But . . ." she said. The words were lost in a fresh wave of tears. The woman swallowed. Her throat clicked. She tried again. "But where—will I spend—tonight?"

Clive smiled.

"Never fear, love," he said. "I've got plenty of room."

Clive Everett lived in the Highgate section of London at a confluence of streets called Pond Square. Along the south side of Pond Square (which was really more of a trapezoid than a square, and which had not been home to a pond since 1860) stood rows of modest houses, Clive's included. Along the north side were larger houses of red brick, including the three-story Victorian that was home to Fritz Meissner.

Katarina stood at Clive Everett's bedroom window, listening to his stertorous breathing—he had finished the sex in record time and promptly fallen asleep—and looking across Pond Square at the three-story Victorian.

Fritz may be there, she thought.

But if so, he was not alone.

She had learned this yesterday, when she had first located the address. It had taken only a half hour of surveillance to establish that shifts of guards were turning over in the three-story red brick Victorian. Two would arrive, two would depart. She had seen the first turnover immediately after arriving, then had gone wandering around the block and come back in time to see another. They were Military Intelligence. She could see it in the jumpy way they looked around, in the way fresh men were delivered by automobile. Never bicycle, always automobile. Who did they think they were fooling?

Her?

Was this a trap set specifically for Katarina Heinrich? Or was it part of some greater deception played by the British on the *Abwehr*? This would not have surprised her. The *Abwehr* were fools. The British, even with their jumpy looks and their glaringly obvious use of automobiles, could have turned the entire network of Nazi agents in England, and the *Abwehr* might not have caught on.

In any event, the house had obviously required more surveillance than she could reasonably give it from the street. So she had turned her attention to the neighboring homes and had noticed the fortyish, foppish man who lived across the way—Clive Everett, even now slumbering noisily on the bed behind her—who dressed snappily, eyed the young ladies lecherously, and evidently considered himself something of a rake.

Contact had gone flawlessly, thanks to a few helpful bombs lobbed by her own country.

Now she had some decisions to make.

The first was whether to kill Clive Everett while he slept.

A ridge of concentration creased her brow.

Clive had told her that he worked in a post office. It seemed reasonable to assume that if he were not to show up for work, somebody might investigate. But would they come right away, or would it take a day or two? If she waited to kill him, on the other hand, how long would it take for him to suggest she find someplace else to go?

Trap or not, Fritz or not, Military Intelligence or not, she was going into that house. She had traveled halfway across the world to deliver the secrets contained in her mind. The shortest and final leg of her journey was at hand, but it would be the most difficult. To achieve it she would need access to the *klamotten*—the AFU suitcase radio set used to contact Hamburg—that was likely inside the house across the way.

Or was it?

The place was crawling with British Military Intelligence. Fritz had clearly been compromised. But if it all was part of a greater deception, perhaps the AFU set was there anyway. Perhaps Fritz was sending regular intelligence back to the *Abwehr* under the watchful eye of MI-5. Katarina knew that Morse code signals were as uniquely identifiable as fingerprints. If they had turned Fritz and hoped to use him effectively, they would have needed to keep him alive.

There was the chance, of course, that he had refused to cooperate. If that was true, he would be dead. But then why keep the house under watch with their rotating two-man teams?

To catch me, she thought. *Because they intercepted my letters. Because they know I'm coming here.*

It was possible, she had to admit, that she was stepping into a trap. But as far as she could see, she had no other options. Fritz and the AFU may have been inside; if they were, she would get to them. All the MI agents in England wouldn't stop her.

She kept looking at the house. It was dark and eerily still. How many of them were in there? How were they armed? Where were they located? How did they communicate with one another?

Part of her wanted to go and do it right then—slip in that night, kill them all, find Fritz and the AFU. During her walk around the block, she had spied several possible methods of entrance. The rear of the house featured a bow window topped by a pierced white balustrade.

There was also a straggly oak that had grown up on the house's left, close to the roof and the top floor. And, of course, there was always the front door. The front door was risky, but then this entire enterprise was risky. She had done well over the past few weeks by taking risks. Taking risks made one unpredictable.

But a wiser part of her felt that another twenty-four hours of surveillance would greatly improve her chances. If she could watch all through the coming day, she would be ready to move by the time night fell.

Behind her, Clive let out a snore. She turned to look at him.

Clive liked her. He would let her stay through the day, she believed, if she seemed appropriately distraught at the loss of her fictional house. Perhaps she would have to sleep with him again . . . but that hardly mattered. Twenty-four more hours of surveillance would be priceless.

She turned again to look at the house. Fritz. So close, but so far away.

I can handle ten, she thought. *Perhaps twelve.*

If there are less than a dozen men in that house, they die tomorrow night.

THE WAR OFFICE, WHITEHALL

"There's no way she's getting past eight men," Taylor said.

"You're the one who warned me not to underestimate her."

"And I meant it. That's why I've wasted eight of our best agents on a job that requires only four. It's not like you to be overdramatic, Harry. MI-Five must be casting its spell."

"Not overdramatic. Cautious."

"But hardly realistic."

"You're also the one who told me that this case has top priority."

"It does, of course. Unfortunately, the day-to-day business of Military Intelligence doesn't grind to a halt as soon as a top-priority situation arises. The war stops for no man. Or woman, as the case may be."

"If she gets past us—"

"If she gets past us, you don't get your chance to play hero," Taylor said. "And, incidentally, we lose the war and eat sauerkraut with schnapps for the next thousand years. Harry, you're not thinking straight. Look at it this way: You've already done your part in helping us capture the Heinrich woman. Truth is, you've been invaluable. But there's no need for you to concern yourself any more. Have you memorized all the information you'll be giving during your rendezvous?"

"The *treff* hasn't even been arranged yet. That's—"

"But when it is, you may have a short time. Take my advice, old chap, and focus yourself on that."

Winterbotham sighed. He reached for his pipe and found himself patting an empty pocket in his vest. He had decided to quit the pipe shortly after hearing that Ruth was alive; he had also decided to quit drinking. The strangest part of it was that the past night, for the first time in longer than he could remember, without his vices and despite heavy bombing, he had slept from dusk until dawn without waking once.

"I just want to make sure that this doesn't go wrong," he said, "so that I *do* get my chance to do my part."

"Harry . . . go home. Get to work on your codebooks. Leave the Heinrich woman to us."

Instead, Winterbotham went to Highgate.

He rode his bicycle. This was only his fourth time on the bicycle since the start of the war, but upon waking that morning he had felt so refreshed, so infused with energy, that he had found it irresistible. He felt as he had during the first war, when he was a boy of twenty-five pedaling messages from trench to headquarters and back again, legs pumping faster and faster, drawing on a limitless supply of power. He wasn't quite twenty-five again, but he felt like a man of forty, or even thirty. When he climbed hills, he half stood on the bicycle and dug into the work with relish.

Keep it up and you'll lose weight, he thought, and smiled to himself. It was about time he lost some weight. How he had kept it on as long as he had, eating just turnips and potatoes and the occasional scrap of meat, he didn't know.

The light had turned golden by the time he reached Pond Square. The scene was bucolic; the bombs had not fallen there. He felt a brief stab of foolishness at having come so far to find everything so calm and quiet. Why, he had taken Taylor's warnings too much to heart, hadn't he? A single woman could not get past eight trained men no matter how capable she may be. Taylor had been right—MI-5 was getting to him.

Nevertheless, he pedaled his bicycle directly to the front door of the three-story red brick Victorian, dismounted, and knocked twice.

Dickens answered—same squat build, same tweed jacket, same bulge in the breast holster.

"Afternoon," Winterbotham said. "Remember me?"

"Taylor's mate," Dickens said, frowning.

"Didn't he tell you I was coming?"

"No, sir, I can't say that he did."

"Ah! He's flighty sometimes. The drink takes its toll. I've come to help keep an eye on Meissner. I understand he's expecting company."

"Yes, sir, we're expecting it. But we're fully prepared to—"

"Perhaps you should invite me inside, Dickens, so we don't call too much attention to ourselves."

Dickens's frown deepened. He nodded shortly, and stepped aside so Winterbotham could enter.

"Sir," he said, "I should tell you that we're—"

"Eight men on the premises, Dickens?"

"Yes, sir. Including myself."

"Arranged how?"

"Two on the first story, front and back," Dickens said. "Four on the second. Two on the top story, front and back."

"Meissner is in his room?"

"Always in his room, sir."

"It seems to me as if you could use one more pair of eyes," Winterbotham said. "Outside, covering the approach."

"The men on the top story are covering the approach, sir."

"Very good, very good," Winterbotham said. "Well, it may be some time yet, eh, Dickens? Look here, old chap, do you play chess?"

It was a position Clive Everett had never found himself faced with before—he had, in his house, a beautiful woman who didn't want to leave.

She was cooking dinner. He sat at the small table in his kitchen, admiring her buttocks through her cotton dress and watching her work. The smells coming from the stove were not bad at all, considering what she had to work with. And she looked every bit as beautiful in the light as she had looked in the gloom of the Underground tunnel. He was almost tempted to keep her around for a few days, if not longer. But that, of course, wouldn't do. The neighbors would talk. Also, the woman did not seem to possess a ration book of her own—not, at least, that she had mentioned. These were trying times. He could not afford charity these days, not even in exchange for the best sex of his life.

Also, she was smoking. Smoke frayed his nerves.

He gathered his courage.

"Catherine," he said.

"Mm?" she said. She was bent over a chopping board, working on some onions. The knife in her hand flew over the vegetables, dicing them finely. Perhaps she was a chef of some kind. She had told him that her husband had died in the war, but that was as far as they had gotten with personal details.

"I know you said that you couldn't bear to go back to your house today," Clive said, "and I understand that. I understand that completely. Yet I can't help but wonder . . ."

He paused, hoping she would spare him the task of finishing the sentence.

"Wonder what?" she said, and set down the knife long enough to take a drag from her cigarette.

"Er, wonder," he said. "Wonder when you think you may go take a look and see how bad the damage is. What I mean to say is—"

"Perhaps tomorrow," she said. "If I feel up to it."

"Er, yes. But the problem is, well . . . did you salvage anything from the house? Anything at all?"

"Oh, damn," Catherine said. An ash had fallen onto her dress; she whisked at it with her fingers.

"A ration book, perhaps?" Clive said. "You did mention that you had been at the market."

She turned and gave him a smile. "I was in such a panic. I don't know what happened to it."

"Yes, yes, of course," Clive said. "Well, let me try to put it another way. And I despise myself for saying this, dear Catherine, please believe me. But we're living in a very difficult time right now, and it's especially difficult—"

"Clive?" she said.

"Yes?"

"Are you asking me to leave?"

"Oh, God, no, of course not," Clive said. "Well, in fact, perhaps, as a matter of fact, I would possibly like to have, er, some rough idea . . . rough idea of when . . ."

She was moving toward him, still smiling, the knife in one hand, the cigarette in the other.

"Catherine," he said, standing to meet her, smiling in return. "You are beautiful. But these are difficult times, my love. You must recognize that."

"Of course," she said. "I don't mean to be a burden."

"I'm not asking you to leave, Catherine. Not at all. I'm just wondering if perhaps you've some idea, some very rough idea, of when you may . . ."

She was drifting up to kiss him, now. He pulled away. If he kissed her, he would lose his resolve. And one could not afford in this day and age to lose one's resolve. These were difficult times. He had done the woman a favor the day before, after all, giving her a place to stay, a warm bed, his companionship. But it could not be allowed to continue. And if she kissed him . . .

"Clive," she murmured.

"Catherine, please. I can't—"

"I'll leave tonight."

"Tonight?"

"Tonight," she said, and slid the knife into his chest between his fourth and fifth ribs, puncturing his heart.

Winterbotham woke with a start.

He sat up, and the chessboard on his lap spilled to the floor.

For a moment he didn't know what had woken him. The house was dark; he had slept away the dusk. How did you like that? Three years of terrible insomnia and suddenly he was drifting off at the drop of a hat. In the middle of a game, if he remembered correctly. Dickens had proven to be a far sharper player than Winterbotham had initially assumed. And where was Dickens? That was what had woken him, he realized; Dickens moving. Dickens had moved—where? To answer the door? Yes, there had been a knock at the door. And now . . .

Dickens came into the room again. He was holding a torch, which shone for a second into Winterbotham's eyes, blinding him.

"God damn it," Winterbotham said.

"Sorry, sir." The light veered away.

"Somebody at the door?"

"Just a volunteer nurse, sir."

"A volunteer nurse?"

"Looking for clean linen. They say the planes may come this way tonight."

"Hm," Winterbotham said. He was still blinking the sleep out of his eyes. The chess pieces had scattered all over the floor, he realized. He got down on his hands and knees—not as easy as it once had been; he grunted loudly—and began to gather them together by touch.

"Need some light there, sir?"

"Why don't you turn on some real damn lights and just pull down the blackout shades?"

"Sorry, sir. Taylor's orders."

"God damn it," Winterbotham said again. "What makes you think the darkness would work for you instead of for her?"

No answer from Dickens. Winterbotham let it go; he knew he was feeling crabby only because he was freshly awoken. He located the rest of the chess pieces, put them inside the board, and then stood, yawning copiously.

"What's the time?" he asked.

"Just past ten, sir."

"Seems I drifted off."

"Why don't you head on home now, sir? We're more than able to take care of things here."

Winterbotham couldn't help but feel tempted. These men were half his age; they weren't drifting off to sleep except in their own beds. They were armed and trained and ready. What good could he really do there, even if the woman did show up? Most likely he would just be in the way. Besides, there was food at his flat. Not just turnips but half a beef pudding he had been saving. He had quit smoking and drinking; the least he could do was allow himself a half-decent meal.

"You're sure you can handle it without me?" he said.

"Quite sure, sir."

"If you're really sure, Dickens."

"Really quite sure, sir."

"All right," Winterbotham said. "I'll stop by in the morning."

"I'll be back at noon, sir."

"Thanks for the game, Dickens. You've a strong grasp of the opening."

"My pleasure, sir."

"Perhaps next time we can play through 'til the end."

"I hope so, sir."

"Good night," Winterbotham said, and went out with his chessboard under his arm.

Katarina watched the old fat man leave.

She was back in Clive Everett's flat, looking out the window. She was naked; she had been in the process of changing her clothes when she noticed the man leaving. It was a stroke of luck. It meant one less person to worry about.

She was fairly certain, after her day of surveillance, that there were between seven and ten men in the house—minus one, now. A variety of trees half obscured the view from her window, but she had been able, by consistently changing her angle of observation, to reach some fairly solid conclusions. There were two on the first floor—three, if you counted the fat one. She had verified this with her own eyes, just minutes before, when she had knocked on the door. There were at least three on the second floor, perhaps more. At least two of them were short and squat. One had a beard. Another may even have been Fritz himself, although it was impossible to be sure.

On the third floor, two more. Of this she was absolutely certain. They were watching for her, looking out the window at regular intervals—covering the approach, they would call it. But by covering the approach so assiduously, they had given away their own numbers and positions.

Since the one who had answered the door had been armed (pistol, breast holster), she would work on the assumption that all of them were armed. But since he had come to the door with the gun still holstered, she would also assume that they were sloppy.

She felt nervous.

After watching the fat man get on his bicycle and pedal away, she resumed dressing. She was putting on Clive Everett's clothes, which were baggy, which was good, and which were black, which was better. She carried no bag, but she held two knives, one in each hand, turned haft-up so that the blades lay flat against the insides of her wrists.

One was the knife with which she had killed Clive Everett. Both were household knives, poorly balanced, and not the perfect weapons for her purposes, although she had sharpened the blades earlier in the day. But she thought they would do the job, if only she could place them correctly. They would not leave her much margin for error.

Around her waist was a length of cord she had cut from a clothes-line in the backyard. The cord was not as dark as she would have liked, but it was thin and it was sturdy. It would fit very well across the staircase she had seen just moments before, when she had knocked on the door and asked for fresh linens.

Why was she so nervous? They were fewer than ten. It should not be a problem.

Panic is your worst enemy, Hagen had taught her.

She took a few moments to get control of herself. Shallow, steady breathing. She was about to risk her life. But she had risked her life before. She had gone into worse circumstances before, although they had been only training missions. There was no reason for this to go poorly . . . unless she panicked.

Suddenly she remembered the dream she had had the night before. The same dream as ever, with slight variations. Fritz was there, but he was wearing an RAF uniform; he had become the enemy, chewing on a Churchill-esque cigar. Clive was there, pawing at her, bleeding from the ears and the eyes. Hagen was there, ramrod stiff, barking out orders, the swastika armband around his bicep brilliant and crisp. And the gallows was there, as always, creaking in the breeze, beckoning . . .

Katarina put the dream out of her head.

There was no more time for thinking.

Now was the time for action.

For the Fatherland.

She knocked twice.

The nervousness tried to rise again, to blunt her edge, to make her weak . . .

No.

The door was opening.

The knife in her right hand turned over, the blade appearing from nowhere like a glittering magic trick.

He had his gun out.

Too late; no matter. The knife flicked across his throat and removed a shallow quarter inch of flesh, and then his blood was jetting into her face like a geyser.

She dropped and rolled left and forward, into the darkness. One more on this floor, to the rear. So far this kill had been silent. Dickens was teetering above her, not yet understanding that he was dead. Katarina took a moment to consider her options. Silent, it had been, absolutely silent, not so much as a gurgle—they still didn't know she was here—but which was more important, penetrating the house, staying in the darkness, or keeping the quiet? She decided to risk keeping the quiet. Instead of moving immediately forward, she took another moment to half stand, put her arms around Dickens's waist, and drag him inside. She laid him on the floor to the right of the door, then reached out and pushed it softly closed with one foot.

A light slashed across the room—somebody's torch.

"Ed?" a voice said.

The light and the voice were coming from the doorway that led to the rear of the floor. She circled, backpedaling, to her left, staying out of the beam. Her rear end bumped against a piece of furniture, but she kept moving, kept sliding, sidling, gliding, and by the time the beam of light had snaked around to the place where she had hit the furniture, she was behind the beam of light, behind the man. Blood was in her eyes; she blinked furiously. This would be as easy as the one at the door had been. A strike from behind. The only question was, ribs or throat? She preferred the ribs when at all possible, but—

He was turning around. The light hit the knife . . .

Instead of trying to draw his gun, he threw himself forward, grabbing for her knife hand. She cursed inwardly, let him get the hand, turned around the knife in the other hand, and tried to put it through his ear—except that he was already moving again. The torch hit the floor and rolled crazily; then they were on the floor together, grappling. God *damn* it, this was all she needed; she had lost one of the knives, and the man's weight was pressing against her chest. He was heavy, he was panting, and now he was punching her—a glancing blow to the temple—God *damn* it—she had hesitated—nobody's fault but her own—and these were the most valuable moments, the moments when she should have been stringing the line across the stairs—how much noise were they making?—God *damn* it, he was punching her again, connecting more solidly this time, and she could suddenly taste her own blood mingled with the blood of the man at the door.

You're panicking, she thought.

She turned off her mind. Let the body take over; let the training take hold. The man on top of her outweighed her by a hundred pounds. She had lost both knives now, somehow, and she was blind with blood. They were making noise, and her chances of penetrating the house successfully had gone down a thousandfold. But none of it mattered.

Panic is your worst enemy.

The man was holding her down with his left arm while his right rose to land another punch. Katarina waited until the blow was moving downward, then delivered an out-to-in cross block, openhanded, just as Hagen had taught her, catching the man on the inside of the right elbow. The blow was deflected; his arm buckled, and his own momentum sent him reeling forward. His hand struck the floor to the right of her head with a sharp *crunch*. She pretended for a moment that she was trying to wriggle out from under him. Instead of fixing his own balance, he threw his weight behind his base arm—the one holding her down—determined to keep her pinned.

It was his last mistake.

She struck three vital points in quick succession: throat, nose, temple.

The man was off her, then, lying on the floor and moaning. She grabbed his torch and swept it around until she had found one of her knives. She picked up the knife and killed the man on the floor.

She switched off the torch.

Breathing raggedly, now. They had made noise. The others would be coming to investigate.

Abort, she thought. *Abort.*

No. Now or never.

She reached the staircase with four huge strides. The cord around her waist came off. She had already tied slipknots on the ends; now she drew the cord tight across the highest step she could easily reach, the sixth step from the bottom, fastening it quickly to the banister supports, operating by touch.

A light flashed at the top of the stairs. She quickly retreated, found the man she had just killed, and patted him down until she found the gun in the breast holster. She held it in her right hand, switching the knife to her left. Her thumb clicked off the safety.

Footsteps coming down the stairs, now. Two pairs. Not calling out; they were being cautious.

This is not according to plan, she thought—she was thinking clearly, coolly, distantly. *This is not according to plan, but we will make do.*

The first one hit the tripwire and came down hard, crying out.

Katarina emptied the chamber, sweeping the gun from left to right, from the middle of the staircase down to the base. In the stuttering powder flashes she could see the man caught on the stairs dancing a crazy jig—hit twice, chest and shoulder, which would probably do the trick—and the one on the floor ducking and covering, his feet up over his head, reaching into his coat, upside-down, until a bullet opened the top of his head and splattered his brains against the front door.

She vaulted toward the stairs.

At least three more. She couldn't wait for them to come to her; she needed to take the initiative. Her most vulnerable moments would be spent climbing the staircase. This was supposed to have happened before they knew she was here. No helping it. She stepped over a body, slippery with blood, and then another one, which was still moving, making a thick sound in the throat—she would take care of him later—and then, thank God, she reached the top riser. There were no lights up there. Her side was stitching painfully—just a cramp, she didn't think she had been hit. Back to the wall, silent, breath wanting to rasp in and out, but no, silent, they were there—somewhere in the darkness—in front of her . . .

There.

A small sound three feet in front of her, one foot to the right.

She tossed the empty gun down the hallway.

As soon as it landed, the man in the hallway opened fire—*men* in the hallway, she saw, two of them. They immediately fired eight bullets at the empty gun sitting on the floor. By then she had moved to close with the nearer one. She kept his body oriented between herself and the other one, a human shield, and damn it, this was not looking so good, not if the two on the top floor were on their way down, but what was there to do? It was too late to turn back.

Katarina stayed *in-tight*, as Hagen had taught her, *in-tight*, drilling it into her head over and over again, stay *in-tight*, so the gun in the man's hand was useless. Her upper, middle, and lower quadrants moved in harmony; her free hand was pressed tightly to her chest, out of harm's way; she feinted, baiting him, classic knife-fighting, brought the knife back around all in one flowing movement, felt his arm in the way to block it, kept the knife moving, economy of motion, staying *in-tight*; he blocked again, and she salvaged the thrust, hitting his pectoral tendon and slicing through it; he cried out, and she opened his brachial artery; then she delivered six horizontal cuts to his face, throat, and forehead. By then she was backing up, and he was going down, and there was a problem here, a genuine problem, because her human shield was down and there was an armed man in the hallway with a gun pointed at her and nothing between her and him—

A door opened. She heard the thud of wood against flesh.

Fritz.

"Fritz!" she cried.

"Katarina?"

"Rückzug!"

She heard the door close. She could see nothing except the flickering afterimages of the gunshots. She put her back to the wall and moved down the hall. A warm mass on the floor. The man Fritz had hit. Alive. Breathing. She knelt down, sent her fingers roaming across his ribcage—

"Damn you," the man said. "Damn your—"

She put the knife between his fourth and fifth ribs. Twisted the blade. Stood up again. Light-headed. How many more? *Two,* she thought, *the two on the top floor.* What were they doing up there? Why weren't they down here yet? Cowards.

The tree, she remembered. *They can come down, come around the outside, come up behind.*

She felt her way in the darkness, found an opening in the wall, felt the shape of narrow stairs. She quickly backed up again and then stood, waiting.

Three minutes passed.

A terrible silence descended on the house. She could feel her pulse thudding in her wrist, in the hollow of her throat. Would they never come down? Cowards. Or were they scaling down the tree right then, coming in through the front door, sneaking up behind? She strained to hear. Perhaps she should forget them. Get Fritz and run. But no. The AFU would be up there. She would need to climb the stairs in the darkness to fetch it. Suicide.

Damn it, she thought. *Damn it all.*

She backtracked, found the nearest corpse, and realized that the gun was not in the holster. Of course not; he had fired when she threw her empty pistol. It was not in his hand either. He had dropped it when Fritz opened the door. Finally she located it a few feet away, in a pool of blood. How many rounds were left inside? She fumbled it open and checked by feel. Three bullets.

She listened. Were they still up there? Were they coming down? Or had they already come down, scaling down the tree? Were they coming up the stairs?

She couldn't stand there all night waiting.

She moved to the door and said, "Fritz. I'm coming in."

The years had not been kind.

She could see him in a shaft of moonlight: pale, emaciated, his hair thinning, his eyes small and frightened.

"Katarina," he said. He sounded awed. "You've come for me."

She stepped past him without answering and looked out the window. Half of the oak that led from the ground to the roof was visible, but no MI-5 agents were climbing down. She stepped back, casting her eyes around the dim room. *Improvise.* She spotted a glimmer: a bottle of vodka, mostly empty. She grabbed it.

"Katarina," he said again, "I thought that it was you they were waiting for. I prayed. But I never—"

"Shut up," she hissed.

She stepped out of the bedroom, took a few steps toward the staircase that led down to the first floor. Her foot landed in a tacky puddle of blood; she slipped, then regained her balance. She smashed the vodka bottle on the top step. Let them sneak up on her, if that was what they intended. Let them try.

She went back to Fritz's room. When she stepped in, he took her by the shoulders.

"I've missed you," he said, and leaned forward to kiss her. His breath smelled of tobacco and vodka.

"For God's sake," she said, pushing him away. "Keep your hands off me. *Verrat!*"

He shook his head.

"Ich bin ein Gefangener," he said.

"A traitor!"

"No, Katarina, it's not so. I had no choice."

"The junk," she said—the *klamotten*. "Is it here?"

"Upstairs, in the attic. They've forced me to—"

Something crunched in the hallway. Katarina pushed open the door, brought the gun up, aimed it at the staircase, squeezed the trigger. Her first bullet went high; the agent was crouched near the floor. Her second took him in the throat. She saw a gout of blood in the momentary illumination of the powder flash. Then darkness and the soft pattering of liquid onto the floor.

One man left. Upstairs?

She spun around again to face Fritz.

"Show me," she said.

"Up—"

"Show me."

He stepped out of the room, then hesitated.

"They're waiting up there," he said.

"No, they're all dead. Hurry!"

She could sense him moving off in the gloom toward the narrow stairs leading to the third floor. She moved up close behind him. He began to climb the stairs. She followed, two steps behind. One bullet left in the gun. She held it in her right hand. In her left hand she turned the knife around so that she was holding the tip between her thumb and forefinger, ready to throw. Not a well-balanced knife, but the only knife she had. Fritz had climbed four stairs now. Five. His head would be coming into the attic—

A gunshot.

Fritz was falling back onto her. She shoved him rudely up the stairs, and two more shots followed. His body jerked twice.

She slipped under him, past him, swiveling, finding her target, firing. At the same time, her left arm came around in an arc and the knife whistled out, following the bullet, *thunk*ing into a man's chest.

Fritz was making a gurgling sound.

She frowned down at him dispassionately.

He had turned weak. And he was a traitor.

But she waited for a few seconds until he was still before climbing the rest of the way into the attic. Somehow she felt she owed him that.

For old times' sake.

THE WAR OFFICE, WHITEHALL

Taylor finished speaking, paused for a moment, and then lit the cigarette he'd been holding. Cold morning light streamed in through the window behind him, pinning the smoke, freezing it.

Presently, Winterbotham said: "How far can she get?"

Taylor looked distressed. "Not as far as she already has, I would say. But her luck's finished now, Harry. We've got CID going door to door, barricades on every road out of the city, and agents watching every railway station in London."

"Have you spoken with the neighbors?"

"Nobody saw a thing, naturally, so we've still got no description since Los Alamos. OSS is working on getting a photograph from New York."

Winterbotham leaned forward. "Andrew," he said, "I was in that house yesterday. I was probably the last one to see those poor blokes alive." He hesitated. "A woman came to the door just before I left."

Taylor blinked. "You saw her?"

"No."

"You heard her?"

"No. But Dickens said she was a volunteer nurse looking for clean linen."

"Bloody hell. That's our bird."

The telephone on the desk chimed. Taylor picked it up, listened, swore, and hung up.

"CID found a corpse in the flat across the way. A man. Knifed."

Winterbotham nodded.

"Perhaps we can trace the path she followed," Taylor said, thinking aloud. "Find out where she met the man, follow her back from there . . ."

He stubbed out his cigarette.

"You understand, Harry, that this means the end of your assignment, at least for the time being. Now that she's seen Meissner in his safe house, the stakes are even higher. She must have gathered some idea of what we're up to here. If she gets in touch with Germany . . . Harry, we *need* Double Cross. We've already started planning the invasion. It depends entirely on deceiving the Nazis."

"So I won't be allowed to complete my assignment."

"Not while she's at liberty, no. I warned you of that before."

Winterbotham paused. Then he said, "How will she get her information to Germany?"

"She'll have to take it there herself. Oh, she could try to wire it with the AFU, but not if she's smart—and she is smart. She must know that if she stays on the air too long, we'll be able to track the signal. No, she would never try to wire everything she has. She'll make a brief contact and set up a meeting of her own."

"You've broken their codes. Can't you intercept her signal, find out where they'll be meeting?"

"It's possible. But don't forget, Harry, even if we did catch the signal, she's been out of touch with the *Abwehr* for a decade. Whatever code she uses, it may well be one we've never seen."

"How will they accomplish the *treff*? Rendezvous with a U-boat?"

"Or a seaplane," Taylor said. "Unless she tries to go through some neutral territory. But I doubt she'll be willing to wait that long."

"How many U-boats are lurking off the shores of England?"

"Not many, of course. The waters are filled with Royal Navy."

"So if *I* were to arrange a *treff* . . . and *she* were to arrange a *treff* . . ."

Understanding dawned in Taylor's eyes. "Good God," he said.

"We might both be instructed to rendezvous at the same place."

"Good God," he said again.

"Schroeder will be sending my sample intelligence in two days, Andrew. If it checks out, they'll arrange a meeting. And that will be at the same place you'll find Katarina Heinrich."

"It's possible," Taylor said. "Yes, it is possible."

"Even probable."

"Good God," Taylor said once more, and reached for the phone on his desk.

CHAPTER EIGHT

BENDLERSTRASSE, BERLIN
JUNE 1943

Hitler paced when he spoke. The more involved he became in what he was saying, the faster he moved. Now he was pacing around Canaris's office so quickly that he seemed to be bouncing from wall to wall. He was speaking just as rapidly, with small dollops of spittle flying from his mouth, and he was gesticulating with both hands so that his spotless gray tunic seemed barely able to contain the explosion of nervous energy.

"Geneva!" he sneered. "Geneva! The pleading of the weak. The trickery of the Jews. Geneva! What do we care about Geneva? Our hands will not be tied!"

Hagen, watching quietly from one corner, nodded to himself. He was in complete agreement with the *Führer*'s "Top Secret Commando

Order" of 1942, which dictated that any captured Anglo-American commandos were to be summarily executed without trial. "Under no circumstances," the Order read, "can they expect to be treated according to the rules of the Geneva Convention."

As far as Hagen was concerned, Hitler had no need to justify himself. War was war, and one did whatever was necessary to win. But several of the other men in the room—most notably Canaris, the traitor—were weak specimens, made nervous and guilt-ridden by the demands of battle. Hitler was taking the opportunity to give them a pep talk. Soon enough, Hagen thought, they would move on to the real purpose of Hitler's visit. The real purpose of the visit, from what he had gathered, was to talk about spies and the upcoming invasion. But the little Austrian corporal could not resist an opportunity for oration.

He flung his words directly at Canaris, who was standing behind his desk. There were two other men in the room. The fourth was von Hassel, sitting on the black leather couch and trying to look bored, as if the words could not possibly have anything to do with him. The fifth was Field Marshal Hermann Goering, who stood looking thoughtfully out the window.

Hitler was working himself into a lather; his voice was turning hoarse.

"We must have the *courage*, the *fortitude*, the *resilience*, the *strength* to strike without mercy!" Each word was emphasized with the smack of his fist into his palm, *smack, smack, smack, smack*. "We must not doubt ourselves! We must not cower! We must not turn back! We must not believe the lies of our enemies!"

Canaris was nodding wearily.

"A thousand years hence," Hitler said, "Germans will look to our conduct on this, our darkest day, as an example of our limitless strength and courage! Stalingrad is our finest hour, gentlemen; for it is there that we face adversity and triumph! We must not falter now! We must not hesitate to use every ounce of our ability!"

Now his hands flew around his head as he spoke, like startled birds. Hagen couldn't help but wonder if his *Führer's* health was suffering. The man was under extraordinary pressure, of course, not only from without but from within—his own generals and followers were always looking for a chance to seize power. But this was precisely what Hitler wanted; he encouraged dissension among his ranks. By keeping his followers at one another's throats, Hitler guaranteed that no given one would become too powerful.

And yet the furious, frantic motion of his hands spoke of more than pressure. It spoke of palsy. He was a man in poor health, and there was no disguising it.

"Soon the Allies will attempt their invasion!" Hitler cried. "Let them! Let them come! Let them charge to their own doom! After their attempt has failed, none will stand in our way! None will dare!"

Hagen felt his patriotism stirring.

"They will never set foot on European soil!" Hitler thundered. *"We will slaughter them on the beachheads! We will slaughter them on the oceans! We will send them to the bottom of the sea!"*

"*Heil* Hitler!" Hagen exploded.

"*Heil* Hitler!" von Hassel and Goering echoed.

"Mein Führer," Canaris said calmly, "it seems possible that the landing force may be too great for such optimism."

"Too great?" Hitler said. "One thousand American dogs are not equal to a single German soldier! The Americans are Jewish pawns! Jewish pawns! *Too great?* If they were ten times what they are, they would not be too great! *Too great?* If they were twenty times, or thirty—"

"And yet one must recognize," Canaris said, "the value of knowing where the invasion will come."

Hitler looked at him, his eyes sparkling.

"Yes," he said. "Of course. That is why we are here today."

"If it would please you, *Führer*, I will make my report now."

"Do so," Hitler said. As quickly as his harangue had started, it was over. He stood straight, hands clasped behind his back, and gave Canaris his full attention.

The admiral reached down, shuffled a few papers on his desk, and cleared his throat.

"Our intelligence from England," Canaris said, "is disconcerting. It suggests an attack within the near future—this year or next. A great number of troops are coming into England and, as we all know, a great number of bombs are falling on Germany."

Several of the men shared rueful smiles; they had had personal experience with the great number of bombs falling on Germany.

Goering did not smile.

"Cowardly behavior from a cowardly race," Hitler said.

"Of course, *mein Führer.* Yet militarily, their logic is sound. Even as the bombing lays the groundwork for their invasion, however, it reveals their intentions. The question that needs to be addressed is where—where will they come? If we can ascertain that, we have won the battle. And if we win this battle, we have won the war."

"Go on, *Herr* Admiral."

"As the Allies begin assembling their troops, we will likely hear of it from our agents in England. But we must take this information with a grain of salt. We must be prepared for an attempted deception."

"Churchill will come at Calais," Goering said from the window.

Hagen glared at him. He felt that he understood Field Marshal Goering, and his understanding led him to contempt. Goering's only concern when the invasion came would be getting his treasures, his jewels, his precious artwork out of Germany. Once he had been a soldier, even a hero, but time and gluttony had made him fat and greedy. He would not trouble himself overmuch with repelling the invasion. He was nearly as bad as Canaris—weak, self-serving, lazy. Why could Hitler, who saw so much, not see the incompetence of his own inner circle?

"*Herr* Admiral?" Hitler said.

Canaris shrugged.

"Calais is certainly the most obvious choice. Which is precisely why we need to be prepared for other eventualities. Dunkirk, or Normandy."

"They will never return to Dunkirk," Goering said. "They fled with their tails between their legs. Normandy? Normandy is ill-suited to attack. No, they will come at Calais."

"And yet," Hitler said. "And yet . . ."

He began to pace again, more slowly, his brow knit with concentration. The men in the room were silent, waiting. Hagen noticed that the *Führer* was displaying a slight limp as he moved. He wondered how bad Hitler's health had really become. It was rare, these days, for Hitler to come to Berlin at all—he spent much of his time in the *Wolfsschanze*, the Wolf's Lair, under reinforced concrete, while Allied bombs rained down on Germany. It would be possible, Hagen thought, for Hitler to become very ill indeed without anybody knowing; the vast majority of the German populace never saw him.

"*Herr* Admiral," Hitler said, "you have over one hundred agents in England, correct?"

"Yes, *mein Führer*."

"You are confident in their abilities?"

Canaris did not hesitate. "Regrettably, none of them enjoys my full confidence."

"Why?"

"The type of individual who spies, *mein Führer*, is a peculiar type. There is often a willingness to deceive, a lack of principle. Few have much allegiance to Germany . . ."

Hagen bristled. The irony of Canaris saying that, of all people . . .

"And so few are willing to risk injury to their own persons. They will not extend themselves as much as we may require. In many cases, we had inadequate time to conduct their training. And do not underestimate the psychological effect of having been behind enemy lines for so long. Many of them may be forgetting exactly where their allegiances lie."

"Worthless," Hitler growled.

"Not quite worthless. But perhaps not as dependable as we require."

"Shall we train more men? Paratroopers? Time is of the essence, and the British are no doubt wary."

"Perhaps there is another alternative, *mein Führer*. One of the last group—a man named Schroeder—has made preliminary contact with a man who works for British Military Intelligence. The man's wife is at Dachau. He has made it clear that he would be willing to offer assistance in return for the woman."

The room was momentarily quiet.

"Military Intelligence," Hitler said.

"Yes."

"That would be helpful."

"Yes."

"You trust this man?"

"He has provided sample intelligence already. It is accurate."

"Then we must secure his cooperation," Hitler said, "at any price."

"I agree, *mein Führer*. He could answer many questions for us."

"But perhaps it is a deception. Perhaps he still works for the British."

Canaris shook his head. "His intelligence conforms with the information we've gotten from our other agents. If he is lying, they are all lying. And I do not believe that is the case."

"Bring this man to me," Hitler said. "Where is he?"

"In London, *mein Führer*. In two days we will be making contact with Schroeder again. At that point, we can arrange a *treff*."

"Do so," Hitler said.

"Yes, *mein Führer*."

"Have his wife brought to Cecilienhof. We will show him that we are prepared to cooperate."

"I understand."

"Churchill," Hitler scoffed. "He cannot even keep his own subjects loyal. It will be his downfall."

Hagen, watching with cold eyes, said nothing.

WOHLDORF, NORTH HAMBURG

Two hundred miles northeast of Berlin, a young man was frowning as he listened to his radio receiver.

He was sitting in a soundproof room deep underground. He wore a pair of headphones, with which he monitored radio traffic to and from England. Twenty feet above, the summer sun shone brightly onto the mansion that stood atop this bunker, but down here the light was artificial and somewhat stale. The air was also somewhat stale, since the man was a heavy smoker. Smoking was not permitted, but the man smoked anyway—at twenty-two he had already developed a chronic, hacking cough.

His frown deepened as he reread the message he had just jotted down. It was in code of some kind, but the code was nothing he had ever seen before. The signal that had carried the message, on the other hand, was a signal he *had* seen before, many times. It was the weak signal of the portable suitcase radios, the *klamotten,* with which *Abwehr* agents communicated with Hamburg.

Perhaps I copied it wrong, the young man thought. He read it twice more but got no more sense from it.

He went to see the man in the next booth, and showed him the message.

This man was five years older, but he also had never seen the code before.

"That's what it is, though," the older man said. "A code of some kind. No doubt about it."

The younger man coughed. "Who could have sent it?"

"Let's ask Krupp. He'll know if anybody will."

They found Krupp in his own booth, listening to his own set of headphones. They showed him the message. By now they were attracting some attention; two other radio operators had appeared from their booths and were watching curiously.

"Know it?" the young man asked.

Krupp frowned, read it again, and shook his head. "I don't know it," he said. "But maybe Neumann will know it."

Neumann was the oldest man working at Wohldorf. He was nearly seventy, with grayish-white hair and a slightly stooped posture. When they went to his booth, they found him sitting with his eyes closed, either dozing or concentrating hard.

"Neumann!" Krupp said. "Got a riddle for you!"

Neumann looked up, then stood creakily and read the message. "It's one of the old ones," he said immediately.

"The old ones?"

"Before your time. Before Enigma. Before the war. Before any of it."

"Can you crack it?"

"Give me a second," Neumann said.

It took considerably more than a second. Finally, Neumann found an ancient codebook, moldy and pungent. He flipped through the pages while the group of younger men gathered around, excited.

"Go back to work," Krupp said, then disobeyed his own order and stood watching.

Another ten minutes passed before Neumann found the code. Then he translated the message, which took five more minutes. Finally he straightened as much as he was able and looked at Krupp with triumph in his eyes.

"Get me Himmler," he said.

HAM COMMON, SURREY

Rudolf Schroeder accepted the package, his lips quirking into a crooked half smile. His lean fingers began to pick at the string tied around the box. Then he paused and looked up at Winterbotham.

"Andrew will be jealous," he said.

Winterbotham smiled. "There's more than enough of you to go around, Rudolf, isn't there?"

Schroeder shrugged. He turned his attention back to the package and opened it delicately. He withdrew a box of candy, a bottle of Scotch, several packs of cigarettes. He immediately opened the box of candy, and his smile broadened.

"How did you know?" he asked.

"Intuition," Winterbotham said dryly.

The box was filled with white chocolates.

"Oh, so naughty," Schroeder said, delighted. He plucked a candy from the box, deposited it in his mouth, and commenced chewing. "Wonderful," he said. "Whatever it is you want from me, Professor, you've found my price."

They were sitting in the same room in which they had first met—dark, damp, draconian. Now, however, there was no AFU set on the table between them. And Andrew Taylor was nowhere to be seen.

Winterbotham had stopped by Latchmere House unannounced this evening, and requested an audience with Schroeder. He had backed up the request with his new alpha security clearance. He had made it clear to the guard that it would not be necessary to keep a record of this visit, and had then given the guard his best alpha-clearance scowl to drive the point home.

"The only other thing I could possibly require," Schroeder went on, chewing lazily, "is a plant. A nice plant to keep me company. Why won't Andrew bring me a plant, do you think? It's not as if I haven't asked."

"Perhaps he doesn't think it's a serious request."

"Why would he think that?"

"Something about a Wandering Jew?"

Winterbotham leaned forward, lowering his voice. "I think Andrew has a bit of that blood himself—somewhere down the line. Do you get that feeling?"

"Why, Professor!"

"I'm simply being honest."

"Professor!" Schroeder said again. "I don't know how I'm supposed to take that."

"Do you know anything of my politics, Rudolf?"

"A bit."

"So you should know that I'm not . . . *patriotic* . . . the way Andrew is."

"Mm," Schroeder said, and popped another chocolate into his mouth.

"In fact, I have sympathy for your cause. Do you believe that?"

"Do you mean the Nazi cause?"

"Is that your cause?"

"What do you think?"

"I think," Winterbotham said, "that we are free thinkers, you and I. Men first, and patriots second."

"Sounds selfish when you put it that way."

"Only honest."

"You're being very honest today, Professor."

"I'll take that as a compliment."

"Does Andrew know you're here?"

"Certainly not."

"Why *are* you here, Professor?"

"Because there are things we can do for each other," Winterbotham said, "of which Andrew would not approve."

Schroeder set aside his chocolates. He lit a cigarette and smiled a humorless smile. "I'm intrigued," he said.

"Tomorrow, Rudolf, you'll be making contact with Hamburg again, yes?"

Schroeder nodded.

"And if all goes well, they will arrange a *treff* with me."

"Yes."

"Do you imagine that you'll be a part of it?"

"I imagine so. They'll probably want me to serve as your escort."

"My thoughts exactly. So you and I, Rudolf, shall be off on an adventure together, correct?"

Schroeder shrugged. "It is possible."

"As a matter of fact, it is not possible. Andrew will never allow it."

"No?"

"No. Not only does he not trust you—"

"He doesn't trust me?" Schroeder said, feigning hurt.

"Not only does he not trust you," Winterbotham said, "but he has a higher priority than this operation. As a matter of fact, Rudolf, I happen to know that *neither* of us will be allowed to honor any meeting we arrange. Andrew is using us as bait . . . to trap a spy."

Schroeder looked at him with slit eyes. He took another long, slow drag from his cigarette. "To trap a spy," he mused.

"Yes."

"So we will arrange this meeting . . ."

"Yes."

"And then not be allowed to keep it."

"Yes."

"Because some other spy, who interests Andrew more than either of us, will be at the chosen place of rendezvous?"

"Exactly," Winterbotham said.

"Why tell me this? Assuming, of course, that it is true."

"Because if we ally ourselves, Rudolf, there's no need for us both to get buggered by Andrew."

"Buggered," Rudolf said. He tasted the word for a moment, then burst out laughing. "Oh, Professor, forgive me! You're so much more colorful when Andrew isn't around!"

Winterbotham, a tight smile on his face, waited.

"Oh! Well! Yes! All right, then, where were we? Ah, yes, there's no need for us both to get *buggered*." He chuckled. "*Buggered*," he said again.

"Rudolf," Winterbotham said.

"Oh, dear. Oh, dear. Forgive me. It's just—"

"Do you want to go home?" Winterbotham asked.

Schroeder stopped laughing.

"My offer," Winterbotham said. "We arrange our own *treff*, you and I, without Andrew's knowledge. It's the only way either of us will ever set foot on that U-boat. Once we reach Germany, we go our separate ways. All I care about, Rudolf, is my wife. As far as I'm concerned, the war can go on without me."

Schroeder was looking at him, nonplussed.

"No doubt you have prearranged coordinates for your rendezvous," Winterbotham said. "When they contact you to set it up, they'll use a number, won't they? Meet at location twelve, or location five, or use method seven, or method three, or go to country six. But you haven't yet told MI-Five the specifics of your system, have you? Andrew really should have gotten that from you by now. But according to the records, he hasn't. He's been lazy, perhaps. Or perhaps he's too fond of you."

"Perhaps he trusts me," Schroeder said.

"Perhaps," Winterbotham said. "But not enough to let you go home, Rudolf, do not doubt that. In any case, my proposal is simple. When Hamburg tells you to meet at location five, you'll tell Andrew that location five is Plymouth. But it's Dover. You and I go to Dover while Andrew and the rest traipse off to Plymouth."

"And how will you get us to Dover, Professor? I seem to be a prisoner here—if you haven't noticed."

"The same way we're speaking right now. Security clearance alpha."

"You're a liar," Schroeder said.

"Do you think so?"

"I know so. Oh, Professor, you must try harder."

"How do you mean?"

"You must have a very low opinion of my intelligence, Professor. You must believe that I'm a very stupid man. I'll admit I do not understand exactly what purpose you hope to serve with this charade—"

"Andrew has no interest in letting me get to Germany. So I've taken matters into my own hands."

Schroeder hesitated.

"Tell me the system you've worked out with the *Abwehr*," Winterbotham said. "What is location one?"

"Lunacy," Schroeder said.

"It's your only hope of getting home, Rudolf."

Schroeder shook his head. He finished his cigarette and ground it out beneath his heel. "You are serious?" he said then.

"I am."

"You must truly love your wife—or truly despise your country."

"What is location one?"

Schroeder grinned. "Location one," he said, "is Ipswich. From midnight to four A.M., Sundays. You stand on the beach, you flash a light two times. They'll send a dinghy to pick you up."

"Location two?"

"You *are* serious, aren't you?"

"I have never been more serious in my life."

"South of Dogger Bank. Fifty-three degrees forty minutes north, three degrees ten minutes east, twenty-six fathoms, midnight to four every Monday. Are you getting this?"

"I'm getting it," Winterbotham assured him.

"You will get me home, Professor?"

"I'll do my best."

"Location three," Schroeder said, and lit another cigarette as he leaned forward.

LONDON

She knew they were looking for her.

She saw them everywhere—bobbies and plainclothesmen, old and middle-aged and youngish, obvious and subtle—but all with too-bright, too-hungry eyes. She had seen several young women being stopped and questioned, and even two being led away for what she assumed was further interrogation. But so far nobody had stopped her. Nobody had so much as asked to check her papers, although she was carrying a suitcase, which must have attracted attention.

Nobody had stopped her, she knew, because of the habit.

Katarina was not quite able to feel confident. She was too intelligent to feel confident, considering her situation and the evident size of the manhunt around her. But she was able to derive a bit of comfort from the habit, which was really a very excellent disguise. It had prevented her from being approached at all. And nobody had even needed to be harmed for her to acquire it, although Sister Abigail Harbert had suffered the unfortunate loss of a piece of luggage.

But the disguise was becoming less excellent with each passing hour. This was due to the simple fact that she was not able to stop anywhere to bathe or to rest. She looked—and smelled—like a woman on the run, if anybody cared to pay close enough attention.

"Excuse me, sister," a man was saying, "can you tell me how to get to St. Paul's Cathedral?"

She smiled apologetically. "I'm sorry," she said. "I'm a tourist myself." Then she put her head down and moved away quickly before the man could take too close a look at her face.

She walked.

She had been walking for more than twenty hours now, all through the night, but there was nothing to do but keep walking. She had dared to return to Clive Everett's flat only long enough to wash the blood off herself, find the suitcase she had hidden, and change into the habit. Then she had felt her time growing short. She had fled.

Now she chided herself for having panicked. If only she had felt confident enough to remain in the flat for just a few more minutes, she almost certainly could have found several suitable outfits for herself left over from Clive's other conquests. As it was, her suitcase contained only the AFU, her purse, and the cotton dress she had worn from Los Alamos.

When the sun went down she would find a place from which to contact Hamburg again. If her message of the day before had gone through, if it had reached the right people, if they had recognized the code, if the British had failed to catch it, if OKW understood the import of the knowledge she was carrying in her head—*if, if, if, if, if;* so many *ifs*—*if* all of those things had happened correctly, then they would have an answer for her that night. They would tell her where and when she would be extracted.

She was tired, but she kept walking.

Two plainclothesmen were speaking with a young woman by the cenotaph near Whitehall. She walked past them. A group of men was digging through a pile of rubble left by the previous night's bombing. One of the men was weeping. She walked past them. It was hard to know which were more tired, her arms or her legs. The suitcase felt like a chunk of lead; her legs felt like strips of raw meat. She had long before passed a level of exhaustion that she had thought was her limit. But there was nothing for it but to keep moving, always keep moving, trying not to draw attention to herself, waiting to make contact again with Hamburg.

She was too tired to feel afraid. She was too tired to feel sorry. She felt nothing but the throbbing pain in her arms and her legs.

From time to time as she walked, she thought of Fritz. Sometimes she saw him as he once had been: young and sleek, standing at the balcony of the hotel in Hamburg. Sometimes she saw him as he had been in Highgate: old beyond his years, emaciated, pale, weak. Soft, and a traitor.

She did not regret his death. She would have killed him herself had circumstances not taken care of the problem. She had no doubt that Fritz—the *real* Fritz—would have wanted this latest incarnation of himself wiped off the face of the earth. The British had done something to him, something terrible. They had indoctrinated him. They had shamed him.

Perhaps it was living among them for so long, she thought, that had affected his brain somehow. She had feared the same effect in herself after so much time spent in America. But Katarina saw little evidence, as she walked endlessly around London, that these were a likeable people. They were pale, as pale as Fritz had been himself, and they were crooked and thin and weak. They had not taken care of themselves after the first war; they had let an entire generation grow up wrong. How different from *her* people in Germany, athletic and handsome and resourceful and idealistic and bright!

The sky was threatening rain. She hoped it wouldn't start to rain.

She walked.

Her people had thrived following their defeat in the Great War. Even in the midst of the poverty and the filth and the self-hatred and the self-denial, they had grown up quick and strong. Perhaps, she thought now, it had been the very adversity of their surroundings that had brought out the best in them. They had not rested lazily on their laurels the way the British had. They had worked, striving for something better. And, of course, they had enjoyed a hereditary advantage. They were Aryan, after all. See how easily she had defeated nearly a dozen British agents! Whatever ability had been in the British had been compromised over the centuries; their blood itself had been diluted through generations of intermingling.

But Fritz had been Aryan. How could he have turned so weak? He not only had allowed himself to be taken alive but had been working in their service.

Perhaps he had simply *absorbed* their inferiority, somehow, through extended contact with them. Or perhaps they had used more nefarious methods over the years, until he was willing to serve their purposes.

She had no doubt that Fritz had been acting as a double agent, sending back false intelligence with the AFU. And if he had been doing it, then it was possible—no, likely—that others had been doing it too. She would have a word or two for the German spymasters, when she saw them again, about how much trust they should continue putting in their agents in Britain.

Thunder rumbled in the sky. She looked up, scowling.

Sometimes she thought that God Himself was against her.

But then she thought about the remarkable successes she had enjoyed so far, in getting out of America, in getting to Fritz—why, in stumbling across the information in the first place—and, to go back even farther, in having been born of pure blood, a white woman, a German, at this particular time in history, when her people were rising up against nearly insurmountable odds to claim their rightful place as leaders, and she knew that God was with her.

And if God would stay with her just a little longer, she thought, she would bear her message to Berlin, and their enemies would crumble before them like dust.

HOLLAND PARK

Winterbotham spent the night sitting in his library, exhausted but unable to sleep. Anticipation of the task that lay before him had sent him back to his vices.

The next day Schroeder would get his answer from Hamburg.

And soon after, God willing, Winterbotham would go into the Wolf's Lair.

The thought scared the hell out of him.

He thought of Ruth, hoping to draw his inspiration there—after all, it would be for her. But to his immense chagrin he was unable to summon the features of her face. He could imagine the shape of her head, the fall of her hair, the scent of her perfume. But the face itself was only a blur. So much time had passed . . .

He suddenly realized that he hadn't even looked at her photograph for months. Why was that? Because it would have been too painful? Or because he had been able to sleep through the night recently and hadn't wanted to take the chance of upsetting that?

In any case, he wasn't sleeping tonight.

He set down his drink, opened his desk, and removed a photograph that had been taken on their wedding day. Ruth was facing the camera, wearing the same odd half smile that had always come to her face so easily. It made one feel privileged to know her, that smile, as if one were being favored with some inside joke.

But the smile meant little. Winterbotham himself had gotten *real* smiles from Ruth, never half smiles. But only very occasionally.

Only when they had been earned.

He wondered how she had done for herself in Dachau. Ruth could be charming when she chose to be; but she did not often choose to be. She wore her contempt for her enemies openly. And the Nazis, in recent years, had been the primary target of her scorn. How bad, he wondered, had they made things for her? How bad had she made things for herself?

Maddening, impossible woman.

He returned the picture to the drawer, slid the drawer closed, and picked up his drink again. Outside, the storm began to taper away. It was, he suspected, only a momentary respite.

There was another photograph sitting on his desktop. He looked at it now over the rim of his glass as he sipped.

The photograph showed an exceptionally pretty girl of perhaps nineteen or twenty, smiling winsomely at the camera. The girl had long blond hair, sharp cheekbones, a long neck, intelligent eyes. She was pixilated with enlargement; he could see the elbows and shoulders of the women who had stood beside her, posing for this office portrait more than ten years before.

The girl was Katarina Heinrich. Taylor had received the photograph, sent by the OSS, earlier that day.

Where was *she* spending the night? In another man's bed, having gotten all she could from Clive Everett? Or was she out in the rain, huddled somewhere, freezing?

The photograph, he thought, was a blessing. Although it had been in Taylor's hands for only eight hours, copies already were on their way to every military policeman, every bobby, every special agent, home guard, and CID in England. Taylor had strung his web; now their task was to sit back and wait for one of the threads to quiver.

Taylor's men were capable. They would surely capture the woman before the *treff.*

But what if they didn't?

She had killed eight agents. Would he able to handle her by himself when the time came?

He shook his head slightly in the loneliness of his study, and smiled a bitter smile.

"Bollocks," he said aloud, and then raised his glass and drank deep.

HAM COMMON, SURREY

Taylor finished writing and looked up triumphantly, first at Schroeder and then at Winterbotham.

Schroeder was giving him a sycophantic smile. Winterbotham, suddenly busy packing his pipe, was focusing elsewhere.

Taylor removed his headphones and looked at the pad before him. " 'Rendezvous four,' " he read, " 'with all urgency.' "

"Whitley Bay," Schroeder said promptly. "The beach across from the Highland Pub. Three to five on Sunday mornings. Flash a light twice, then wait to be picked up."

"Highland Pub," Taylor repeated, making a note on his pad. "So we've got her."

Schroeder kept giving him the same sycophantic smile. Winterbotham kept working on his pipe, eyes downcast.

"We won't make the same mistake as last time," Taylor said. "This time we'll be prepared. No chance she'll get away again."

"Surely not," Schroeder said, "eh, Professor?"

"No chance," Winterbotham agreed without looking up.

CHAPTER NINE

ESSEX

Katarina, frowning, stared out her window.

The passing landscape consisted mostly of pastures and fens. Here and there, a low green hill, sometimes featuring a small farmhouse, rose from the shallow water. Farther off toward the horizon she could see a tangle of briar, a scatter of beechwoods. The sky overhead was a vibrant, steely blue.

He recognized me, she thought.

Impossible.

Well, not *impossible*, exactly. But extremely improbable. During the past ten years, she had disposed of every photograph of herself, or so she believed. She had learned to cover her tracks as a matter of course.

But the way the man in the train station had looked at her . . .

She felt nervous.

After gazing out the window for a time, she turned her head and took the measure of her compartment mates. An older man beside her, deeply suntanned on his face and arms, was dozing. His head banged against the oak paneling in time with the train chugging across railroad ties. Two children and a young mother sat across the way, reading from a book of Mother Goose. A thickly-set man with black hair, squeezed awkwardly beside one of the children, was browsing through a copy of the *Illustrated London News*. He was handsome, muscular, a bit on the short side.

He caught her looking at him.

He smiled.

She smiled back, demurely, and turned to look out the window again.

At Northampton, the young mother and her brood left the compartment. For a few moments, Katarina thought that she and the black-haired man would be left alone. Then an elderly man entered, followed by a well-fed young woman wearing an oversized anorak.

The train began to move again, chugging slowly at first, then gaining speed.

If the man in London truly *had* recognized her . . . But no, they wouldn't have been able to reach Northampton before the train, would they? It would take time to find transportation, to find available agents.

Unless, of course, they'd already had some men at Northampton.

The nervousness was beginning to curdle into panic.

She looked at the man across from her again.

They shared another smile.

Katarina crossed her legs, and the cotton dress inched up on her thigh.

The conductor came up to the two men standing between cars. Both men were holding tightly on to whatever handholds they could find, feet spread, trying to maintain their balance as the train rocked along.

"Gentlemen," the conductor said, "if all compartments are occupied, then make some space in the corridor; but you can't stand here."

One of the men flashed his ID. "Knox," he said. "Boyle. Military Intelligence."

The second man held up a photograph. "Seen this woman on the train?"

The conductor leaned forward. He peered at the picture, scowling because Boyle was not doing a very good job of holding it still as the train lurched around.

"A pretty little bird," Boyle said, "around thirty. Traveling alone. Her hair may be dark now, just above shoulder-length. She would have gotten on at Liverpool Station. Ticket to Leicester."

"Yes," the conductor said. "She's on the train, in the next car. Shall I show you?"

Knox and Boyle exchanged a glance.

Knox shook his head. "She's dangerous, mate—more dangerous than you'd imagine. We're just here to keep an eye on her until we reach Leicester."

"Let us know if she goes anywhere," Boyle said. "And for God's sake, man, don't let on that she's caught your interest."

"Right, sir. I understand."

"Good," Knox said, and nodded to Boyle. "We've got her now," he said.

Katarina was on the verge of addressing the thickly set young man—she would compliment his youthful appearance and wonder aloud why he was not in the service—when she noticed the conductor staring at her.

He was making a pretense of moving down the corridor outside her compartment, picking his way carefully over the scattered kit bags. But his eyes were locked directly on her face. When Katarina glanced up, he looked away quickly, flushing, and hurried past.

A chill ran through her. She stood, stepped over the elderly man's legs, and reached for the compartment door.

"Leaving us?" the thickly set man asked brightly.

She smiled back at him. "Just for a moment," she said.

She stepped out into the narrow corridor, walked calmly to the end, and pushed open the door leading to the space between cars. There was nobody standing in the drafty chamber; only hot air and the stink of burning coal. A loud *chuff-chuff-chuff* filled her ears as she stepped onto the swaying, precarious tongue of metal that served as a floor.

She looked around. The vestibule was flimsy, so that it could flex as the train went around a turn, with a door set on either side. Both doors were secured with padlocks. Katarina raised her hand and hammered it down onto the handle of the door on her right. The lock held. She repeated the motion, and the lock sprung open with a tiny *pop*. She hit the handle once more, and the door swung open and she found herself staring at watery green earth rushing past at thirty miles per hour.

It would ruin the dress, no doubt about that.

But beggars couldn't be choosers. She drew a breath and then jumped, tucking and rolling as she came out of the train, pinwheeling over the rushing earth.

Knox was whistling "South of the Border."

Boyle, who had heard Knox whistle "South of the Border" more times than he cared to count, was trying to ignore him. He lit a cigarette, looking out the foggy window at the passing landscape. He saw—

or thought he saw—some kind of colorful tumbleweed moving past the train.

He blinked, staring. That was exactly what it had looked like: a tumbleweed, straight out of a Gene Autry flick, except that this one had been an unnaturally lively yellow.

"Did you see that?" he asked after a moment.

"What?"

"It looked like . . ." He kept staring out the window. "Bollocks," he said. "I think my eyes are going in my old age."

"I wouldn't doubt it," Knox said. "Give me one of those fags."

Boyle gave him a cigarette.

"I'm going to stroll down to the other end of the car," Knox said, tucking the cigarette behind one ear. "Take a peek and make sure our bird's still in her nest."

Boyle watched as Knox opened the door, stepped over the threshold, and began to make his way down the corridor. The train was coming out of a turn; Knox kept one hand pressed against the wall as he moved, to maintain his balance. He passed the first compartment, then the second, then the third. At the end of the car, he turned around and started to come back.

Boyle frowned. The fool was going to give them away, he thought, if he kept walking back and forth past the compartment. And not only was he walking past the compartment again, he was gazing into it, directly into it, without even trying to conceal his interest.

Now he was opening the door. He was saying something to whoever was inside.

Boyle swore, pushed his way into the car, and went to join him.

"Don't tell me," he said.

Knox looked at him, tight-lipped, and drew his gun.

CHAPTER TEN

HUNTINGDON, SUFFOLK

Katarina invested five minutes by a shallow pond, stripping off her dress, soaking it, then spreading it on a rock to catch the sun while she soaked and scrubbed herself.

She would have liked to dawdle a bit by the cool water in the late-afternoon sun, but of course she could not afford the delay. She struck off again, heading in a direction that she considered to be north-northeast, walking through fields of heather, keeping her eyes and her ears open, wondering how many men were looking for her and whether they had dogs, whether she might find a weapon or food or shelter in the near future, whether she had any realistic chance of staying free to see the nightfall.

In a peculiar way, she felt wonderful.

She was tired and she was hungry; her nerves were on edge, and she was, or at least she should have been, afraid. But she was also alive, engaged in a mighty challenge, dependent once again on nothing but her own resources. She was bringing the secret of atomic fire to her people, who would value it and celebrate her for her accomplishment. She was on a mission to change the course of history. Chance was against her, but she had known that when she started on this—she had already gotten farther than she had ever expected.

And as an added bonus, Richard would never touch her again.

She had been walking for more than an hour when she saw a man standing at the edge of a field. The man, several hundred yards away, was facing the opposite direction, looking out across the waist-high grass. Katarina moved quickly but calmly into a shadowed copse of pale-blossomed trees. Then she stood and watched for nearly thirty minutes, stock-still, as the man made his slow and methodical way across the field.

When he had disappeared from view, she waited another five minutes and then recommenced walking.

As she walked, she pondered the significance of the man in the field. He had been heading in the direction from which she had come. It was a squeeze, then. And she had just slipped through it. She would be able to continue in her direction, now, and remain unmolested—unless they had set up a second perimeter farther out.

She wondered if a description of her had been circulated to the locals. It could prove a crucial question. After all, she could not walk all the way to the arranged place of rendezvous. Even if she made it in time, which she doubted was possible, she would remain too exposed in the open countryside, for too long. No, she required transportation. Perhaps if she could change her appearance again, she could board another train. Or perhaps she would be forced to settle for a stolen car, or even a bicycle. Whichever; the priority was getting off her feet, getting out of this immediate area, and getting through the second perimeter, if there was such a thing.

She kept walking. When the sun was just beginning to sink behind the horizon, she spied a scatter of low houses less than a mile away.

She turned toward them.

Taylor spread the map on the hood of the Bentley. The men clustered around in the dimming light to follow the cigarette in his hand as he pointed with it.

"She left the train here," Taylor said, stabbing at the map, "or somewhere near it. She's heading to Whitley Bay—here. Unfortunately, we've no guarantee she'll go directly from point A to point B."

He used the cigarette to describe a circle in the air above the map.

"She seems to have evaded our squeeze, gentlemen, but she doesn't know about the second perimeter set up by Special Forces. So our task is simple. We must find her, and eliminate her, before she stumbles into that perimeter. We can't have SF taking credit for catching our bird, now, can we?"

Several men snickered.

"We have two dozen agents at our disposal. The area within the second perimeter is approximately ten miles in diameter. That means every group of two men will cover a space of less than one square mile. Each third team will have a bloodhound. We have a strong scent from the luggage she left on the train. The odds are fantastically in our favor, gentlemen. I will brook no excuses for failure."

A rustle moved through the men. The dogs, straining at their leashes, whimpered quietly.

"You will notice that quadrant one is mostly farmland; quadrant two is a lovely stretch of countryside consisting almost entirely of bogs; quadrant three contains the oil refinery and the railroad tracks; and quadrant four contains A Three-eighty, the edge of the forest, and a few holiday houses. Shoot to kill. Any questions?"

A young man cleared his throat.

"Yes, Kendall?"

"Sir," the young man said, "begging your pardon, sir, but . . . a couple of the lads are wondering, sir—"

"Speak your mind, lad."

"Well—it's Highgate, sir. If she was able to kill eight . . ."

Winterbotham stepped forward. "Go on," he said.

Kendall looked at him with huge eyes.

"Go on," Winterbotham said again.

"Sir, the lads are thinking that if she was able to kill eight, sir, and we're moving in groups of two—"

"In Highgate she had conducted surveillance of the target area, gentlemen; but here she is stranded in countryside she has never seen before. On the other hand, this is *our* country. We outnumber her twenty-four to one, without counting the Special Forces patrols at the perimeter. So what, precisely, frightens you?"

Now the young man was blushing. "Nothing, sir."

"Do you not feel comfortable with groups of two?"

"No, sir. I mean, yes, sir."

"You'll be with me, Kendall. I'll hold your hand, if you like."

More snickers, nervous laughter.

"Well, then," Taylor said, "if that's settled. Quadrant one: Lee, Weaver, Davis, Cooper, Bennett, Nuffield. Quadrant two: Hardwicke, Lipton, Lewis, Sayers, Kemsley, Benson. Quadrant three . . ."

Katarina approached the houses carefully, staying as much as possible in the shadows of the encroaching dusk, listening.

There were six houses, cheaply made from plain wood, arranged in a loose semicircle. They were not farms, although all possessed large, if scrubby, gardens. They reminded her of houses she had seen while driving from Los Alamos to Ohio. Poverty was not there, not at the moment—but it was close. She could see it lurking in the rows of yellowish unhealthy tomatoes, in the dilapidated roofs, in the homemade blackout shades on the windows, black paint on cardboard. What could they have here that would possibly help her? She would do better to move on.

Then she saw the lorry.

It was sitting on a patch of grass in the center of the semicircle, looking forlorn. She approached it warily. From somewhere not so far away, over the murmur of summer insects, she could hear a voice singing "Kiss Me Goodnight, Sergeant Major."

The bed contained empty buckets, a coiled hose, a cork helmet. It was a makeshift fire-fighting vehicle, manned, no doubt, by volunteers from the small village around her. Pitching in and doing their part for the war effort, just like everybody else—when they were sober enough. These were the "heroes with grimy faces" whom Churchill had praised so vocally when the London Fire Brigade had been absorbed into the National Fire Service in 1941.

Katarina looked around. A chicken was strutting importantly across the dusty yard in front of a nearby house; otherwise there seemed to be nobody watching.

She opened the lorry's door, slipped inside, and bent down to have a look at the ignition.

Winterbotham drove.

Kendall sat beside him up front, drumming his fingers on the windowsill. They dropped off agents in groups of two: Lewis and Hobbs at the fringe of the forest; Richards, Temple, and a bloodhound named Sad Sack near A380. Then they headed back toward the center of the quadrant, and the holiday homes.

"Try to relax," Winterbotham said.

Kendall's fingers immediately stopped drumming. "Sorry, sir."

"I hope you don't think I came down on you too hard back there, Kendall. I was hoping to make a point in front of the men."

"Yes, sir."

"Between you and me," Winterbotham said, "you're absolutely right. There's no reason at all to believe that two-man teams will suffice."

Kendall stared at him.

"Can you reach in the glove, Kendall, and hand me the pistol there?"

"Um . . . yes, sir."

The Bentley drifted to a stop fifty feet away from the nearest house.

Winterbotham counted six of the little hovels arranged in a loose cluster—hardly more than shacks, really, with their two rooms and their scrubby gardens. The irony was that these pathetic houses would be inhabited, for the most part, by exiles from the tonier neighborhoods of London. When the bombing had grown thick, in the midst of the Blitz, those who could afford to buy a plot of land and leave the city had done so. But their new "holiday houses" had been necessarily modest. First had come a lack of supplies—metals, rubber, textiles, woods, paint—and then, as time wore on, a lack of even the most basic amenities.

"We'll stay together," Winterbotham said softly. "Sweep from one house to the next, starting with the closest one."

"Yes, sir."

"Nervous, Kendall?"

"No, sir."

"Hm," Winterbotham said, and threw open his door.

They began to stalk toward the nearest house, side by side, pistols in hand. As they drew close, Winterbotham heard the sudden cough of an engine turning over. He frowned. Where was that coming from? Now it was revving, spiraling up and down. Close by, he thought. Out of sight—but very close by. In fact . . .

He caught movement out of the corner of his eye. He grabbed Kendall and pushed him down, flinging himself after in the same motion.

The lorry swept past within inches, headlamps off, the stench of oil following in a thick cloud.

Winterbotham gained his feet, brushing at himself.

Kendall, beside him, stood more slowly.

"Check the houses," Winterbotham said. "Somebody may need help."

Kendall showed no sign of having heard him. He was looking off after the lorry, dazed.

"Check the houses, Kendall, God damn it!"

Winterbotham gave him a push in the direction of the nearest house, then turned and hurried back toward the Bentley, cursing under his breath.

The engine labored audibly, sending up clouds of sooty black smoke.

Katarina blocked out the noise. She needed to think.

Should she try to keep the lorry? Or should she make a go for it on foot?

Keep the lorry, she decided, at least for the time being. They would be closing in. If she was on foot, they would nab her immediately.

She turned right—north—and opened up the engine. The lorry bumped along the old road under the deepening twilight, sounding pained. Twice she nearly slipped off into a ditch that paced the road on the right. Both times she dragged the lorry back onto the road with clenched teeth, amid tremendous gouts of dust. If she dared turn on the headlamps she would have felt a bit safer—but even with the blackout hoods, she couldn't risk it.

Don't panic, she thought. *Think!*

Maybe she should dump the lorry, hide in the countryside. But what if they had dogs? She was afraid of dogs. Hagen had trained her to handle them anyway—but no, the wind was shifting too frequently for her to be confident of keeping the correct orientation. The best thing to do . . .

Who knew the best thing to do? Not she.

She was finished.

"Damn it," she said aloud. "*Think*, God damn it!"

She wanted a cigarette. But her purse had been left behind, on the train, with the suitcase.

She moaned low in her throat and kept driving.

She was *better* than they were, she could handle any given dozen of them. But they would overwhelm her with sheer numbers. They would pile on, tear her apart like dogs fighting over a bone.

She wiped her hand across her nose.

Don't panic, for Christ's sake. Think, for Christ's sake.

No. It's over.

It's never over, she thought.

Roadblocks? Most definitely. And sooner rather than later. And even if she could barrel through the roadblocks—not that she could, but even *if* she could—there were thousands of troops assembling in this part of England. Along with the thousands of troops came hundreds of tanks and half-tracks and Jeeps. They would block the road with something that couldn't be rammed.

Leave the lorry and you'll get the dogs. Keep the lorry and you'll hit a wall.

Take the lorry off the road?

The going would be even slower driving over fields. The trick might buy her a minute or two as they tried to figure out where she had gone, but she'd be no closer to breaking through the second perimeter.

A low whining sound reached her ears. As she listened, it climbed higher to a piercing shriek. She began to tremble. *An alarm,* she thought. Because of her? Was every person in this godforsaken stretch of country going to be looking for her now? She would hang, no doubt about it, hang, hang, hang. For a moment she believed it, and the panic that had been nibbling at her began to slaver.

Then spotlights poked up into the night. Four, six, an even dozen. She heard the first coughing rattle of antiaircraft fire: *ack-ack-ack-ack-ack-ack.*

Not an alarm, she realized.

An air raid siren.

Then she could hear the planes themselves, far away. She craned her neck out the window as she drove, searching the sky.

Why bomb out here, in the middle of nowhere?

The railroad. They would be trying to bomb the railroad.

The bombs would smash the perimeter for her.

She spun the wheel, and the lorry bounced off the road into a rocky field, heading west.

When the first bombs hit, Winterbotham pulled the Bentley to the side of the road and watched.

The bombs were falling in a scythe pattern some distance away—seven or eight miles, he guessed, to the west. The railroad tracks, then. Some of the planes would probably also make a go for the oil refinery, if they had the fuel and the bombs to spare.

He sat, hands on the wheel, watching the geysers of flame rise up into the night, and he tried to think.

If she hadn't turned off the road, he would have caught up to her by now. The Bentley could outrun that lorry; he had no dcubt of it. And so she *had* turned off the road. But why? She must have known that her progress would be severely impeded by the fields. How far could she hope to get?

Put yourself in her place, he thought. The net closing all around; time running out; nowhere to go.

Another carpet of bombs exploded far away. Pillars of brackish smoke began to rise. He thought of all the wildlife, the varied flora and fauna, being destroyed—*Abies grandis, Taxus baccata, Cerastium glomeratum, Pteridum aquilinum.* Countless others. The creeping buttercup, however tenacious, could not hold its own against a bomb.

This goddamned war, he thought.

And how would *she* feel, witnessing this?

Proud of her country for penetrating England's defenses? He rather doubted it. The bombing put her in danger, after all—a few miles was a small distance with this kind of operation. All it would take was one Heinkel, one Dornier drifting slightly off-course, and bombs might saturate this very spot. Her own people could be the ones who kill her.

When she saw the planes, then, she would turn away. East was her direction, in any case. It led to the coast, her ultimate goal.

But she's not one to lose her head, he thought then. *She's not one to run blindly away from danger. On the contrary. She* embraces *danger, simply because it makes her unpredictable. Perhaps when she sees these geysers of flame she does not see them as a threat. Perhaps she sees them as just the opposite—a curtain of fire to shield her from the prying eyes of MI-5.*

In that case, she heads toward them.

Winterbotham turned west.

The lorry jounced over a ditch, nearly got hung up on a bush, tore free, tilted up onto two wheels, balanced precariously, and then righted itself.

The explosions were moving east and north. Katarina twisted the wheel hard, pointing herself toward them, and jammed her foot down on the accelerator. The trick would be to get close enough to slip through any gap made in the perimeter, but not so close as to become incinerated.

She crashed through a hedgerow, splashed through a fen, then broke out into an open field.

She saw the explosions marching toward her. She held the wheel with both hands, squeezing hard, and kept on. At the last instant, she would turn—but not before. If she lost her nerve now, she would lose her last chance.

The noise was deafening, apocalyptic, night turned to day.

Her hands started to twist the wheel, to veer away.

Her mouth formed a tight line.

She turned the wheel back.

Kept on.

They were perversely beautiful: multicolored spouts of earth and flame, trees and debris and grass and stone and funneling smoke, sixty feet away, forty feet, thirty . . .

She spun the wheel—too late.

The world became a slow and sweet place.

Winterbotham saw the lorry an instant before it vanished into a wall of flame.

He stepped on the brake. He blinked, then reached up and rubbed his eyes.

He prepared to follow her—to drive the Bentley into the inferno.

Instead, he found himself sitting where he was at an almost-safe distance, engine idling, heart thudding in his wrist.

The perimeter, he thought, would have crumbled. Even the most stalwart SF man wouldn't stand still while a Junker dropped a bomb on him. They would close ranks as soon as the barrage had ended, plugging any hole; but if she survived, she would find her chance. They wouldn't be able to reorganize effectively until dawn.

He kept watching. He raised his thumb to his mouth and nibbled on the nail, a habit he had vanquished forty years before.

The explosions continued.

Nobody could survive that, he thought.

Katarina watched, feeling pleasantly high.

She felt as if she had been swatted with an especially large, soft pillow. Tiny somethings rained on the car all around her, on the undercarriage and then the roof, undercarriage and then roof, as she rolled again and again, slowly and sweetly.

Then something happened, very loud. The world went dark. A huge rushing filled her ears.

Time passed. She decided that she was thirsty. It was hot out here, after all. Hot sitting on the beach, the sun baking the sand all around her . . .

Then the lorry rolled again and she was flung against a door made of tissue paper, a door that parted as she fell against it, spilling her out onto the ground. The ground was covered with molten metal. Still, better than the two-ton burning coffin on top of her. She huddled as close to the ground as she could manage as the lorry rolled away, and somehow God was with her and she managed to avoid sticking her face into any pools of molten shrapnel.

The rushing in her head became a rushing in the sky.

The planes overhead, banking, coming back for another pass.

Katarina, she thought calmly, *stand up and move.*

Hadn't she been in a truck a moment before?

What happened to the truck?

She was still wondering this when something happened yet again, not very far to her left this time. There was a furnace there, and somebody had flung the door open, and now she was getting a bad sunburn here on the beach—it was a very hot beach, after all, and . . .

Crawl.

She pulled herself forward, ignoring the inferno all around her, ignoring the terrible sunburn she had gotten from the furnace.

A few moments later, she encountered a cool eddy of air—a single eddy slipping away almost the moment she sensed it. But it had been cool nonetheless, and that gave her hope. Blessed coolness, blessed relief. She managed to stumble up onto her feet. She staggered forward, dizzy, and found another cool spot. This time the coolness was coming from below. It was grass. Cool grass, not even scorched. She collapsed onto it.

She rested.

After a few moments, she rolled over onto her back and looked behind herself.

The fires were already dying down, but the smoke was growing thicker, ever thicker. She could see the remains of the lorry, upside-down, perhaps thirty feet away. It was burning.

I crawled away from that, she realized.

She allowed herself a few moments of congratulations. Then she gained her feet again, carefully. Her head was ringing and she felt weak, but she was alive, in one piece.

She found more grass leading away from the fire.

Cool, damp, blessed grass.

She followed it.

In the light of dawn, the devastation looked minor.

The land was scorched; cool chunks of shrapnel were scattered hither and yon; the lorry was a crumpled box. But the railroad tracks themselves were intact, and as the sun came up, a bird was singing merrily from somewhere off in the trees.

Taylor and Winterbotham held tin cups of coffee and smoked cigarettes, surveying the area. Around them, agents poked and prodded the greenery, searched through the wreckage, spoke softly among themselves. Two dozen bloodhounds pulled on their leashes, mewling.

After a time, Kendall separated himself from the rest, approached Taylor, and saluted.

"No sign of her, sir."

"Any chance she was incinerated?"

"I don't see how anything could have gotten out of that lorry alive, sir."

Winterbotham snorted.

Taylor turned to him, raising an eyebrow. "She would need the luck of the devil to drive into that and walk away."

"If she was in the lorry, Andrew, where's the body?"

"Perhaps we'll find it if we beat the bushes a bit."

"But you won't. We need to establish another perimeter—the sooner the better. How many more men can you raise?"

Taylor considered. "Another two dozen, perhaps, between CID and Special Forces."

"If you went to the board and called in all those old favors you're so fond of cultivating, how many?"

Taylor smoked his cigarette. "Four score," he decided. "Not for long, of course. Twenty-four hours."

"Do it," Winterbotham said.

CHAPTER ELEVEN

PETERBOROUGH, NORFOLK

The air raids, in Gladys Lockhart's opinion, made the rest of the war worthwhile.

Every time the Germans sent their planes winging over the Channel, Gladys and her employer, Sir John Frederick Bailey, left their brick, ivy-covered farmhouse and went to wait in the Anderson shelter in the yard. They sat together in the darkness, talking in low voices, listening to the wireless he kept on a shelf there. From time to time, their legs brushed in the close confines; and then Gladys thrilled, silently, and bit her lip, and tried not to blush, and prayed to herself that the war would never end.

Each time the alarm sounded, she felt the same flood of nervous exhilaration. She would promptly put aside whatever duty she was engaged in and meet her employer at the back door—he was, invariably, coming from his study. Together they would leave the little country house, walking quickly past the small garden, the few prickly rosebushes, the twin hedgerows. Then Sir John Frederick Bailey would, with an air of great chivalry, allow Gladys to enter the shelter before him. She would duck her head and climb in, as often as not stepping into a pool of water collected from the previous night's rain. But who cared? Damp feet were a small price to pay for minutes, and sometimes even hours, spent alone with Sir John Frederick Bailey.

Eventually, of course, the raids would end. Then they would go back into the farmhouse, which was, of course, a much more modest domicile than Sir John could have afforded—Sir John's modesty, in Gladys's opinion, was one of his most winning features—and return to their respective roles of master and maid. Sir John Frederick Bailey would return to his study to pore over his books and his papers and try to meet whatever deadline was hanging over him on that particular evening.

And Gladys, polishing a divan or emptying a dustbin, would begin to look forward to the next night's raids.

Tonight had been an especially good night.

Sir John had started to talk about his work. He rarely spoke to Gladys of his work; whenever the subject did arise, he tended to speak in only the broadest generalities. Tonight, however, he had become involved with the telling—post-war reconstruction, Gladys could clearly see, was his greatest passion since the death of his wife. He had lost track of the time. Nearly an hour had passed after the last Nazi plane had lumbered back over the Channel before he realized what had happened.

Then he laughed, taking off his glasses and polishing them on his sleeve.

"I apologize, dear Gladys," he said. "I've become carried away. I must have been boring you terribly."

Gladys smiled. "Not at all," she said.

"You are a patient darling, aren't you? But, no, I know that you're only being polite. Come on, then. Just time for a cake before bedtime."

They climbed out of the shelter—he let her go first, as always; in Sir John's world, chivalry took precedence over class—and strolled back to the house. Gladys, walking out front, allowed herself a moment of hope. It had been such a good night, such a *wonderful* night, as Sir John Frederick Bailey had forgotten himself and spoken with intensity about his work. He had spoken to her as an equal, and now it seemed impossible, simply unimaginable, that they would revert to their old roles the moment they stepped over the threshold of the ivied farmhouse. They had passed some crucial watermark in their relationship. After tonight, everything would be different.

She reached the door and paused for a moment so that he could catch up with her. She could smell smoke, but only faintly; the bombs had fallen far southwesterly. She could hear the hum of cicadas and the slow thumping of the gate around the front of the house. She would need to go latch the gate before bed, she reminded herself. But first she would wait to see how Sir John Frederick Bailey treated her, after they stepped inside. Perhaps he would ask her to join him in a cake instead of simply expecting her to serve him, as was the routine. How could he not? They had *connected*, sitting in the shelter, in an intimate and personal way. She had served the role of—well, of a *wife*, if that wasn't too presumptuous: listening, supporting, occasionally facilitating with a particularly apt comment or question. Surely that level of profound *connection* did not vanish in an instant.

But he turned to her as they stepped inside, and said, "I'll take the cake in my study, please, Gladys, just as soon as you've finished with the dishes."

He turned and shuffled off down the hall. After a few seconds, she heard the door to his study close with finality.

She drew a breath, wiped absently at the corner of her eye, and went to finish with the dishes.

She was not an unattractive girl.

On the contrary: Boys had always seemed to give her plenty of attention, when there had been boys her age around. Now, of course, she was older—she would be eighteen the next month—and there were no boys her age around anymore. They all were crouched in muddy foreign fields somewhere, fighting the war.

But she didn't think she had lost her looks yet. In the past year, as a matter of fact, her legs had grown longer, more graceful and womanly; her waist had risen and narrowed; her hips had plumped pleasantly; her bosom had grown large and firm and now pushed at her uniform in an undeniably mature fashion. Her skin was milky, her cheeks rosy, her hair long and blond and shining.

So why would Sir John Frederick Bailey never try for a kiss?

She examined herself from different angles in the mirror above her dresser, holding in her stomach, thrusting it out, pouting into the glass, frowning, smiling. Perhaps, she thought, the trouble was with her teeth. They were a bit yellow. But Sir John Frederick Bailey's teeth were mottled themselves—far more mottled than hers.

His wife had been dead for twelve years; he must have been lonely. He must have had needs. And yet he had never even looked at her, not so much as *looked* at her, with anything like lust in his eyes.

Outside, the gate banged against the fence.

Perhaps her breasts had grown *too* large. She frowned at the thought, which had the ring of truth. She had always believed that men were fond of large breasts—that had been the conventional wisdom at school, which she had left at age fourteen, and in Bristol, where she had worked as a shop girl before coming to the agency. But why must it always be so? Perhaps men had different tastes for breasts, the same as they had different tastes for opera, or for the cooking of meat. Perhaps Sir John Frederick Bailey preferred small-breasted women.

She sighed, held her breasts up in the mirror, pressed them down, and wondered if she could possibly create some kind of device to hold them flatter to her chest.

On the other hand, perhaps her body wasn't the problem. Perhaps it was her face. She hollowed her cheeks, checking her profile from both sides. As far as she could tell, she was pretty. But how would she truly know? How would one ever know if one were truly pretty or not? The boys had paid her attention, true enough; but boys lacked standards. Boys . . .

She frowned. Something had changed.

Something outside. The wind? No, it continued to whistle around the little farmhouse.

The gate, she realized then. The gate had stopped banging.

She moved to her window and looked out at the road. She saw, in the starlight, a woman collapsed at the foot of the walk. The gate, oblivious to the woman's presence, was banging soundlessly against her, again and again and again.

They had intended to bring her to the guest bedroom on the second floor, but carrying her up the stairs proved to be too much trouble—the woman was less petite than she looked. Finally, they gave up on the idea and took her into Sir John's bedroom. They lay her down on the bed, then stepped back in unison and regarded her.

And there you have it, Gladys Lockhart thought sourly. *In the house five minutes and already in Sir John's bed—which is farther than I ever got.*

Sir John removed his glasses, wiped them on his sleeve, put them on again, and said: "Quite a beauty, I'd venture, beneath all that grime."

The woman was perhaps twenty-seven or twenty-eight, Gladys estimated; and she *was* pretty, prettier than Gladys herself, although in a different way. She had short dark hair, stylishly cut, and clean cheekbones, and a taut thin body that suggested curves rather than describing them. But she was also filthy, covered with soot, scratches, burns, and dried blood. Her right hand was bleeding, wrapped in a sordid strip of cloth. She stank of perspiration and something else, something worse—cooked flesh. Her dress was torn in at least a dozen places. Her breathing was ragged and shallow; and, as they carried her, she had drooled on herself rather uncharmingly.

"Where did she come from?" Gladys asked.

"Caught in tonight's raid, from the look of those burns. Must have lost her bearings and wandered. Beyond that, I couldn't say."

"Will she be all right?"

He frowned, leaned closer, picked up one eyelid, and peered into her pupil. "I'm no doctor, of course," he said, letting the eye close again. "But—yes, I'd say so. The burns don't look too severe. She's probably suffered a concussion. Let's clean her up a bit so the scrapes don't have a chance to get infected, and give her a good night's sleep. Perhaps in the morning I can give her a lift back to wherever she's wandered away from. That's a fair use of petrol, wouldn't you say?"

"I would think so," Gladys said.

"It must be some distance," he said thoughtfully. "I know everybody in Peterborough, or so I thought, but I've never seen her before."

"She's very pretty," Gladys said.

"She may not take kindly to a stranger undressing her and cleaning the wounds. But one assumes she would feel more comfortable with a woman than with a man. Would you mind terribly, Gladys?"

"No, sir. Not at all."

"Excellent," Sir John Frederick Bailey said. "Well, then! I'll be in my study if you need me."

"You'll spend the night in there, sir?"

"Yes, I think I can manage."

Gladys summoned her courage. "I'd be glad to let you have *my* bed for the evening, sir, if you like."

"No, I'll struggle through," he said. "But thank you for the thought, Gladys." He peered at her through his glasses with his hazel eyes. "Such a thoughtful girl," he said. "Your mother would be proud."

Gladys, whose mother had died when she was two years old, said nothing.

"Well," Sir John said, "you know where the washbasin is, Gladys. I'll leave you to it."

THE WAR OFFICE, WHITEHALL

Taylor put a cigarette in his mouth. He lit it and dropped the match into a glass ashtray on his desk. He sucked on the inside of his cheeks for a moment before exhaling, which, to Winterbotham, indicated that something had not gone well.

"Out with it," Winterbotham snapped.

Taylor exhaled. "She's gone," he said.

"Impossible."

"So one would think. But we've checked every square foot within thirty miles of the lorry and found neither hide nor hair. She couldn't cover more distance than that, Harry, in the time she's had, even in the peak of health. If we're to believe that she walked away from that wreckage—"

"Of course she did," Winterbotham said.

"Then she must have drowned somewhere. Otherwise, the dogs at least would have caught her scent. I'm canceling the search effort while

I still have a favor or two left to call in. Tomorrow we'll start to drag the lakes and streams."

"For God's sake, Andrew, we've almost got her."

Taylor shook his head. "What we've got, Harry, is a hundred men working on a single case. Their agencies want them back, and I can't justify keeping them any longer. Don't forget, there's—"

"I haven't forgotten."

"We can't keep extending the perimeter to forty miles, or fifty, or sixty, until we get her. It's simply not feasible. Besides, if she's still alive, we'll nab her at Whitley Bay—five days from now."

Winterbotham leaned forward. "Do it now, Andrew. Extend the perimeter to a hundred miles and knock on every door."

"Harry, I know you'd like to have your chance at Ruth—"

"That has nothing to do with it."

"We'll get her at Whitley Bay, and that's that. If you were in my place, I've no doubt that you'd do the same."

Winterbotham regarded him icily. He seemed on the verge of speaking. Then he leaned back in his chair and produced his pipe. He began to pack it.

"Agreed?" Taylor said.

Winterbotham didn't look up. "Agreed," he said.

PETERBOROUGH, NORFOLK

The woman had been cleaned, dressed in fresh clothes—Gladys's clothes, of course—and bandaged in half a dozen places. But even with a bandage on her temple, a terrible burn on half of her face, and a bloody scratch across her nose, her beauty shone through.

Gladys, standing in the bedroom doorway and watching the woman sleep, felt her heart sink. What hope could *she* have with Sir John with a vision such as this around?

Gladys stared at the woman until she heard the kettle whistling from the kitchen. When she went to catch it, she bumped into Sir John, who was staggering out of his study looking somewhat crumpled in the previous day's clothes.

"Oh!" she said. "I beg your pardon, sir."

"My fault," he mumbled, "entirely my fault." He stepped aside so that she could move into the kitchen ahead of him.

"I was just looking in on our guest," Gladys said, moving to the kettle.

"How is she?"

"Still sleeping. But more easily than last night."

"Good. What can you manage for breakfast, Gladys?"

"Porridge," she said with a smile. "Perhaps a bit of sausage mash, if you like."

"I would, very much. For some reason I've quite an appetite today."

"Shall we wake her and have her join us?"

"No, let the poor thing sleep. But make some extra, Gladys. We'll give her a shake as soon as we've finished."

Sir John snapped his fingers directly under the woman's nose. He did it twice, then gave her a quick, short pat on the cheek.

"Here she comes," he said. "Here she is. Good morning, young lady. How do you feel?"

The woman's eyes went from Sir John Frederick Bailey's face to Gladys's. They sparked with something like panic.

"Never fear," Bailey said soothingly. "You're among friends. You must have gotten a bit too close to a pickle barrel last night—but you're fine, just a bump on the noggin. Here, now, don't look so distressed. You're among friends, I tell you. Can you sit up?"

The woman sat up slowly, helped by his arm around her shoulder. "Where am I?" she said.

"You are in Peterborough, madame, in my house, and I am Sir John Frederick Bailey, a fellow of the Royal Institute of British Architects. And in reply to your next question: You arrived here under your own power, last night. We had nothing to do with it whatsoever."

She blinked muzzily.

"As I said, you've a bit of a bump, and a bit of a burn. But nothing more serious than that, I assure you. The bandages are mostly for show. I expect you'll make a full recovery."

The woman looked again from Bailey to Gladys—with less panic in her eyes, Gladys thought, and more genuine interest.

"You took me in?" she said.

"It seemed the only decent thing to do."

"That's very Christian of you, sir."

"It is my honest pleasure, young lady. Do you mind if I ask your name?"

"Agnes, sir. Agnes Bevin. From Cardiff."

"Cardiff! What on earth brings you to Norfolk?"

"I was on my way to pay a visit to my sister. In Leicester."

"By railroad?"

"Yes."

"I wonder," Sir John said. "Were any trains derailed last night? Do you recall, Miss Bevin, the circumstances of your accident?"

"The last thing I remember . . . now, let me think. We were on the train; we had just passed through Huntingdon; then the lights went down and we slowed; they told us that the planes were coming, we pulled the shades . . . "

"Huntingdon!" he said.

"Yes."

"You've wandered all that way?"

She pressed a hand to her temple. "I can't quite . . . To be honest, I've a bit of a headache."

"My apologies, Miss Bevin. I am remiss in my duties as host. We have a breakfast for you, if you feel up to it. The interrogation can continue after you've eaten."

She gave him a wan smile. "I'll try, sir," she said.

"There we go. Gladys," he said, standing, "take our guest's other arm, if you don't mind, and we'll get her to the breakfast table, where we can talk like civilized people."

Agnes Bevin ate like a horse.

Gladys Lockhart, finding excuse after excuse to remain puttering around the kitchen, took a bit of dark satisfaction from the woman's appetite. She wouldn't keep her figure long, not if she made a habit of eating like that. When she realized the direction her thoughts were going, however, Gladys cut them off guiltily. When had she become so vindictive? It wasn't right to take satisfaction from another person's hunger. Perhaps things were worse in Cardiff than they were in Norfolk. In any case, Sir John, as Gladys well knew, had it better than most. He received eggs every single week, and four ounces of meat, which was, in most places, the ration for an entire family. Not that he didn't deserve the special treatment. After all, he was a knight of the empire, a brilliant and accomplished—

"Architect," he was telling the woman now. "I don't mean to boast, of course. But I was educated at Uppingham, and immediately upon graduation became a lecturer at the Liverpool School of Architecture—the youngest lecturer in the distinguished history of that institution." He smiled, took off his glasses, and rubbed them on his sleeve. "In short enough order I became a fellow, specializing in civic design, and then a full professor. Now, you must be wondering how I received my title. I established a council, you see, for the preservation of rural England. My ideas were really quite roundly embraced . . ."

The woman, forking another bite of sausage mash into her mouth, hardly seemed to be paying attention.

"In any case," Bailey said, clearing his throat, "let me apologize, Miss Bevin. I've become carried away. I must be boring you terribly."

She glanced up. "Not at all," she said, and then returned her attention to her plate.

Gladys couldn't find any other task in the kitchen that required her continued presence. She left, giving Sir John a slight bow, which he ignored. He was already moving on to his conference with Chamberlain, one of his very favorite stories.

"You could see that the man had just about had it, Agnes, from the way his hand trembled when he reached out for the handshake . . ."

Gladys made several trips between the house and the backyard to fetch laundry, detergent, and a washboard. Then, kneeling in the grass near the Anderson shelter, she began to scrub. Flecks of soap danced around her in the wind.

As she worked, she looked up from time to time through the small kitchen window. The woman—Agnes—and Sir John Frederick Bailey were still at the table, both sipping cups of tea. Gladys frowned. How had that happened? She had never seen Sir John prepare his own cup of tea. She hadn't even believed that he possessed the necessary skills.

Perhaps Agnes had done it for him.

How wonderful of her, Gladys thought.

A few minutes later she looked up again, expecting that Sir John would have proceeded to his study by now. Work, after all, was his highest priority. He was not likely to dawdle too long after breakfast over cups of tea, no matter how attractive his houseguest.

But Sir John, she saw, was still at the table, laughing at something Agnes had said. As Gladys watched, he reached out and placed his hand, for a moment, on Agnes's thigh. Agnes was wearing one of Gladys's skirts; the material bunched up between his fingers when he squeezed. After another moment, he took his hand back, still laughing. Agnes began to laugh with him, musically.

Gladys bit her lip.

She bent over the washboard again and scrubbed until the shirt in her hand tore with a loud burr.

CHAPTER TWELVE

THE FINCH PUB, WHITEHALL

The dart left Officer James Kendall's hand, described a wobbling arc, and then, to great general laughter, missed the board altogether and lodged itself in the wall.

"One pint too many!" somebody called jubilantly, and another said, "Fifty-one-by-Fives not your game, eh, lad? Perhaps cribbage!"

Kendall took a step back from the line, smiling. "I'm all in," he announced.

"Thank God. Now, let's play some darts!"

Kendall pointed at the heckler, still smiling, and wagged his finger back and forth in mock warning. Then he found his pint, abandoned at the bar, and watched as a game of '01 got underway.

He became slowly aware of a presence standing just behind him—

a large man smelling vaguely of citrus. After a few moments, the man said: "There's no need to throw so hard, lad. Leave your back foot on the floor. If she's sticking in the wood of the wall, she'll stick in the bristle without a problem."

"I appreciate the advice," Kendall said tightly. "But the fault isn't mine. It's the darts. They're brass."

"Strange, then, that the others don't seem to have any problem with them."

Kendall turned, opening his mouth. The words caught in his throat when he saw that it was Winterbotham standing behind him, a pint of bitter in one hand, an orange-scented pipe in the other. Kendall had last seen Winterbotham out in the countryside, surrounded by debris, organizing a search party with Taylor. He had not expected to see Winterbotham here, tonight, standing in the Finch.

He choked nonsense for a moment, then stammered: "Forgive me, sir—please—I didn't realize it was you."

"No need to apologize, Kendall. You hadn't said anything yet."

"Er—yes, sir."

"Let's find a booth, lad, if you can spare a moment."

They found a booth under a row of windows covered with gas shades. Kendall piled into one side, Winterbotham the other. They lifted their pints, clinked the rims together, and drank. Kendall pro-duced a pack of papers and a small pouch of tobacco. In one corner of the pub, somebody started in on "Roll Out the Barrel," drunkenly off-key.

"I'm a bit surprised to see you here, sir. Mingling with the commoners and all that."

Winterbotham smiled. "I would take offense at that, son, if it wasn't true. As a matter of fact, I'm only here because of you."

"Because of me?"

"Your wife informed me that you were working late. So of course I came directly to the Finch."

Kendall flushed. "Begging your pardon, sir, but I *was* working late. I only just arrived here."

"I believe you, Kendall. Settle down."

"Sorry, sir."

"You've got to stop apologizing, Kendall."

"Yes, sir. I . . ."

He caught himself.

"Good," Winterbotham said. He drew on his pipe; it had gone out. He lit it again, exhaled a smoke ring, and said: "What is it you're working on at the War Office that requires you to stay so late?"

Kendall finished rolling his cigarette, licked it, put it between his lips, and leaned forward to let Winterbotham light it for him.

"I'm not certain I'm at liberty to discuss that, sir—no offense intended."

"None taken. Tell me if I'm in the vicinity, Kendall. You're preparing a trap for the woman, to be sprung on Sunday morning at Whitley Bay. I'm part of the effort myself, although Taylor and I are at odds, just a bit, on how exactly to proceed."

"At odds?"

"I feel that we should be trying to apprehend the woman now, before she reaches Whitley Bay. Taylor would rather wait."

"If you don't mind my saying so, sir, I can't imagine why we'd try to find her now. We know where she's going, and when, and just keeping the roadblocks up is putting quite a strain on Mr. Taylor's resources." He puffed on his cigarette. "Besides," he added, "she's almost certainly dead. Otherwise the dogs would have got her."

"Dogs can sniff out a corpse as well as a living woman, Kendall."

"Not if it's underwater, sir. Begging your pardon."

"Hm," Winterbotham said.

He blew two more smoke rings, concentric.

"I have my own reasons for wanting to apprehend the woman

before she reaches Whitley Bay," he said. "Personal reasons. Do you know what role I serve for MI-Five, Kendall?"

"Not precisely, sir, no."

"My wife is a captive of the Nazis. I've offered to betray England in exchange for her—with Taylor's blessing, of course. In other words, I've been groomed as a double agent."

That stopped Kendall. He looked at Winterbotham for a long moment. Then he picked up his pint and took a slow sip.

"But as long as the Heinrich woman is free," Winterbotham said, "my mission has been suspended."

"Taylor's orders?"

"Yes."

"My condolences, sir."

"Kendall," Winterbotham said, "that lorry was headed right for us. Do you remember?"

"I'll never forget it. If you hadn't knocked me aside . . ."

"Do you consider yourself to be in my debt?"

"You saved my life, sir."

"Then help me, Kendall. Help me find the woman before Sunday. We'll organize our own search party and comb the countryside within, say, a hundred miles of Leicester."

Kendall raised his eyebrows. He saw that Winterbotham was serious; the eyebrows lowered. He thought for a few moments, in silence.

"I couldn't get more than two or three from MI-Five, sir, without Taylor's becoming aware of it."

"I've found that one can accomplish a great many things under Taylor's nose, son, without Taylor becoming aware of it. Surely you could scrape up more than two or three."

"I'm sorry, sir. But I don't believe I could. Besides, even if only *I* were to disappear, it would raise questions."

"I'm willing to let questions be raised. If we hand the woman to them, it won't make any difference."

"How many would you require, sir?"

"A dozen, at least. More if at all possible."

Kendall shook his head. "I don't count half that many men in MI-Five as true friends."

"What about some other lads? Boyhood pals?"

"They're in the war, sir."

Winterbotham sighed.

"Sir," Kendall said, "if I were able—"

"Yes, I know. Just shut up and let me think for a moment."

Kendall shut up.

A few minutes passed. Winterbotham finished his pint, puffed on his pipe, sent one smoke ring through another. Presently, he said: "If I were to find some small favor you *could* do for me, in the future, could I depend on you to come through?"

"No doubt of it, sir."

Winterbotham gathered together his pipe and tobacco, and stood. "Don't dally too long here, Kendall, if you don't mind the advice. That's a fine young woman you've got at home. Even if she does wear trousers."

Kendall smiled. "I'll tell her you said so, sir."

"Very good. Cheers, then."

He turned and began to move away. Suddenly, he stopped and came back to the booth.

"Kendall," he said, "there may well come a time when I will hold you to your word."

"I'd appreciate the chance to cancel the debt, sir."

Winterbotham looked at him for another moment. Then he nodded once and turned again to leave.

"Sir?" Kendall said.

"Yes?"

"The back foot, you say?"

"The back foot, Kendall."

He left Kendall looking after him. After five minutes, Kendall stirred, finished his pint, produced his tobacco and papers, and began to roll himself another cigarette.

WHITLEY BAY, NEWCASTLE

Peter Faulkner disliked Taylor and Winterbotham even before they began asking him questions.

It was their clothes that caught his eye. They were city clothes, not designed for work in the shipyards nor on the fishing boats. When they sat down at the bar, he noticed their hands—city hands, smooth and uncallused. When they ordered their pints, he noticed their accents. City accents, and not the poor part of the city at that.

They had all sorts of questions, Faulkner told his wife later that night. They asked about the shipyards and the weather patterns and the local inns. They showed him a photograph of a pretty young woman with long blond hair who looked, to his eyes, rather Nordic. They wanted to know if the woman had been seen around town lately. They asked him to imagine her with her hair a different length, or a different color. They asked him to add ten years to the face in the photograph.

Scotland Yard, he told his wife. They must have been from Scotland Yard, on some sort of a manhunt.

His wife laughed. You've some imagination, Peter Faulkner, she said. You should be writing dreadfuls for a living.

What else could it be? he demanded. When mysterious men show around photographs of a beautiful woman . . .

Probably just a cheating wife, Faulkner's wife said. Probably just a jealous husband and his mate, hoping to come across as official. Why in the world would Scotland Yard be looking for a lone woman out here, of all places, at the end of the earth?

By evening, Taylor and Winterbotham had visited no fewer than twelve pubs.

They both were feeling weary, bloated, and a bit tipsy; and to make matters worse, the sky above them was clouding over rapidly. They settled down in a thirteenth tavern, Kirk House, to eat kidney pies that did not seem to have any kidney in them whatsoever. As they ate, they discussed what they had learned during the day.

"If she stays at an inn, we've got her. There are only the three—York House, Brown, and the Bay. Therefore—"

"Therefore, she won't stay at an inn," Winterbotham said.

"Right. And if she *is* alive, she'd be in no shape to spend a week outdoors. She'll find somebody to take her in."

Winterbotham nodded. "Some kind, unsuspecting Geordie."

"So we'll have to wait until she comes out of hiding. We'll nab her on the beach."

"At which point we'll also have a submarine full of Nazis to contend with," Winterbotham pointed out.

"Peterson is bringing a corvette in today and anchoring her up the coast. Midnight Sunday he'll slip down and give the bastards something to chew on."

Winterbotham took a sip of his ale. It was Newcastle Brown—Dog, to the locals—tangy and strong.

"Harry," Taylor said after a moment, "I owe you an apology. I raised your hopes, and now I've dashed them. I promise you this: As soon as the woman is in custody, your case will take priority."

Winterbotham nodded. "Thank you, Andrew."

"I only wish I could do more."

They ate and drank for a few moments, in silence.

"If you don't need me," Winterbotham said, "I won't stay around for the operation itself. I'd like to get back to London. Back to my books."

"Whatever you like, Harry."

"Perhaps when this is all over you'll swing by for a game of chess."

"That would be Sunday evening."

"God willing."

"I'm feeling optimistic," Taylor said. He reached over and gave Winterbotham's shoulder a fraternal squeeze. "Thanks to you, old chap. You've been invaluable. I want you to know, Harry, that I've submitted your name for the Order of the Bath."

Winterbotham started. "A medal," he said.

"A medal." Taylor turned his attention back to his kidney-free kidney pie. "I can't think of anybody who deserves it more."

CHAPTER THIRTEEN

PETERBOROUGH, NORFOLK

"Who cuts your hair, darling?"

Gladys Lockhart flushed. She handed the plate she had just washed to Agnes, who accepted it and began to wipe it dry.

"You do it yourself," Agnes pressed. "Don't you?"

Gladys, mortified, nodded.

"Not anymore, you don't. Let's choose you a new look, darling. Have you got any magazines? You've got a Dorothy Lamour kind of face, but here you are with a Greer Garson kind of hairstyle. Where do you keep your movie magazines, Gladys?"

"In . . . in my dresser," Gladys managed.

"Then let's get these dishes done and have a look, darling, what do you say?"

They finished the supper dishes with expediency, then Agnes followed Gladys upstairs to her bedroom. Gladys, still blushing, removed a stack of movie magazines from the lower drawer of her dresser. They spread them on the bed and then browsed through them together, sitting side by side.

"Never underestimate the power of a good bob," Agnes said. She looked up and then reached out and touched Gladys's hair. "Have you ever considered changing the color?"

"Coloring my hair?" Gladys said.

"Yes, coloring your hair! You've got to think *modern*, Gladys. Just consider how nice you'd look as a brunette. As a matter of fact, it's about time for me to make a change myself. Why, let's swap!—I'll go blond, and you go brunette. *Then* let's see Sir John Frederick Bailey not pay any attention to you! Let's just see it *then!*"

Gladys giggled.

"And for *me*," Agnes said thoughtfully. "Mmmm, let's see . . . I'm already too short to do very much, aren't I? Pity. But we could go for a feather cut, I suppose, and dye it blond, or maybe red. . . . You don't happen to have any hair dye, Gladys, do you?"

Gladys shook her head.

"What about one of your friends? Or perhaps there's a shop nearby?"

"Most dye goes straight to the army," Gladys said, "for their uniforms."

"Mm," Agnes said. "Yes, of course it does."

She thought for a moment; a crimp of concentration appeared between her eyes.

"What about bleach? For the laundry?"

"Why—yes, we've got that."

"But of course that would only work for me. Going blond, I mean. It's not apt to turn you any darker."

"We could still change my style, though," Gladys said hopefully, "couldn't we?"

"Of course, dear. I'll cut you, and you cut me."

"But I'm not very good at cutting."

"We'll work together," Agnes said, "and go very slowly."

She reached out and took Gladys's hand, squeezing it once.

They made a surreptitious foray downstairs. Sir John, still using his study as a bedroom, was snoring audibly. Gladys quickly found bleach and scissors and a washbasin; as an afterthought she picked up an old copy of *The Standard* to catch the fallen hair.

Back in the bedroom, Agnes began to cut, separating a few locks of hair at a time between her index and middle fingers, snipping, then moving along to another clump. Gladys watched in the mirror, fascinated, as the hair framing her face fell away.

"I'm going to look fat," she decided.

"Nonsense. You'll look beautiful."

"Please don't cut too much, Agnes."

"Don't *worry*, Gladys. Have faith."

After another ten minutes, Agnes stepped back, shook out Gladys's hair—cuttings tumbled to the newspaper, pattering softly—then fluffed it up. They regarded it in the mirror together.

"Very fantastic," Agnes assured her.

Gladys turned left and right, inspecting herself. "Really?" she said.

"Very grown-up. Very glamorous. He'll love it."

"Really, truly?"

"Really, truly. Come on, now it's my turn."

They changed positions. Gladys tried to take the scissors, but Agnes stopped her. "I can do the bangs myself," she said.

As it happened, she navigated the bulk of her own haircut, working with near-surgical precision. When it came time to even out the back, she let Gladys take over, stopping her every few moments to check the progress in the mirror.

"You've got to be very careful," Agnes said, "because it's already so short. I don't know how much time I'll have to grow it out before he comes back."

"Before who comes back?"

"Philip, of course. My fiancé."

"You're engaged!"

"Well," Agnes said, "not *officially*. But I've got a feeling . . ."

"Where is he now?"

"In Sicily. He's a lieutenant."

"Tell me about him, Agnes, please."

Agnes smiled at her reflection in the glass. "Let's see," she said as Gladys snipped at a stray lock. "He's handsome, of course. But not *too* handsome. You want to stay away from the *very* handsome men, Gladys, darling. They think altogether too much of themselves, and when they lose their looks, they've got nothing left."

"What does Philip look like?"

"He's tall," Agnes said. "Six feet tall. He's thirty-four years old, and his hair is starting to gray a bit, but just around the temples. He's thin, but not *too* thin. His nose and chin are a bit sharp, but strong; and his eyes, Gladys, are simply amazing. His eyes can make your heart stop in your chest. They change color, depending on his mood. Careful, there, darling, you don't want to—thank you. But you know, I think that's enough. We can bleach it now, but we must dilute the bleach first."

They mixed a concoction of bleach and water in the washbasin. Agnes lay on the floor, her head resting in the basin, as Gladys worked the liquid into her hair, the ends, the roots.

"How long have you known one another?" Gladys asked.

"Hm?" Agnes said. "Nearly two years." Her eyes were closed. Her face, Gladys thought, looked very peaceful.

"Have you . . . ?"

"Mm?"

"You know," Gladys said.

"What?"

"*You* know, Agnes. Don't make me say it."

Agnes opened one eye, then closed it again. "Yes," she said. "We have."

"Was he your first?"

Agnes opened both eyes. She gazed abstractedly at the ceiling for a moment before closing them. "No," she said.

"Who else?"

"I'd rather not discuss it, Gladys."

"But it *is* better with somebody you love, right?"

"I'd rather not discuss it, I said. Now, just concentrate on what you're doing."

"But, Agnes, please. You must tell me—"

"Quiet, Gladys. Concentrate."

That night Katarina lay awake in bed, trying to will herself to sleep—and failing.

She rolled over angrily and pressed her head deeper into the pillow. She *needed* to rest. The entire purpose of her *staying* in Peterborough was to rest.

Why couldn't she sleep? It made no sense. She was spent—utterly and completely spent, emotionally, mentally, and physically.

She had realized, following her encounter with the *Luftwaffe*, that she needed to get outside of whatever new perimeter her pursuers established. That meant a hike—and not the leisurely sort. She had struck off on foot, setting a nearly impossible pace for herself, despite her dizziness. This, she had recognized, was her only real chance: to get farther from the crumpled lorry than they would think possible.

The very worst of it had come near the beginning, during a one-mile hike down a shallow river. Simply submerging oneself in a creek, she knew, would not throw off a bloodhound. The scent rose to the top of the water. One needed to travel a good distance, slogging through a brook, for it to be worth anything. And she had done it, though her body—exhausted, battered, and burned—had cried bloody murder.

Somehow the dogs had never quite caught up to her, although she had heard them, more than once, baying in the distance. After leaving the stream, she had walked all through the night, all through the following day, keeping to the woods whenever possible, giving wide leeway to the towns she encountered; then, after a few hours of fitful rest, she had walked all through the night again. She had pushed herself to the very point of collapse.

But she had made it. That was all that mattered. She had come far enough to slip through the third perimeter. Now they wouldn't find her unless they conducted a house-to-house sweep.

Which they surely would, considering the import of the knowledge in her head.

She wondered, not for the first time, why they hadn't come yet.

Perhaps they were focusing themselves only on roadblocks and railway junctions. But this explanation, while tempting, did not satisfy her. She knew the secret of the bomb; would they really be content to pursue her in an essentially passive way? Not, she was forced to concede, unless they possessed some backup plan, some perceived likelihood of catching her farther down the line.

The *treff*?

Would they be waiting for her there?

But how could they possibly know where the rendezvous would be? Even if they had broken her codes, the chances that they could have isolated and identified the particular burst of wireless noise from Hamburg that had been her instructions . . .

Could Fritz have betrayed her? She would not have doubted it. Yet she couldn't figure out how. He was dead before she had ever learned the location of the rendezvous.

Then what?

She heaved another sigh and rolled over again, burrowing into the sheets. It did not particularly matter, she thought, one way or the other, if they were expecting her at the *treff*. It did not matter because she was already committed. She would go ahead with the rendezvous in any case, trap or not.

Then she had the strangest thought of all:

What if she *wasn't* already committed?

What if she changed her mind? Took herself out of the game?

She opened her eyes, considering.

It would be possible, she decided. Lay low in Peterborough for a week or two, until things cooled a bit. Then move on. Elsewhere in England, or up into Scotland; or to Lisbon, or Tangier, or Casablanca. Eventually the war would end, and then the world would open itself to her. Perhaps, she thought, she could even return to America. The Jitterbug. The Big Apple. The Lindy Bop. Yes, it could be done. She was still young enough to start over.

She thought of Philip, the fictional Philip, whom she had described to Gladys in such detail out of whole cloth. Then she thought, somewhat wryly, of Oscar Wilde: *Man is least himself when he talks in his own person. Give him a mask and he will tell you the truth.*

But was that really what she desired—a safe, conventional, boring situation? Had she forgotten so quickly what life had been like for Catherine Danielson Carter?

No, she hadn't forgotten.

Better to be true to herself and perish than to risk returning to that—or, even worse, to risk what had happened to Fritz.

And don't forget, she thought, *if you make it, you'll be a hero. You'll return to Germany with the secret that will win the war. You'll have your pick of men. You'll live out your life with the victors in splendor, with honor, in luxury.*

And yet . . .

And yet.

And yet she did not believe, deep down, that the secret in her head *would* be enough to win the war.

Or, more precisely, she did not believe that her people would use it that way.

Every time she tried to picture the result of her delivering her secret to Hitler, she envisioned *Götterdämmerung*—the twilight of the gods. That was the Germanic way, after all, from times of legend: Valhalla ablaze in an orgy of death and destruction, friends and foes perishing as one; Siegfried, Brunhilde, Wotan all drowning in blood and flame—yet satisfied, somehow, with what they had wrought. It was, she believed, the true essence of Hitler's war: not to conquer the world and acquire *lebensraum*, not at its core, but to fight against impossible odds and to conquer, for a time; and then, when his enemies had beaten him back, to burn everything he encountered. His foes, his followers, and finally, gloriously, himself.

Blasphemy.

Blasphemy and propaganda.

She was exhausted. That was the problem.

She tried again to force herself to sleep. She would need her sleep in the days to come.

Then she thought of the girl.

Another betrayal. Another murder.

She had not allowed herself to grow close to anybody, to make any sort of real personal connection since her time at Owen and Dunn, ten years before. The marriage to Richard had been a study in keeping chilly distance; she had not let him past even her outermost line of defense.

The last time she had grown at all close to anybody, in fact, she had ended up killing her.

Now history seemed on the verge of repeating itself.

Gladys was kind and sweet, naïve and friendly. But of course she would have to die—both she and Sir John—so that no alarm would be raised once Katarina had stolen the car.

She would eliminate Gladys on Thursday, she thought, when Bailey went into London on business. Then Bailey himself, when he arrived home that night. Then she would take the car and drive, keeping under cover of dark, hiding and sleeping during the day, reaching the point of rendezvous well before Sunday morning, rested and fed, ready for anything.

Her hand wandered absently to her hair. It was bristly, not only from its great shortness—what a fright she must have looked—but from the bleach, which had proved harsh and desiccating.

Still, it was an extreme change, an effective disguise. She guessed that very few of the male British Military Intelligence officers who were looking for her would make a connection between her current self, the dark-haired woman with the mid-length bob who had been on the train, and the Katarina Heinrich of the flowing blond locks. Especially not if she was able to show them Gladys Lockhart's National Registration card. They did not share a perfect likeness, she and Gladys; but if the light was poor, it should be good enough.

And God damn it, why didn't he *come* to her, the old fool? She was in his bed. She would accept him if he came. It would be, at least, a distraction. But he was too much of a coward.

When sunrise was a mere hour away, she decided that she had no chance of sleeping that night.

Then her body played a trick on her. She slept through the dawn.

THE NORTH SEA

Kapitänleutnant Schmidt did not know which was worse, the hovering SS man in his glistening black uniform or the fact that they were out of coffee.

The SS man, named Hagen, was making a point of staying aggressively close to Schmidt. The submarine, U-403, was claustrophobic enough, in *Kapitänleutnant* Schmidt's opinion, without an SS man dogging his every move. If the man was still following him so closely when they approached the coast, Schmidt would have no choice. He would have to ask Hagen to cease and desist.

Except that he wouldn't, and he knew it.

He was terrified of the SS man, who wore the Twelve-Years-Long Service Award prominently displayed on his lapel, just below the double slash of lightning. Twelve *years* in the SS, Schmidt thought—the man must have been truly immune to pity.

Schmidt knew that he was not alone in his fear of Hagen. The *Abwehr* representative on board, the nominal leader of this mission, was a man named Klaus Gruber. Gruber positively cringed every time Hagen so much as glanced at him. The rest of the crew simply kept their heads down and avoided making eye contact, perhaps imitating the conduct of their captain.

If only there had been a decent supply of coffee on board, Schmidt thought, he would have felt more alert, more able to handle the SS man. But he had been told just as they were putting out: There was no more coffee to be spared for the U-boats. Things in Berlin must have been going badly indeed, if they couldn't even rustle up a few pounds of coffee for the brave boys in the wolf packs. The U-boats, after all, were Germany's first line of defense.

He sighed heavily, then folded up the periscope and turned around.

And immediately bumped into Hagen, who was sticking close, as usual.

"Excuse me, *Herr* Hagen," Schmidt said.

"Of course," Hagen said in a voice that was almost a purr.

"I'm going up to have a look at the weather," Schmidt said. Even as he said it he wondered why he felt the need to justify himself to this man, who was officially nothing more than an observer.

"The weather concerns you?"

"It does. It should concern you, too. If that storm doesn't come in, we'll make a fine target for the British corvettes."

"Do you not expect the storm to come in?"

"In fact," Schmidt said, "I expect just the opposite. But I'll feel better when I've seen it break with my own eyes."

Hagen nodded.

"So if you'll excuse me," Schmidt said, and waited for the man to step aside to make room.

Hagen did so, but slowly, contemptuously.

"Herr Kapitänleutnant," he said as Schmidt brushed past, "if by chance the storm does not break, what, may I ask, are your plans then?"

"If the storm does not break," Schmidt said, "we will postpone the rendezvous for one week. Let the English traitor return when circumstances are in our favor."

Hagen's mouth turned down at the corners.

"I am afraid that is not possible," he said softly. "Perhaps now is the time for me to inform you, *Herr Kapitänleutnant*, that there is more at stake here than you are aware."

Schmidt tried to look the man in the eyes, but he was unable to hold his resolve. Instead, he quickly looked down at the bulkhead beneath their feet.

"More at stake?" he muttered.

"*Herr* Gruber's mission is only one of the missions we are undertaking. We will be rendezvousing with two agents during this *treff*."

"Two agents," Schmidt repeated.

"Correct."

"Why was I not informed?"

"The second mission is confidential. Even *Herr* Gruber is not aware of it."

"Who is the second agent?"

"That does not concern you. Suffice it to say that I am reporting directly to *Reichsleiter* Himmler on this matter."

Schmidt straightened up. "If you compel me to approach the coast in clear weather, *Herr* Hagen," he said, "I believe it does concern me. This is my vessel, after all. As captain I am responsible for her well-being."

Hagen's frown turned up into a dull smile. "*Herr* Schmidt," he said, "so long as the storm breaks, there will be no need to determine who possesses the ultimate authority onboard this vessel, hm?"

Schmidt, with an effort, continued to stand at his full height.

"If you would care to force the issue," Hagen said, "you will find me willing. But since it seems that we will have the storm we require, is that truly necessary?"

Schmidt said nothing.

"I thought not," Hagen said. "Now, come, *Kapitänleutnant* Schmidt. Let us go and have a look at your weather . . . together."

PETERBOROUGH, NORFOLK

Gladys's lips were moving. "Whhh . . ." she said.

Katarina put her hand over Gladys's mouth. She watched the confused light in the girl's eyes fade, fade, and then die.

Katarina took her hand back, put it in her lap, and sat for a moment on the kitchen floor, thinking. The craving for a cigarette hit her, momentarily enveloped her, and then passed. She looked at the corpse lying next to her. *Not yet eighteen,* she thought. Gladys's mouth was open; her tongue looked unnaturally red. She had begun to vomit blood before she had died.

Her eyes also were open, staring bleakly.

Not yet eighteen, Katarina thought again.

She reached out and closed the girl's eyes.

After another few minutes, she gained her feet. She felt suddenly old. Her back hurt. She looked down again at the corpse, then bent over—her spine popped loudly—and picked up the knife.

After straightening again, she hesitated. The kitchen windows were open; she could hear the pleasant buzzing of insects in the garden.

The garden earth would be soft, easy to dig.

She set the bloody knife down on the counter, got her hands under Gladys's arms, and began to drag her.

When Sir John Frederick Bailey arrived home that evening, he found Katarina Heinrich standing in his kitchen, alone in the semi-darkness, holding a bottle of wine.

At the sound of his footsteps, she turned. She swayed, regarding him. Her clothes were muddy; her face was slack.

Sir John Frederick Bailey looked her up and down.

"Where did that bottle come from?" he asked sternly.

Katarina didn't answer. She raised the bottle and drank from it.

"Where's Gladys?" Bailey said. He took a step forward, into the kitchen. "Where did that bottle come from? Answer me, Agnes. From the cellar?"

Katarina nodded.

"Did Gladys tell you that you could—"

"John," she said. "Come here."

He stood there, staring at her.

"Come on," she said, and smiled. "I've got a secret."

Bailey snorted. "You're drunk," he said.

He reached for her, meaning to take the arm that held the bottle. But somehow the bottle ended up on the floor, and her hand ended up closing around his wrist. She turned him around forcefully; a bone in his arm splintered with a loud, dry crack. He opened his mouth to cry out, and her other hand came up, the fingers sliding between his lips, choking him.

Then her first hand moved and did something soft in his side, near his kidney, spreading warmth up into his ribs. He felt a delicious agony that shaded, very quickly, into wet, and dark, and quiet.

"Verzeihen Sie mir," Katarina murmured, lowering him to the floor.

She waited for full night to fall, just in case the neighbors happened not to mind their own business. Then she dragged Bailey to the garden, slit his throat, laid him upside-down over a sharp rock, and watched him bleed into the freshly turned earth.

After watching him drain for a few moments, she went inside again and collected her baggage. She piled it into the Aston Martin parked in the driveway: a four-seater with two doors, built in 1938 but still in near-perfect condition. A nice step up from the lorry, she thought. And all she'd had to do to get it was—

She cut the thought off.

She entered the house again and conducted a final quick search to make sure she'd missed nothing of value. She was rewarded by the discovery of several dozen small white tablets in a vial in Bailey's desk drawer. They were amphetamines, produced by the American army to keep its soldiers alert and awake. Bailey, it seemed, had his vices.

Katarina took a handful and pocketed them. Then, with sudden inspiration, she took another handful and, using the flat blade of a letter opener, ground them to dust on the desktop. She tore a piece of paper from a notepad, folded it into a packet to hold the powder, and tucked it into her shoe. If she needed a sudden burst of strength, she would forsake the pills and simply snort the powder. It would travel directly to her bloodstream, providing intense energy and increased alertness—for a few minutes. Then, of course, she would crash.

For emergency only, she thought.

She went around to the backyard again, checked on Bailey, and saw that he had another few minutes of draining left in him.

She stood in the garden and waited, carefully thinking nothing at all.

She struck off an hour past dark.

She drove north. She would avoid turning east, toward the coast, until it was absolutely necessary. The ten-mile strip bordering the water was a restricted area; it would be heavily patrolled.

She felt nervous.

After driving for perhaps twenty minutes she noticed that the road seemed to end very abruptly two hundred yards ahead. As she drew closer, she realized that she had reached her first roadblock: two sedans, parked in a V. She slowed, thinned her lips, then came to a full stop.

Two young men appeared from the brush at the side of the road. One came to shine his torch in her face, while the other went around to the passenger seat to take a look at Bailey. Out of the corner of her eye, she saw light glancing off the ascot wrapped around Bailey's throat, off the brim of the hat pulled low over his face—

"Get that light out of his eyes," she snapped. "Can't you see he's sleeping?"

The lads, neither of them older than nineteen, hastily obeyed.

"Sorry to trouble you, miss. But may we see your papers, please?"

She passed the papers over, then sat drumming her fingers impatiently on the wheel.

The man by her door looked at the first identity card. He flipped to the second. He flipped back to the first.

He handed the cards back through the window, and waved her on.

She passed Spalding, then Newark-on-Trent, then grazed the eastern border of Mansfield, then entered a stretch of country leading toward Doncaster. She drove for another hour without encountering a second roadblock.

Her nervousness increased.

What did they know that she didn't?

Finally, in the small hours of the morning, she decided not to push her luck. If she came upon a roadblock now, she would be the only car to have passed within recent memory. They would pay far too much attention.

She began to look for a place to wait out the rest of the night. After twenty minutes, she reached a small road running roughly northeast, into thick woods. The way was marked by a signpost featuring a wood carving of a pheasant. *Private property,* she thought. With any luck, they owned a lot of land and would leave her alone until morning.

She doused her headlamps and took the turn.

Once surrounded by trees, she drove for another thirty feet, then pulled the Aston Martin as far off the road as possible. She killed the engine, got out, and spent ten minutes arranging loose brush to screen the car.

She climbed back behind the wheel and tried to settle down for the night.

Sir John Frederick Bailey, even bled, was beginning to smell. She turned away from him, putting her face near the open window. But she couldn't escape it: a ripe, sour odor, already rich with decay. She tried to close off her senses. Discipline. She had hoped to keep Bailey through the second night of driving, until she had reached York, in case she encountered more roadblocks. He shouldn't have started to putrefy for another day at least.

But the stench proved too great to bear. There was something about Bailey, it seemed, that lent itself to rapid decomposition. After a half hour she admitted to herself that his use to her was finished.

She got up, dragged the rigor mortis–stiffened corpse out of the car—upsetting much of her screen in the process—pulled him two dozen feet away, and left him lying facedown in a streambed. She had to bury him, of course. But she suddenly felt too exhausted even to move.

She went back to the car and slipped behind the wheel again. In just a moment, she would get up and dig a shallow grave. She wondered if the ground of the streambed would be easy to dig. Or would the forest floor be better?

God, but she was tired.

The interior of the car still smelled like a corpse. When had she become so soft? she wondered. When had she turned so weak that something as trivial as a bad smell could upset her?

She had rested long enough. It was time to get up, leave the car, and bury the corpse.

She would take an amphetamine. Get herself going again. That was what she would do.

In just a moment, she thought.

In just a moment.

In just one more moment.

She woke to the sound of a truncheon rapping on the windshield.

A man was standing beside the Aston Martin, waving her out of the car.

She bought herself a second by rubbing at her eyes. Then she obeyed slowly, leaving the suitcase in the back untouched—he was watching her too closely.

The man was tall, on the far side of sixty, smelling powerfully of hair tonic, wearing a faded waistcoat. It was a cane in his hand, she realized, not a truncheon. In his other hand was a leash. A mottled gray-black terrier strained at the end of the line—not in her direction but toward the dry streambed.

Toward the corpse.

"Morning," the man said.

"Good morning," Katarina said.

"You won't mind if I ask what you're doing here, sleeping in a car on my brother's property, now would you?"

Katarina looked around for a moment before answering. If there was a brother in the vicinity, he was keeping to himself. Nor could she see a house or a farm; only the woods, the deep wet shadows, and the bright morning sun.

She looked back at the man, judging distances.

"I ran low on petrol," Katarina said. "I pulled off the road. A girl can't be too careful these days."

The terrier turned its head and looked up at its master. It barked twice, pipingly, then strained again toward the streambed.

"I suppose not," the man said. "Where are you headed, all by yourself?"

Katarina heard twigs snapping. She turned her head and saw another man coming from the direction of the streambed. He was perhaps a decade younger than the first, wearing a dark roll-neck sweater, holding a shotgun.

"Body in the stream," he said.

"Bloody hell!" the man with the dog said.

"Raise your hands," the man with the shotgun said, and put the gun on Katarina.

She hesitated, then put her hands above her head.

"You know what we've got here, George? One of those Fifth Columnists, I'll wager."

"You've gone daft. This bird?"

"*You* explain why she's out here, then, with a body in the stream not two dozen feet away. The car's stolen, I'll wager, and what's more she's got no papers."

"What about it?" George asked Katarina.

"On the dash."

George moved to the car, opened the front door, and leaned in. After a moment he stepped out again, holding the papers. He carried them to the man with the roll-neck sweater, riffling through them as he walked.

"Gladys?" he said.

Katarina nodded.

"Don't take this the wrong way, love, but you look a shade over seventeen."

She said nothing.

"And who's this? Fellow in the stream?"

"Aye."

They both looked at Katarina.

"Turn around, lass," George said. He came forward, unlooping his belt from his trousers. "Put your hands behind your back."

Katarina turned, lowered her hands, and put them into the small of her back.

She watched the man's shadow on the forest floor.

As he reached for her wrists, she pivoted on the balls of both feet, dropping, sending a mirror block to his right hand, striking the ulnar nerve on the inside of the wrist, deadening that arm. Then, rising again, she delivered a left hooking arc with the heel of her palm, hitting the small bony ridge just under his right ear, dislocating his jaw.

She seized him by his shoulders, spun him around to face his brother, threw him forward, and took cover behind the car.

Roll-neck sweater held his fire—God damn it.

Katarina crouched behind the Aston Martin, peering beneath the undercarriage. She could see George sprawled on his side, on the ground, looking at his dead arm with wonder.

She opened the back door of the car and started to climb in.

The shotgun thundered. The windows on one side of the car blew out, spraying glass.

A shard grazed her temple. She ignored it. Her fingers snagged the suitcase and she quickly slithered back out of the car. She hit the latch, found the haft of the knife. Except for the shallow wound on her forehead she was unhurt. One barrel left in the gun. But where was he? She peered beneath the undercarriage again. She could see George, still down—and the dog, still with its master—but where was the second man?

A soft crunch.

To her left. Coming around the Aston Martin.

She rolled under the car, rolled over crackling pieces of glass, and came up lightly onto her feet.

Roll-neck was in the process of sneaking around the front. She turned the knife over in her hand as she stood, taking aim.

" 'Ware!" George cried, his voice cracking.

Roll-neck spun, bringing the gun up. At the same instant, the knife flew from Katarina's hand. She immediately dropped onto the forest floor again. She did not see the knife find its target; but there was a choking sound, a drizzle of blood in the air, a belated explosion from the gun, then a sudden hissing, squealing, steam-venting from the front of the car.

The dog was coming for her.

She reached for its throat, but it gave her teeth, trying to bite her hand. She managed to spin the thing over in the air and drive it into the earth head-first. The terrier let out a yelp. Katarina picked it up again. She drove it into the ground again, and its neck snapped.

She turned her attention back to George. His eyes were huge. He began to try to drag himself away across the ground, his dead arm flapping uselessly.

She finished him.

Then she considered her next course of action. The Aston Martin was ruined; steam was pouring from it. How long would it take for these men to be missed? She looked for wedding bands, saw none. Which didn't mean a thing. If the alarm was going to be raised immediately, then she would not travel on foot; she would risk hitchhiking. But if the alarm would not be raised for half a day, she would rather gain some distance from this place before showing her face to anybody.

She decided to proceed on foot—at least for a time. She ate a quick breakfast, not looking around herself, chewing thoroughly, so the food would stay down. She went through her baggage and chose only the most necessary items—the knife, water, the torch. She splashed water on her wounds, changed the bandages again, and left the medical supplies behind with the suitcase.

How far left to go?

All the farther, she decided, for not having gone yet.

She looked at the two bodies for a moment before she struck off. Looking at them made her gorge start to rise.

She looked away.

She went.

CHAPTER FOURTEEN

FLAMBOROUGH HEAD, YORKSHIRE

The lighthouse was no stranger to storms.

She had stood here, on Flamborough Head, for more than a century. During that time, she had seen far worse storms than the one that was gathering now, out over the North Sea.

She stood eighty-five feet from the ragged cliffs that sloped down to the water's edge. Originally, she had been built one hundred feet from the precipice, but in the intervening century the storms had eroded the land. The sea was hungry for her, nipping closer with each passing decade. Eventually it would claim her—but that time was still far away.

For four years now she had lain dormant. One day very near the start of the war, the government had come and told old Rupert that they were borrowing her. From now on, they'd said, she was not to be lit unless they ordered her lit; and once lit, she was not to go dark until they ordered her dark. Old Rupert was to remain living there, ready to be of use.

And he had ever since, but the government had never returned.

Perhaps they had forgotten her.

The Nazis, however, had not forgotten her.

Even unlit, she served as a fine landmark. Her gray stone façade was painted with red and white stripes. At forty-odd feet she was not a particularly tall specimen of lighthouse, but perched up on the cliffside she was tall enough.

Rudolf Schroeder knew her as rendezvous four. From three o'clock to five o'clock on Sunday mornings, she would be watched by a U-boat at sea. If a light was to flash twice, the U-boat would dispatch a dinghy to the rocky beach below.

Old Rupert had been manning the lighthouse for thirty-five years.

Tonight he stood on the balcony that encircled the lantern, holding a bottle in his hand, peering up at the sky. Any moment now, he thought, the storm would break. It would be a real storm, a humdinger. Not the worst he had ever seen, not by a long shot—he had seen quite a few storms in his thirty-five years keeping the lighthouse—but a humdinger nonetheless; and the cliff would crumble that much faster, and the sea would creep that much closer.

This pleased him, somehow.

The air was heavy and hot and clung irritatingly to his skin. Even the cool breeze coming in off the water couldn't cut through it. In an hour, perhaps, when the breeze was no longer cool but had turned viciously cold . . . but old Rupert didn't care to wait. He turned and moved inside, stepping carefully past the mercury baths (more than once he had slipped, when drunk, and mercury was not a good thing to be slipping in), and then cautiously descended the narrow stone staircase.

Rupert moved into his tiny, gloomy kitchen and fetched a glass. Why a man should need to drink from a glass was beyond him, especially when the man was alone; but Marion, he knew, had always disapproved of his drinking straight from the bottle. Marion had considered it unseemly.

He carried the glass and the bottle into his study. The room was windowless, cramped, fragrant with old books. He lit the kerosene lamp and settled into his chair. A small framed photograph of him and Marion sat on the desk beside a quill and inkwell, a rusted old compass, and a five-inch rack and pinion sextant. A chessboard beside the quill had gone untouched for at least three years; a thick layer of dust lay atop the pieces.

Rupert poured himself a tot, toasted to nothing, and knocked it back. He poured himself a second, set it down, then looked around and wondered what book he should read tonight.

There had not been a lot for Rupert to do since the government had forbidden him to operate his lighthouse and Marion had gone away. Most nights he drank. For the first few hours of drinking, he would read, or study old maps, or play solitaire. Then, when sufficiently intoxicated, he would start to sing. Sometimes he would go up to the balcony and sing out at the sea, daring his drunk limbs to betray him, to send him tumbling over the railing. That would be a relief, in a way. But so far his legs had always held him. Perhaps he simply needed to get more drunk, he sometimes thought, before going up to the balcony surrounding the lantern.

It seemed like a fine night for singing to the sea—the storm and all. He knocked back his second drink, refilled his glass, and turned his attention again to the rows of books.

He had read them all before, many times over. Even when the lighthouse had been operating, Rupert had suffered no shortage of free time. Once every four hours he had needed to crank a large weight up the center shaft of the tower to keep the lens turning; but except for that simple task, his days, for the most part, had been his own. Marion had left nearly eight years before, when she'd married the boy from over near the Tyne. Rupert had approved of the boy. Then he had been shot down in the Battle of Britain, a true pity. Rupert had hoped that Marion would come home after that, but she'd chosen to stay in London. Not that he blamed her. A young woman didn't want to be stuck in a lighthouse with her old, drunk, half-mad father; even he understood that.

He realized that his eyes were misting over. But there was nobody there to see it, so he didn't care. He knocked back his third drink, refilled the glass, and dabbed at the corner of his eye.

Then he made his selection for the evening: *King Solomon's Mines*, by Haggard. A fine selection for a Saturday night, he thought. Adventure and so forth. He would barrel through it, and by the time he reached the end he would be drunk enough to go up to the balcony and dare the ocean to take him.

Maybe he would even be drunk enough, tonight, that it would actually happen.

He turned to the first page. Outside, the clouds split open and spilled out the first drops of summer rain.

PART THREE

CHAPTER FIFTEEN

WHITLEY BAY

Taylor swept the binoculars across the night-shrouded beach, left and then right, right and then left, in ever-widening arcs. He took them from his eyes and puffed on the damp cigarette hanging between his lips. He checked his wristwatch. He put the binoculars to his eyes again. Left and then right. Right and then left. It was too soon for the Heinrich woman to be on the beach, of course. It was raining with ever-increasing force, and it was the dead of night. All of which meant that he wasn't seeing much of anything through the binoculars. But he wasn't yet ready to give up. Perhaps, if he was watching closely enough, he could apprehend her before the *treff* proper and avoid a bit of complication. Perhaps—

"Sir," somebody at his elbow was saying.

Taylor took the binoculars from his eyes again. He turned to look at Kendall. Kendall looked nervous, but then, Kendall always looked nervous.

"Sorry to disturb you, sir. It may be nothing. But we've got a call from Wells—"

"Who?"

"Wells, sir. At Latchmere."

"Yes, yes."

"He says that Schroeder is extremely anxious to speak with you."

"What's it about?"

"He refuses to tell anybody but you, sir. But he seems to have convinced Wells that it's important."

Taylor took another drag from his cigarette, then pitched it into the sand at his feet. "Tell him he'll have to wait. I'll be at Ham Common on Monday."

"Wells asked to speak to you himself, sir, if you said that."

"For God's sake, why?"

"He seems to feel it's important."

"Bloody idiots," Taylor muttered. "All right. Cover the beach, Kendall."

He handed Kendall the binoculars and then turned on his heel and strode off toward Faulkner's Pub, moving briskly under the cold plump drops of rain.

They had taken over Faulkner's Pub for this particular operation, with Peter Faulkner's grudging consent. Faulkner's was perfect for their needs. Only the Highland was closer to the expected scene of the *treff*; but since the Highland was also a landmark for the meeting, Taylor had considered it a bit too close for comfort.

On this summer midnight, Faulkner's Pub was filled with men cleaning guns, men studying maps, men talking in low voices. The one thing none of the men was doing was drinking, which frustrated Peter Faulkner, standing by the bar, to no end. But he was able to take some satisfaction from their presence nevertheless. He was looking forward to explaining to his wife the next morning that the marital problem that had brought these men to his pub must have been a corker indeed. Twenty-five government agents were apparently after the woman in the photograph, armed to the teeth, with seemingly limitless resources.

Taylor moved to a corner in the rear of the pub and accepted the phone that was offered him.

"Taylor," he said.

"Wells here, sir."

"What's the problem?"

"Schroeder's been sick all night. Now he's demanding to see you immediately."

"Sick?"

"Vomiting, sir."

"Pity. Why does he want to see me?"

"He won't say."

"Put him on."

"He says he won't speak over the phone, sir."

"I haven't time for games, Wells. Tell him it's that or nothing."

"Hold on, sir."

Taylor held on. He considered lighting another cigarette as he waited, then decided against it. Not only was he running low, but he hadn't eaten in hours; all the smoke was making him feel a bit nauseous.

After a few moments, Wells was on the line again.

"Sir?"

"Yes?"

"He still won't speak over the phone, sir. But he says that you're wasting your time there. He demands that you come to Latchmere and speak to him immediately."

"Wasting my time?"

"That's what he says."

"God damn it, tell him no more goddamn chocolate if he doesn't get on this goddamn phone right now."

"Hold on, sir."

Another, longer, pause. This time Taylor gave in to temptation and lit a cigarette. He took a deep drag; his head immediately began to swim.

"Andrew," a voice said. Dour, lazy, heavily accented.

"Rudolf. What the hell is this about?"

A hesitation.

"Winterbotham," Schroeder said then.

"What about him?"

"He's buggered us both."

"What on earth are you talking about?"

"The old cocksucker," Schroeder said distinctly, "was meant to come here and fetch me. But he never came. And the chocolates he gave me were poisoned, I'm sure of it. I've been sick as a—"

"Slow down, Rudolf. Go there and fetch you for what?"

"For the *treff*."

"Rudolf, you had—"

"We deceived you," Schroeder said. "He promised to take me with him if I helped to throw you off his track."

"Throw me off his track?"

"If I lied to you, Andrew. Lied about the location of rendezvous four."

Taylor's cigarette fell from his mouth.

"Fuck," he said.

FLAMBOROUGH HEAD, YORKSHIRE

A lamp was on inside the lighthouse, blazing out through the sheeting curtains of rain.

There would be food in there, and dry beds. Compared to the gray night, the whipping winds, and the evil rain, the light inside looked brighter than it must have actually been. It looked as if a sun were glowing inside the lighthouse, a miniature sun, beckoning her . . .

No, she was hallucinating. That was all. How many miles had she gone, in the past few days? Too many.

Ten steps left to the door. Nine steps. Not too late to be strong . . . to turn and burrow under a bush and wait out the storm and the night . . . but she was so hungry, so tired, so cold and wet . . . Besides, she was feverish . . . eight steps . . . Suddenly she realized that she could not make it. She could not even make it to the door. She was finished.

Then she had made it, somehow, and was rapping the brass knocker against the hoary wood, over and over again.

Then the light was growing brighter, ever brighter.

Then the door opened, and hands were pulling her inside.

The old man was very drunk.

Katarina was sitting in Rupert's study on a creaky wooden chair, with a tattered blanket around her shoulders, listening to the old man talk about his daughter. A nearly empty bottle sat on the desk before him between a book and a dusty chessboard. The old man was trembling and slurring his speech—but this, she thought, was not necessarily from the liquor. This could have been from prolonged exposure to the mercury baths. Most lighthouse keepers were half mad, at least.

She took a sip of her tea. It was hot and strong and made her feel almost like herself again.

" 'Round your age," Rupert said, and reached for the bottle. He started to bring it directly to his mouth, then paused, squinted, and moved the neck of the bottle unsteadily toward a glass.

"Where is she now?" Katarina asked politely.

"London," the old man said. "Hell, I don't blame her." He raised his glass. "To London," he said.

Katarina smiled weakly.

He drank, peering at her over the rim of his glass. "Care for a tot?" he asked.

"Thank you, no."

"Some grub?"

She hesitated.

"Got a bit of bubble and squeak someplace. Hold on."

Rupert levered himself out of the chair without waiting for an answer, stumbled, righted himself, and moved past her, toward the kitchen.

Katarina sat without moving. She felt drowsy. How long had it been since she'd last slept? Forty-eight hours? Seventy-two? The room was warm; the storm outside seemed distant. The blanket across her shoulders was dry and smelled old, but old in a good way.

She looked around and found a clock tucked onto a shelf between books. Nearly half past twelve. Sunday morning; and earlier than she had thought. In just under three hours she would be standing on the beach outside. She would need to find a light of some kind, to give the signal—she had left hers abandoned in the countryside, along with everything else she had been able to drop, to lighten her load. But the old man must have a torch around there somewhere.

And then she would be back in Germany. After so long away, more than a lifetime . . . it was difficult to believe. What was Berlin like these days? Was it anything like the Berlin she remembered?

She wanted to sleep. She could easily drift off right there, sitting in that uncomfortable chair. But sleep was a luxury she could not yet afford. Less than three hours, she thought. Besides, she had to kill the old man, didn't she? Leaving him alive would be taking an unnecessary risk.

Not that he could really do her any harm . . .

What had happened to her, that she thought that way? What had happened to her sense of duty, her sense of *efficiency*?

He came back and handed her a plate. On the plate was a dull knife, a hunk of bread, stale but not moldy, and a small chunk of cheese. Beside the bread and cheese was a dollop of cabbage and potatoes, lightly fried.

"I'm sorry," Rupert said. " 'Taint much."

"It looks wonderful."

She devoured the food in a few bites, then picked the crumbs off her plate with her fingers. The old man wasn't paying attention. He was back behind his desk, drinking again, misty-eyed, talking about his daughter.

There was no need to kill him.

Just thinking it made her scorn herself even more. How had she lost her edge? She had seen what had happened to Fritz; she should have been more wary than ever of commiserating with the enemy.

But her mind kept coming back to the thought. There was no need to kill him. He was old, drunk, and kind. He was half mad with mercury poisoning. He was helpless.

On the other hand, any unforeseen quantity presented a possible danger. The safe route . . .

"Aha!" the old man cried. "She gets that, too!"

Katarina blinked. "What?" she said.

He leaned across the desk, pointing. His finger stopped an inch short of her forehead and hovered there.

"The worry line," he said. "Marion gets that, too. When she's thinking about something, thinking hard, she gets that line right down the middle of her forehead, just the way you've got it there."

"I'm just trying to figure out how on earth I'm going to get to Bridlington tomorrow, with my bicycle gone."

"You and Mare would like each other. I know you would. She's a fine young woman."

"I'm sure she is."

"Fine young woman," Rupert said again. He reached for his glass and found it empty. He reached for the bottle and found that empty, too. He grinned foolishly. "Hell," he said.

He pushed himself out of his chair, swayed for a moment, then carefully knelt on the floor, his back to Katarina, and reached for his liquor cabinet.

She picked up the knife.

Afterward, she vomited up the bread, the cheese, the cabbage and potatoes, and the tea. Waves of dizziness rolled over her like surf over the beach below.

But she got her hands under his arms anyway, and dragged him up the narrow stone staircase. He was heavier than she would have thought. People took on weight, in death. Sixty stairs wound up. By the time she reached the top, her breath was coming short and hard. A film of chilly sweat covered her face.

It was, she feared, the first stirrings of pneumonia. If only she could lie down, close her eyes, just for a few hours . . .

She placed old Rupert, with some effort, in the mercury bath under the great lens. The lens was a two-ton beehive of layered glass; the mercury filled the huge tub beneath it. Rupert settled into the viscous substance tentatively, but refused to sink below the surface. For several minutes, Katarina tried, without success, to prod him down. Time after time, he rose again. Finally she gave up.

She stumbled back downstairs. Sleep was coming for her; she couldn't pretend otherwise. She was on the verge of . . . on the verge of God only knew what. An hour or two was all she needed, that and some food that would stay down. Then she would return to the Fatherland and save all her countrymen and there would be parades and flowers and music and dancing and perhaps Fritz would be there, holding her, gently kissing her, as flashbulbs popped and the gallows swung in the background . . .

No, Fritz was dead. She had seen it herself.

Delirious, she thought. *You're delirious.*

The thought of food was tempting, but the demands of finding and eating it seemed altogether too daunting. She staggered off the bottom step and moved past the study to see what else was in this hovel. She found one bedroom with a small bed neatly made. Better than the chairs in the study. She collapsed onto it face first. Stripped off her filthy, sodden bandages, dropping them on the floor. Lying on a dead man's bed. A man she had just killed. A man who had taken her in, taken her out of the storm . . .

The storm, she thought.

She could hear it raging.

I wonder, she thought, and then slipped into a deep, dreamless slumber.

She swam back to consciousness slowly, clawing her way up through layers of sleep.

Somebody was standing over her. Watching her. She could feel the eyes boring into her. Whose eyes? Richard's? Where was she? Princeton? New York? Or was it Hamburg? No . . . She remembered. She was in a lighthouse on the eastern coast of England, and—

She opened her eyes.

A man was standing beside the bed.

She sat up and immediately scooted away, staring up at him with panic-bright eyes. She had fallen asleep. *Stupid, weak, clumsy, soft . . .*

How had they found her?

Lightning flashed; she saw that the man held a gun.

The old fat one, she realized. The old fat one from Highgate.

A sheet of rain slapped violently against the window, making the pane rattle in its frame. The man turned his head reflexively a few degrees toward the sound.

She went for him.

CHAPTER SIXTEEN

HAM COMMON, SURREY .

Taylor was sitting at the table, smoking a cigarette, when Rudolf Schroeder was shown into the room.

The guard behind Schroeder prodded him toward the empty chair with the butt of his carbine, evidently low on patience even after the brief walk from the barracks. Taylor said nothing as Schroeder fell into the chair. The man's usual insolent grin was painted on his face, but Taylor thought there was a forced element to it tonight.

The guard turned toward the door.

"A-*hem*," Schroeder said. He lifted his hands above his head again and shook them. The cuffs there made a small, musical sound.

The guard looked at Taylor, who shook his head.

"Oh, dear," Schroeder said as the guard left. His insolent smile was replaced by a mock, exaggerated pout. "Have we fallen so far, Andrew, that you need me handcuffed when we speak?"

Instead of answering, Taylor reached down and found the package he had brought from Whitley Bay. He put it on the table between them—a small white parcel loosely wrapped with a piece of twine.

Schroeder eyed it suspiciously. "What is it?"

"Open it and find out."

"I've had enough chocolate, Andrew, thank you very much. Your friend tried to poison me, you know."

"It's not chocolate, Rudolf."

Schroeder reached for the box, hampered somewhat by the handcuffs around his wrists. His fingers manipulated the twine until it fell onto the table; then he poked the flaps of the package open and upended it.

Nothing came out.

He shook it twice, then turned the package over again.

"Empty," he said.

Taylor nodded. "I hoped to make a point. No more gifts."

Schroeder pulled a face.

"You said that you would speak to me in person," Taylor said. "Here I am. I've traveled a fair distance, Rudolf, when time is of the essence, to hear what you have to say. I don't suggest you try my patience any more."

Schroeder leaned back in his chair, seemingly sober.

"Andrew," he said, "I apologize for dragging you all the way out here. But you must understand . . ."

Taylor brought the cigarette to his mouth; Schroeder's eyes followed it.

"I'm out of cigarettes," Schroeder said. "Can you spare one?"

Taylor shook his head.

Schroeder, licking his lips, rearranged himself on the chair.

"You must understand," he went on. "You hold all the cards, so to speak. Except, Andrew, for one. One card. The true location of rendezvous number four."

"Mm," Taylor said.

"If I had told you that over the telephone, what would I have? Nothing. So you can see, Andrew, why I need to play this close to the vest, as they say—that is how the expression goes? Close to the vest, yes. Because once I tell you my bit of information, I will *truly* have nothing."

"But you will tell me?"

"In exchange for a promise," Schroeder said.

"What promise is that?"

"The same promise the professor made me. Except in your case, Andrew, I'll expect you to keep it."

"To bring you along for the *treff*."

"Exactly."

"I can't make that promise. Let you go, back to Germany?"

"Then you won't catch your spy."

"Spy?"

"He told me that much."

"Ah."

"He made it sound important."

"It is."

"I wish I could help, Andrew. I like to think that we're friends, you and I. I like to think that under different circumstances . . . But you must understand, I require something in return, hm? That is only natural. It is what makes the world go 'round, hm?"

"Hm," Taylor said.

"I see two possibilities," Schroeder said. His eyes were still on the cigarette in Taylor's hand. "I could reveal the location to you en route. That way I would be guaranteed, at least, of being brought there. But I would have no guarantee of actually being allowed to go aboard the U-boat, hm? So there is a second option, hm? Which is that we trust each other. I will tell you where it is, and then trust you to bring me along—once you've given your word, of course."

"Hm," Taylor said again.

"I *do* trust you, Andrew. And I hope that you trust me—this one unfortunate exception aside, of course."

"Of course."

"It goes without saying that upon my return to Berlin I will not mention your operation here. As far as the Old Man will know, I found work at the pub near Whitehall. I arranged the *treff.* But Winterbotham, the agent of my choosing, was apprehended at the last moment by MI-Five. I escaped—barely."

"I see."

"Do we have an agreement?"

Taylor took another drag of his cigarette. He inspected the fingernails on his right hand.

"Why should I believe you now," he asked, "when you've just finished lying to me?"

"Because you have no choice. But better: because it is in my best interest to tell the truth once you've promised to take me along."

"Hm."

"Surely you can see the wisdom," Schroeder said, and grinned slavishly.

Taylor shook his head.

Schroeder watched as he tapped out another cigarette, stuck it in his mouth.

"Tell me something else I can do for you, Rudolf. Anything else."

"There is nothing else."

"Money?"

"Please."

"Women?"

Schroeder laughed. "I just want to go home."

"But I can't allow that."

"But you must."

Taylor lit the cigarette in his mouth. He ran a hand over his pate.

"You'll find a way," Schroeder said.

"God damn it, Rudolf."

"I'm sorry. It's that or nothing."

"All right. Where?"

"You are promising?"

"Yes," Taylor said. "I am promising."

"I'm trusting you, Andrew."

"And I you. Where?"

"Yorkshire."

"Where in Yorkshire?"

"Flamborough Head. There is a lighthouse. The window is Sunday mornings, three to five."

"Three to five," Taylor said. "Good Christ."

He stood so suddenly that the table rocked. He turned, heading toward the door.

"Andrew," Schroeder said.

Taylor paused, his hand on the doorknob. After a moment, he turned back to face Schroeder.

"You promised," Schroeder said reasonably.

Taylor said nothing.

"Andrew," Schroeder said, and manufactured a laugh. "You promised."

"I lied."

"You can't leave me here. I go crazy here. The walls close in on me. I was never meant for this."

"You won't be here much longer."

"I'm being moved?" Schroeder said. "God damn it, one cell is the same as the next. Take me with you, for God's sake! You promised! You promised me!"

"You'll never spend another night in a cell, Rudolf."

Schroeder stared at him. "Andrew," he whispered. "You wouldn't."

Taylor left the room, closing the door behind himself.

CHAPTER SEVENTEEN

THE NORTH SEA

The U-boat surfaced to find a storm turned to fog.

The fog was thick, palpable, impenetrable, choking the sporadic lightning into a diffuse alabaster glow. *Kapitänleutnant* Schmidt could barely make out his own hand held at arm's length from his eyes. But Hagen was peering off into the haze as if he were seeing something of great import.

It came as little surprise when he turned to Schmidt and said: "If she were to signal, we would not see it."

Schmidt held his tongue.

"We must move closer," Hagen said.

Schmidt shook his head. "*Herr* Hagen," he said, "I will not."

He felt, more than saw, Hagen bristling.

"If we cannot see the signal, *Kapitänleutnant*," Hagen said, "then we are not fulfilling our duty. I would take that as—"

"If we move closer, *Herr* Hagen, we will lose this vessel, your spies, and our own lives. I will not brook argument on this matter. If you wish to try to take control of the boat, do so now. If not, you must respect my wishes."

Although Hagen was only a few feet away, Schmidt was unable to make out his face. He could only wonder how his stand had gone over.

Nearly half a minute passed. Then Hagen said, "You are right. It does not make sense to risk the boat."

Thank God, Schmidt thought. "We will send the dinghy to shore," he said. "Two men will look for the signal. If they see it, they will make contact."

"Indeed. Those two men shall be *Herr* Gruber and myself."

Schmidt managed not to grin. "I will prepare the dinghy immediately, *Herr* Hagen," he said.

FLAMBOROUGH HEAD, YORKSHIRE

In the dream, the bullet passed through her shoulder and lodged in the wooden doorjamb and she barely felt it and she was fine and life went on.

But in reality, the bullet was still inside her.

She could feel it every time she pulled herself up another stair. It was wandering around inside her body, prodding at the muscle and tissue and skin from the inside out. Sometimes the pain of the shifting bullet would become so fantastic that she would actually lose consciousness for a moment. She was on the verge of losing consciousness anyway, between the stairs, the fever, the exhaustion. But it was the bullet in her shoulder that kept pushing her over the edge—kept pushing her into the dream even when her attention was sorely needed here, in reality.

In the dream they were leading her to the gallows. Fritz held one of her arms, and the old fat man held the other. Both were smiling at her with expressions of condescending pity, or perhaps it was pitying condescension. They were walking to the gallows between throngs of British citizens who were howling for her execution. Even the children were howling. The children, it seemed, were howling loudest of all.

Then thunder broke and she found herself back in reality, halfway up the staircase in this goddamn lighthouse, bleeding, sobbing, unable to continue.

She pulled herself up another stair.

The fact that she was climbing the tower in the first place illustrated just how poorly she was doing. She should have gone the other way, outside, to the beach. Then she could possibly have given the signal, somehow, and perhaps even gotten some help from reinforcements.

She had kicked up at the old fat man, from the bed; the gun had barked twice. One of the bullets had slammed into her left shoulder, spinning her around. A lucky shot. She had rolled off the bed, rolled onto the floor, and kept rolling. Not realizing yet that the bullet was still inside her. Before he could find her in the gloom, before he could fire again and finish it, she had slipped away into the corridor.

And stumbled in the wrong direction.

There had been a time, she knew, when her training would have gotten her through the worst of the shock, when her reflexes would have proven sound. Even in bad circumstances she would have acted correctly.

It's not too late, she thought. *You still have a chance to make things right.*

Yes—because her body was an instrument, and she was its master.

She forbade her body to pass out again. There were things to do, in reality. Like climbing this staircase, like killing the old fat man, like staying alive long enough to tell her secrets to the crew of the U-boat floating at this very instant off Flamborough Head.

She pulled herself up another stair. The bullet moved again in her shoulder. She didn't cry out, but her face scrunched into a mask of agony. For several seconds, the rictus remained on her features. Then the lines slowly vanished as her muscles relaxed—except for the deep groove between her eyes.

She achieved another stair, and then, despite her noble intentions, drifted away again.

She was Catherine Danielson, not yet Carter, getting off the train in Princeton ten years before. Richard was there, coming to meet her. She had seen in his eyes from the very first that he was attracted to her. He was leading her back through the campus, back to his little university house, carrying her suitcase, giving her a tour that felt more like a lecture. A group of young men in frayed gowns was ogling her, but Richard didn't seem to notice. Richard was explaining something about . . . wages . . .

But it was the gallows he was leading her to, of course, not the house; no, not the gallows but the . . . yes, the gallows. How could she have thought otherwise? He was leading her up the stairs, and the crowd all around was chanting. She was frightened, terribly frightened. They were going to kill her, these people. A priest stepped up, unfolding a piece of parchment. The priest charged her with espionage. Then he named her—her real name. Her given name.

"Heinrich," he said.

Except she was back in the lighthouse again.

"Katarina Heinrich," the voice repeated, and echoed.

She blinked, sucked in a pained breath, and pulled herself up another stair.

"Katarina Heinrich," the man said yet again. His voice, warped by the acoustics of the tower, sounded hollow and otherworldly.

"That is your name, isn't it?" he said. "Katarina Heinrich."

How many more stairs to the top? She couldn't bear to think about it. She pulled herself up again.

This time the dream was different. This time she was bounding up the stairs, whole again, capable, perfect, hiding in the vat of mercury. Deadly poison, mercury, but in the dream it was harmless; and in the dream she sank into it easily, like a bath. In the dream she killed the fat man when he stepped into the gallery, flinging the knife in her hand with deadly accuracy, skewering him through one eye.

The knife. Did she have it?

She opened her eyes. Looked at her hands. No, the knife was only a dream.

Thunder exploded again, farther away. The storm was moving off.

She decided, suddenly, that she was dying.

Not over yet, she thought. *Not over yet, God damn it.*

She managed another stair.

In the dream, it was the last stair. She had reached the gallery. The final dregs of the storm were beating at the windows. A slash of lightning illuminated old Rupert, facedown, floating in the mercury bath beneath the tremendous Fresnel lens. In the dream she dragged herself halfway across the floor and then collapsed, utterly spent. She could no longer feel the bullet in her arm. The arm had gone numb. *Dying,* she thought. She felt like a very little girl who had stumbled into a Grimm fairy tale, with the storm trailing off outside, the bogeyman coming up the stairs behind her, and nowhere left to run. It was cold up there. The middle of the summer, but somehow it was cold up there. Or perhaps the coldness was inside her. The numbness had spread from her arm to her chest. Perhaps it wouldn't stop at the boundaries of her body. Perhaps her last act in this world would be to bring the coldness out, from her body to the world . . . Oh, but she had hoped for fire. She had hoped to bring atomic fire out into the world, instead of cold. But there was no fire to be found.

"Not . . . dreaming," she muttered.

It was true. This was no dream; it was reality. And if she died now she would never bring fire to the world, only cold. And so she could not lie there on the floor. She needed to get moving. To find a weapon.

Her body was an instrument, and she was its master.

She tried to sit up, to get moving again, and her body, politely but firmly, refused.

She collapsed again, with a small sob.

In the dream, then, she rolled over onto her back to wait for him to come. He was directly behind her on the stairs, after all; probably being overcautious—he didn't know how badly she was hurt. But any second now she would see his shadow looming on the wall as he reached the top of the stairs. . . . Why, there it was now . . . in the dream . . . he was coming for her . . . she wished for poison. If she had possessed a poison capsule she would have swallowed it. Better death than capture. Or would this man kill her?

He came into the gallery.

He looked as frightened as she felt. His eyes were darting into every crevice, as if she had some last trick, some last spectacular trick, hidden up here. He must have heard about Highgate, she thought. *He must think I'm dangerous, even now.*

But there was nothing she could do as he slowly came into the room, the pistol in his hand pointed at the crease between her eyes.

"Katarina Heinrich," he said.

She nodded, or tried to.

In the dream, then, his finger was tightening on the trigger. Not going to arrest her after all. He was going to kill her, right there and then. Not weak, this man. Hard. Willing to do whatever it took. She could respect that.

In the dream, then, Hagen came to her rescue. He emerged from the staircase behind the man, the same old Hagen, gaunt and rangy and encased in sheer black, which he wore only when he was working. In the dream, Hagen was holding a Luger, which he pointed at the old fat man's head. In the dream, Hagen said, "No, please."

Which was a funny touch for a dream, she thought. Of course,

Hagen's English was not particularly good, and of course, that *was* pretty much the way he would speak, were he to speak in English at that moment. But since his role in this dream was as savior, as *deus ex machina*, she would have thought that he would have been forgiven his deficiencies in English. She would have thought that he would have spoken flawlessly.

The old fat man froze.

"Set down the gun," Hagen commanded.

The old fat man bent, carefully, and set down his gun. He raised his hands over his head.

"Take two steps back, please," Hagen said.

The man took two steps back, hands still raised. Katarina watched, bemused. Not such a bad dream, she thought. She wondered if she was dead yet. Not such a bad way to go out, with a nice dream like this. If only Hagen would shoot the old fat man in the head, everything would be perfect.

But Hagen wasn't shooting him.

"Professor Winterbotham?"

The man nodded once, shortly.

"My name is Hagen," Hagen said. "This is Gruber."

Katarina saw, then, another man behind Hagen—a mousy little man who emerged from the shadows, looking excited.

"Professor," Gruber said, mincingly. "On behalf of Admiral Wilhelm Canaris, please accept my invitation to return with us to Berlin immediately."

Katarina closed her eyes. She felt confused, and extremely spent. What was going on? What was this odd turn her fantasy had taken? Who was this mousy little mincing man?

When she opened her eyes again, Hagen was crouching next to her, examining her shoulder. He saw her eyes open, and the ghost of a smile traced his lips.

"Katarina," he said. "You came home."

Katarina nodded.

"Rest," he said.

She nodded again.

She closed her eyes.

And rested.

CHAPTER EIGHTEEN

The car rumbled to a stop in the fog.

"What is it?" Taylor asked, leaning forward.

The driver cleared his throat before answering. "I believe this is it, sir," he said.

"This is what, Fitz?"

"*It*, sir. As near as I can guess."

"The lighthouse?"

Fitz nodded.

Taylor leaned forward even farther, trying to peer through the windshield. "Can't see a bloody thing," he murmured.

"The road ends just ahead."

"Can't you pull up a bit?"

"There's no road, sir. I can drive on the grass, if you like."

"Hold on," Taylor said.

He threw open his door and marched past all four cars in line, rapping on the windows. They formed a huddle in the misty night: Taylor, Kendall, Colonel Fredricks, and two men from the Criminal Investigation Division of Scotland Yard, called CID.

"We're here," Taylor said. "We just don't know it yet."

Colonel Fredricks was frowning into the night around them.

"Bloody hard to see anything in this soup."

"I'm aware of that, Colonel. Unfortunately we've no time to spare waiting for it to lift. Does everybody have a sidearm?"

They all had.

"We'll make straight for the beach," Taylor said. "Once the beach is secure, we'll send a party back to the lighthouse. By the time our contingent arrives from Whitley Bay, we'll either have them in the lock or cut off with their escape route blocked."

"Sir?" Fredricks said.

"Colonel?"

"What about Winterbotham?"

"What about him?"

"What are we to do if we run into him, sir?"

"What do you think?" Taylor said, checking the load in his pistol.

"But . . ."

"Any *sensible* questions?"

There was none.

"God be with us all," Taylor said.

They struck off toward the beach in two groups.

Taylor led the first, with Colonel Fredricks on one side and Kendall on the other. They passed an abandoned Sunbeam Talbot—Winterbotham's car, Taylor realized suddenly, although he hadn't seen it for years—and then angled left, away from the lighthouse.

The two from CID went to the right, around the lighthouse's other side.

The ground was marshy and wet. It squelched softly with their footsteps. The fog stole the sound as soon as it was made, spreading it thin. When Kendall spoke, the same thing happened to his voice: "Sir," he whispered, "a path. Leading down the cliffs."

It seemed to Taylor as if the voice was coming from all around him. When he tried to look at Kendall, he could see nothing but a smudge among the rest of the haze.

"Where?" he whispered back.

A hand touched his.

"Come on," Kendall said. "I'll lead you."

Taylor reached out to his left, to take Fredricks's hand. He found himself grasping at air.

"Fredricks," he hissed.

There was no answer.

"Fredricks!"

Nothing.

"I've lost Fredricks," he said.

After a moment, they went on anyway, Kendall leading the way, Taylor holding his hand like a schoolgirl. The path led down a rough, steep cliff that Taylor would not have cared to negotiate even under good circumstances. As they descended, however, they began to get beneath the fog. Soon Taylor could see Kendall in front of him; he let go of his hand. Soon after, they were stepping onto the rocky beach itself, grateful to have avoided sprained ankles or worse. Far out above the black sea, Taylor could see a loose toss of stars very low to the horizon, very distant, in a place the storm had not touched.

The beach was deserted—except for the shadow of an empty dinghy resting on the sand.

Taylor and Kendall exchanged a glance without speaking. Then

Taylor turned and looked back up the cliff. The fog thickened as his eyes moved higher; but from there he was able to make out the lighthouse, a black blur behind the mist. The occupants of the dinghy, he supposed, were up there.

If that was the case, they soon would be back.

He indicated, with a gesture, that Kendall should take cover farther down the beach. Then he himself crept back, silently, to the path leading up the cliff. He positioned himself about a dozen feet from the base in such a way that he would not be visible to anyone coming down until they were directly beside him.

He checked his gun again.

He considered lighting a cigarette, and decided he couldn't risk it.

He waited.

As soon as Hagen heard the engines burring softly over the distant sound of the surf, he silenced his companions by raising a hand. They were just coming off the foot of the spiral staircase—Hagen in the lead, Gruber behind him, Katarina supported between them, the British traitor bringing up the rear.

He cocked his head, listening. Although his hearing had deteriorated a bit, lately, it was still sharp. At least three cars, he decided, and possibly more.

Schmidt would not wait for them any longer than he deemed safe. In fact, he would probably relish the opportunity to strand Hagen there, in the heart of enemy territory.

He waved the men in close, and spoke in a whisper.

"I will lead," he said, "and clear the path. You follow behind with Katarina. Keep off the beach until I have given my signal. And protect her at all costs. Your lives are valuable only as long as she remains alive."

"Signal?" Gruber said. He was breathing hard, winded from the menial task of carrying Katarina down the stairs. Hagen felt a flash of disdain for this sallow little man, so soft and weak, such an apt emissary for the traitor Canaris. He dismissed it.

"A whistle. Wait two minutes before following me."

He put Winterbotham's pistol into Winterbotham's hand, then vanished.

Gruber and Winterbotham looked at each other.

"Can he do it?" Winterbotham asked.

Gruber nodded. Winterbotham could smell his fear, ripe and sour.

"He can do it," Gruber said.

Hagen listened.

Two groups, he decided. One directly in front of him moving through the fog toward the water. Three men in that group. Amateurs, whispering among themselves, squelching through the damp grass. The second group was behind him, circling around the back of the lighthouse. Professionals, or at least men with experience not limited to desks. He couldn't immediately know how many they were; they trod softly.

The three in front of him, however, would be easy.

He holstered the Luger before moving forward. If he could take the three silently, it would make the second group that much easier.

He fell into step behind the amateurs. He could see nothing, but he could *feel* them, feel their energy on the fog. Two were drifting off to the right. As a result, the other, continuing straight, was separating himself from his companions. None of them seemed to realize what was happening. Hagen followed the one who was continuing straight. The man was nervous, very nervous. Hagen could feel his nervousness crackling like electricity. He would have his gun in his hand, this nervous amateur, and he could not be given a chance to squeeze the trigger. But Hagen did not think that would be a problem.

He waited until the man in front of him had paused, perhaps

realizing for the first time that he had become separated from his companions. Then he stepped forward, slipping his arm around the man's throat, inserting his fingers into the man's mouth. At the same time, he took the man's other hand, the one holding the gun, and applied sharp pressure to the inside of the wrist with his thumb until he heard the gun fall into the grass with a soft *flumph*. The man was beginning to choke. Hagen adjusted his balance, planted a strong grounding foot, and then bent the man over his knee, holding the head steady with one arm, and twisted.

He lay the corpse down soundlessly.

He drew a knife in case one of the man's companions had heard the short scuffle.

"Sir," one of the other amateurs said. Perhaps ten feet away, perhaps fifteen, directly to his right, "a path. Leading down the cliffs."

"Where?"

"Come on. I'll lead you."

"Fredricks," the other hissed.

Hagen froze.

"Fredricks!"

Hagen raised the knife, preparing to throw it.

"I've lost Fredricks," the voice said.

A moment later, they were moving away down the cliff, scrabbling, making so much noise that it almost seemed as if they were making noise on purpose. Hagen let out his breath. He would let these two stay on the beach, he decided, where he knew their location, until he had finished dealing with the professionals.

He began to proceed forward, keeping near the edge of the cliff. He moved slowly, pausing after every two steps to listen. The professionals must have been somewhere in front of him, coming in his direction.

Unless, he thought suddenly, they had gone to the lighthouse instead.

No. He had heard them moving around the outside of the lighthouse, coming toward the beach.

But if he had made a mistake, Katarina would be the one to pay the price.

The thought made him frantic. He knew very well that panic was his worst enemy, but at that moment he gave himself over to it—after all of this, he had left Katarina behind, guarded by an idiot and a traitor. After all of this, after finally being reunited with her after more than ten years apart, he had immediately let her out of his sight. But it was not too late to correct his mistake.

He began to walk briskly toward the lighthouse, reminding himself to move silently, telling himself at the same time that as soon as he had satisfied himself that Katarina was out of harm's way, he would move silently, but for the time being—

"Scotland Yard!" someone cried.

In the next instant, somebody fired a gun.

Hagen cursed himself even as he dropped to the ground, even as he pulled free the Luger. He was old; that was the problem. He had decided that the men had been moving around the lighthouse and he had then doubted that decision, for no good reason at all. These men were professionals—Scotland Yard, as they had so considerately informed him. They had taken advantage of his mistake.

Another report sounded. A bullet whizzed close past his ear. Hagen rolled to his right, keeping the Luger close to his body, *in-tight.* How many? Now his own heart was pounding too loudly in his ears for him to be sure. He rolled four times and then sprung into a crouch, bringing the gun up, oscillating the barrel back and forth, still cursing himself. The knife had fallen somewhere. He forced himself to set aside the recriminations—there would be time for those later. He listened, extending his senses past his own thudding heart.

One, at least one, in front and to his right. His Luger was immediately trained on the man. But until he knew how many he faced, Hagen would not fire. He would not make the amateur's mistake and give away his own position by firing.

Instead, he began to backpedal.

Vanish, he was thinking. *Vanish, then reappear. Seize the—*

"There!" someone cried.

Three more shots thundered in the night. Hagen gave up any pretense of backpedaling.

He turned and ran.

Gruber was standing in the narrow front hall of the lighthouse, peering outside through a small window. When the sound of the first shot came, he uttered a surprised yelp.

"Hörst du das?" he cried.

He kept looking out the window, licking his lips compulsively. Another shot sounded, and then, a moment later, three more in rapid succession.

"Lass die Frau hier und beeile dich," Gruber said. *"Komm mit verstärkung von dem Boot zurück."* He turned toward Winterbotham. *"Komm mit verstärkung . . ."* He trailed off.

He began to raise his hands over his head.

Winterbotham fired.

Taylor heard one shot, a second, three more; then, distantly, a sixth.

"Stay here!" he called to Kendall.

He began to charge up the slope without waiting for acknowledgment. The soil under his feet seemed looser going up, somehow, than it had coming down. He found himself having trouble finding dependable footholds. Perhaps he needed somebody's hand to hold, he thought.

He kept moving anyway, doggedly, until his breath was rasping through his lungs.

Somewhere in the distance, a foghorn wailed.

A cramp stitched his side. He kept climbing, gritting his teeth. *Too old for this,* he thought. *Too old, too heavy.* Oh, but it all had gone to hell. He wanted to blame Winterbotham—Winterbotham, the old fool, God damn him to hell—but he could not blame Winterbotham without blaming himself. After all, he had been the one who had brought Winterbotham into the game. He had known his friend's reputation. He had taken a chance, and now it was coming back to haunt him.

Perhaps he should have made directly for the lighthouse upon arriving, he thought, instead of for the beach. But how could he have known they would be in the lighthouse? No, his logic had been sound. Secure the beach, prevent the escape, then work his way back to the lighthouse. And Christ, the cramp in his side hurt. Christ, but it burned like fire. Christ, but he was out of shape. He kept climbing anyway. Should have scuttled the dinghy, he realized suddenly. Should have scuttled the dinghy so it wouldn't matter if they made it to the beach. He should turn around and do it now. But something wouldn't allow him to move away from the sound of the gunfire, no matter how legitimate his reason. To move away from the fight would have been to admit his failure as a man of action—to admit that his only contributions to the game would be limited to intellectual acrobatics, forevermore.

Finally he came off the path, onto the clifftop. He was panting loudly. He staggered through the fog on legs gone spongy, panting like a dog on a hot afternoon. *Worthless,* he thought. *Worthless in a fight.* Look at him. He was . . .

A man passed in front of him no more than two feet away.

Taylor stopped, staring. He had caught a glimpse of lustrous black.

None of the men in his party had been dressed in lustrous black.

The SS, on the other hand, were known to favor it.

Still panting, he gave chase.

Katarina Heinrich, witnessing the murder of Klaus Gruber, experienced a sudden rush of adrenaline.

She blinked, lifting her head. She blinked again and then suddenly she remembered the packet of amphetamine dust tucked into her shoe. She had forgotten it. Stupid, lazy, weak . . .

She clawed it out, fumbled it open, brought it to her face, inhaled sharply.

She managed to get her leg under herself, to throw her weight against the wall, to begin pulling herself to her feet. Gruber, the *Abwehr* man, was tumbling backward. In the muted kerosene glow coming from the study, Katarina could see his face—what was left of it—sliding off his skull like snow sheeting off a mountainside under a hot sun.

Now Winterbotham was turning, the gun coming around to bear. Katarina had no illusions about what would happen if he was allowed to complete his turn. She would be shot down in cold blood.

So she attacked.

She flung herself at Winterbotham, and the bullet moved inside her, and she went soft and weak all over. Her legs fell out from under her. The blow, which had been intended for his face, glanced harmlessly off his chest. Then she was on the cold, mossy floor again, waves of vertigo rushing over her. All of her wounds, it seemed, had reopened; she was slicked with blood. She moaned thickly. She rolled over, onto her back. Her eyes wanted to close. She felt tired, so tired . . .

Her heart thudded, double time. The amphetamine had reached her central nervous system.

Winterbotham was stepping away, aiming the gun at her.

She kicked up. The kick cost her; she felt something tear inside. But her foot hit the gun solidly, spinning it out of Winterbotham's hands, sending it end over end into the shadows.

Katarina used the momentum of the kick to roll herself over, onto her feet. There was so much agony inside her that she had given up trying to keep track of it all. She hurt, very badly.

She pushed the pain away.

Focused.

Came at Winterbotham, snapping a kick at his face, ignoring the ripping sensation in her belly.

He raised a hand to defend himself. The kick connected with his forearm. She immediately aimed a sharp jab at his head. This time she hit her mark. He staggered backward, dazed.

She took a moment to check her balance, and went for him again.

She sent a round kick toward his chest. He pulled back, cowering into the wall. Then, as the force of her kick turned her around, he moved forward, thinking that she would be most vulnerable when her back was facing him. Just as she had hoped. She leapt up immediately, spinning 180 degrees in the air, and caught him across the bridge of the nose with a crescent kick.

He went down.

She landed heavily on the balls of her feet. Bleeding everywhere, pain running through her body in an intricate network, breath rasping in and out of her lungs. But she had done it. He was down.

A wave of nausea took her; she stumbled.

He was up again.

They circled each other.

Blood poured down his face. His massive hands opened and closed. His eyes were small and bright and hot.

He feinted; she backed off. She feinted, and he blocked. Biding his time. She would have done the same, had she been in his position. He could see how badly she was hurt. Each passing second meant lost blood.

Run, she thought. *Run for the beach.*

But she would never make it, not if he gave pursuit. Either she dealt with Winterbotham now, or she gave up and surrendered.

She went for him again.

A feint with the left, another feint with the left, a jab with the right. He moved back quickly, ducked the first, ducked the second, and grabbed for her wrist after the third. Too slow; she spun, stepped into him backward, and drove her elbow into his kidney. He gasped. She reached over her shoulders and grabbed his throat. Threw her weight forward, trying to roll him over her shoulder, to hurl him to the floor on his back.

But he outweighed her by more than a hundred pounds, and he had set his bulk solidly on wide-spread feet. She pulled for a moment, to no effect. Then he landed a blow on the side of her head, spilling her to the cold floor.

She heard bells ringing, distantly.

She gasped, swallowed blood.

Tried to stand up, couldn't.

Her eyes were closed. She could feel her grandmother stroking her face. Getting her ready for bed.

Open your eyes, Katarina.

She tried. Couldn't. Tried again.

Winterbotham's back was facing her. He was crouched over, digging through the shadows. Looking for the gun, no doubt, so he could put an end to her.

She struggled up. Dizzy. But if he got the gun . . .

She dove for him.

He turned and then they rolled to the floor together, hands at each other's throat.

Hagen was improvising.

He was running, but running could also be considered leading, and so he was *leading*, leading the men away from Katarina. There were three men behind him, two professionals and one amateur. The amateur, who was closest, was breathing so hard that Hagen thought he must be on the verge of a heart attack.

He had been running (*leading*) long enough to have come off the grass, to have crossed briefly across a strip of road, and to have entered the edge of a forest. Now, surrounded by fragrant trees, with his pursuers having fallen temporarily behind, he was able to take stock of his situation.

He could hear the clumsy amateur blundering through the foliage. He changed direction, moving a few steps at an angle perpendicular to the one he had been following. Then he stopped, and took refuge behind a tree. He regulated his breathing and listened. Once the amateur had blundered past, Hagen would walk a circle back through the forest—a wide, cautious circle, which would put him behind the pair from Scotland Yard. Then, assuming he had thrown off the pursuit, he would return to the lighthouse and Katarina. It would rankle him to let these men escape, but he needed to put such superficial concerns aside. He needed to stay focused on the mission.

Now he could hear the amateur approaching, trampling branches. The man was still unable to catch his breath, it seemed, although the dense trees had forced him to slow to a walk.

Hagen waited. Instead of moving past, the amateur was slowing . . . slowing . . . and then stopping, not very far away. From the tortured sound of his respiration, Hagen guessed that he was simply unable to go any farther.

Hagen leaned cautiously out from behind the tree. He could see the man's silhouette in the gloom, bent at the waist, hands on his thighs just above the knees, very nearby.

Hagen turned and slipped away through the forest.

He had taken but a single step before his foot landed on a twig. The twig snapped, more loudly than he would have thought possible.

He flung himself down even as he was aware, vaguely, of the amateur raising his gun and firing.

The gun went off very close to Hagen's head, but the bullet drove harmlessly into the underbrush. Before the man had a chance to fire again, Hagen had skittered away, snaking between the trees, disappearing into the forest.

He began to thread his way back toward the lighthouse. He could hear nothing except a ringing tone that seemed to emanate from the base of his skull.

He cursed bitterly to himself. He had no luck tonight, it seemed. The gunshot had been too close to his head.

He was deaf.

Katarina dug her fingers into Winterbotham's throat.

She was on top of him. He was trying to roll her over, to reverse their positions, but that would be the end of it—she couldn't let that happen.

She squeezed as hard as she could, pressing her thumbs viciously into his trachea. His face was red, turning redder by the minute. But her own face must have been red, too, because his hands also were wrapped around *her* throat, squeezing just as hard as she was—if not harder.

She hissed, willing him to die.

Winterbotham's eyes were calm. How could he look so calm?

Die, she thought.

But he was too heavy, too strong. She was too small, too weak, too soft . . .

Veils of gauze dipped over her vision. The bullet was still inside her, wandering.

Now he *was* turning her over, settling his weight on top of her. She was helpless to prevent it.

And still his fingers dug into her throat mercilessly.

Suddenly, Gladys was there, watching quietly. Fritz and Hagen were standing beside each other, applauding. A spring breeze was blowing, teasing the fields into motion. Lilac and lavender, campion and convolvulus . . .

She was back on the mossy floor of the lighthouse. She could hear her own breath raking in and out of her lungs.

His hands ever tighter around her throat.

She felt suddenly sad. To have come all this way and have it end like this . . . But the sadness was not without a sweetness. She wrapped it around herself, this strange, unexpected melancholy, and inspected it curiously. She had tried and failed, but at least she had tried. She had been true to herself. And she had avoided the gallows. That was something.

She looked into Winterbotham's face. It was no longer red; now it was gray and translucent. The wall behind it looked the same. Her own hands, beating weakly against his chest, were the hands of a ghost.

She sighed in sudden ecstasy. Why, there was no more pain! All of the pain had vanished!

She tried to open her mouth, to thank him for taking away the pain. No words came out; the breath rattled in her throat.

Winterbotham kept squeezing.

Her thoughts turned very cool and clear, very precise. She could feel herself slipping the last few degrees into death. She saw, with terrible clarity, her mistake: She had tried to strangle him. But strangling was inefficient. If she had not been wounded, feverish, and exhausted, she never would have tried to strangle him.

Perhaps, she thought then, it was not too late to correct her mistake.

She decided to execute a back roll, flipping him over her head. She would roll with him, of course, landing with her knees on his biceps, rupturing the muscles there. Then a driving palm heel to his chin, snapping his neck.

She tried; but she had no strength. He barely rocked on top of her.

Just the palm heel, then.

She drove the heel of her palm into his chin.

He ignored it.

That left the eyes.

She tried to poke Winterbotham in his left eye.

He took one hand away from her throat to block the strike. She immediately executed an out-to-in cross block on his other arm, spilling him forward.

She kneed him in the groin.

Then he was off her, gasping.

She half stood, stumbled to the door, collapsed, half stood again, found the doorknob, sucked in an agonized breath, twisted the knob, threw her shoulder against the door, tumbled out into the fog, and collapsed again.

She got to her feet again.

Drew another breath, which burned.

And ran, stumbling, for her life.

On the road between Hagen and the lighthouse, six Wolesley sedans pulled to a stop behind the five already there.

Special agents poured forth, twelve in all. They had come from Whitley Bay. Many held firearms; all milled about in confusion. There was not a leader among them, not even a man of higher rank than the rest. They spoke among themselves in normal voices, debating the best course of action.

Thirty feet away, and approaching rapidly, was Hagen.

Winterbotham stood, dazed.

He needed to get to the beach. But the woman had gotten away from him. Must he follow her? Or would Taylor take care of her? He had heard more cars pull up outside. He had heard another gunshot from far away, in the direction of the forest.

Taylor had found him somehow. Schroeder, he thought. Schroeder must have survived and told him about their arrangement.

Follow the woman? Or try for the beach?

The clock continued to roll forward; the U-boat would not be waiting forever.

The beach, he decided. And Ruth.

He found the pistol on the floor and checked the load. Two bullets.

He stepped out into the foggy night.

Activity to his left, invisible through the mist. He turned right.

He strode toward the ocean, feeling surprisingly calm.

He reached the path leading down the cliff and began to negotiate it cautiously.

Lunacy, he thought. *Lunacy, what you're about to do.*

Perhaps, and perhaps not. In any case, he was doing it.

He reached the beach proper. He spied the dinghy, abandoned on the sand, oars glistening. He began to move toward it.

Then Kendall materialized from behind a low pile of rocks, gun in hand.

When Hagen emerged into the midst of the Special Forces, both were surprised.

Hagen recovered first.

A round kick sent the man closest to him onto the ground, dazed. A spinning hook kick put another man down with a broken neck. Then, before the agents could figure out quite what was happening, Hagen followed the second man onto the ground. He rolled beneath the undercarriage of the nearest staff car, and kept rolling until he came out the other side. He calmly drew his Luger and stood.

He fired six shots.

Six men fell.

Again, Hagen followed them to the ground. Now the remaining agents were realizing what was in their midst; their guns were drawn, and they were falling into combat stances. Hagen could hear them yelling, but the words themselves were lost in the rush of white noise filling his head.

The Luger was empty. He discarded it, rolled under the car again, and came up onto the balls of his feet lightly, inhaling from his *tanden*, focusing with a silent *kiai*.

He struck the man to his left with a reverse jab, and felt the cartilage of the man's nose being pushed into his brain. He continued with the roundhouse movement, flowing into a crescent kick that caught the man to his right even as the man's pistol was coming around—close, too close—spilling the man down; and now Hagen could sense two others coming at him, two others who had gained their bearings.

Too many, he thought.

He tried to strike the closest one, but he missed.

Cold metal crashed against the back of his skull.

Hagen fell onto one knee. He steeled himself to rise again, shaking his head, trying to clear it. He turned his face up to the night and found himself staring down the barrel of a gun.

He dropped onto his back, hooked the man's ankles with his feet, and twisted. The man went cartwheeling down, firing at the same time. Hagen felt the bullet pound into the ground by his throat. He rolled, wondering where the other one was, why he hadn't fired yet—

The bullet took Hagen in the small of his back.

His legs went immediately numb. He tried to keep rolling, but it was not possible to roll with numb legs. His spinal column had been severed, he thought. So it was over. But perhaps—

The agent shot him three more times. The final bullet opened Hagen's head and splattered his brains on the grass in a crazy Rorschach.

Then the agent looked around himself, wiping his hand across his nose.

Three men were standing, dazed.

"Christ," the agent croaked.

One of the men vomited noisily.

"Christ," the agent said again, and fainted.

Winterbotham walked toward Kendall, not slowing, across the rocky beach. Kendall nodded. Winterbotham, without preamble, raised the gun in his hand and then brought it crashing down across the bridge of Kendall's nose. Kendall sank to his knees, clapping his hands to his face. When he took his hands away, they were wet with blood.

Winterbotham moved to the dinghy and began to pull it across the sand toward the water. Kendall watched, nursing his bleeding nose. When Winterbotham reached the shore, he clambered into the dinghy, then used an oar to push himself out into the North Sea.

Kendall, still kneeling, watched as the dinghy worked its way out over the dark water. If there was a U-boat out there, he couldn't see it.

But there must have been, because the professor did not come back.

Nearly twenty minutes had passed before Taylor worked his way down the cliff again. He walked to Kendall and looked down at him and, for the moment, said nothing. He dug in his pockets, found his cigarettes, put one in his mouth, and lit it.

Overhead, the sky was beginning to lighten with the first rouge of dawn.

At the sound of the engine turning over, Katarina snapped back to consciousness.

Her first impulse was to sit up; and she very nearly did so. Then, just as she was lifting her head, she heard voices.

"I'll tell you one thing, mate. If an *army* man screwed things up this way, he'd have jankers for a month."

"Right. When you're enlisted, they watch you like a hawk. But as soon as you're the one giving the orders . . ."

"You've pegged it. Where'd you serve?"

"Dunkirk. You?"

Now the car was pulling onto the road, gravel crunching beneath its tires. Katarina carefully lowered her head again. She snuggled as low as she could in the backseat of the Wolesley sedan. She wished for a blanket or a tarp—*something* with which to cover herself—but there was nothing at hand. She was forced to make do with the inky shadows.

Just as long as the lads didn't crane around for the next five minutes or so, she thought. In five minutes or so, after they had gained some distance from the lighthouse and the other British agents, she would kill them both. Then she would take the sedan back to the beach. There might still be time. She might still have a chance.

Not that she was in any sort of shape, she realized, to handle resistance if she encountered it. The amphetamines had faded, leaving her with one hell of a hangover: blurred vision, cold sweats, jackknife heartbeat, tremors racking her body. She felt ravenously hungry, and more exhausted than ever.

But the bullet, at least, had stopped moving around—for now. Thank God for small favors.

She closed her eyes, lulled by the steady motion of the car. The lads up front were still talking; their voices sounded soothing, and very, very young.

Too late, she thought. Too late to make the *treff.*

But what other option did she have?

Stay here, of course. Sleep. If they reached London without the lads finding her in the backseat, slip away when nobody was paying attention. Find somewhere to hole up for a couple of weeks until she gained a bit of distance from death's door. Then find a ship—a ship going anywhere.

Anywhere but here.

A tear burned the corner of her eye; she wiped it away absently.

And what about her people? How would she feel when they finished the bomb and dropped it on Germany, if she turned away now? Like a coward.

But would she feel any better if she delivered the bomb to Hitler and he used it to bring on *Götterdämmerung*?

A crease appeared between her eyes.

Her mind was in a jumble. Her mind, it seemed lately, was always in a jumble. Who was to know what was right or wrong? How was she supposed to know *what* to think?

Treason, she thought darkly.

Take the car, return to the lighthouse, and honor your rendezvous.

But it was too late for that. Her eyes were closing.

Go on, she thought. *Rest. Sleep.*

TREASON! her mind shrieked. *TREASON! WAKE UP!*

So very tired . . .

If she gave up now, would she ever be able to look at herself in a mirror?

Would she ever be able to sleep again?

Still wondering, she dozed off.

CHAPTER NINETEEN

10 DOWNING STREET, LONDON

Winston Churchill stood on the garden terrace of Number 10 Downing Street, a paintbrush in one hand, looking critically at the easel before him.

The prime minister possessed something of a permanent scowl; the critical look on his face fit the features well. Looking at him now, one could easily imagine the recalcitrant schoolboy who once had lived inside this body, who had been described by his teacher as "a constant trouble to everybody, always in some scrape or other."

Kendall, who had gotten into his own share of trouble growing up in London's East End, could hardly believe he was in the prime minister's presence—or was, more precisely, about to be in the prime minister's presence. He, Andrew Taylor, and Major Robertson were just now stepping into the half-acre garden from the Cabinet Room, all three simultaneously raising hands against the glaring sunshine.

Taylor whispered, "Don't interrupt him while he's painting."

So they stood and watched, for the better part of ten minutes, as Churchill added a large blue mountain to his barely above average landscape. During this time, the remnants of Churchill's lunch were taken away, his flute of champagne was refilled, and a cigar was set out for him on a table underneath a sun umbrella. He looked like a man on vacation, Kendall found himself thinking, not like a man involved in a desperate fight against an aggressor who already had captured most of Europe. But this should not have been surprising—not from Churchill, who was known to deal with the most serious official matters from his bed, his dinner table, even his bath.

Presently, Churchill set down the paintbrush, turned to the men, and offered the suggestion of a bow.

"Forgive me, gentlemen," he said. "The mountain wouldn't wait. Have a seat. Champagne?"

They sat around the table under the umbrella, accepting flutes of champagne. Kendall felt terrifically nervous, even more so than usual. Taylor, however, seemed calm, if weary; and Major Robertson, the soft-spoken head of Operation Double Cross, seemed almost bored.

"A fine day," Churchill said, lighting his cigar. "I hope the news you've brought me isn't bad, gentlemen. It's far too fine a day for bad news."

Major Robertson, running his finger around the rim of his glass, gave a smile. "I'm afraid there is a bit of bad in with the good, sir. Or I should say, that's the way it seems at first. The reality may be more complex."

"That is the problem with modern times," Churchill said. "They are unnecessarily *complex*. Two things have disappeared in my lifetime: Men no longer study the classics, and men no longer ride the horse. Times are now too *complex* for such simple pleasures, one supposes. But if you ask me, we have lost a good deal in these two things."

Kendall had to remind himself not to stare too hard. Something about the way Churchill spoke was utterly mesmerizing; it was nearly impossible to look away.

"In any case," Churchill said. "Major?"

"If you don't mind, Mr. Prime Minister, Mr. Taylor has been more involved with this case than I."

"By all means. Mr. Taylor?"

Taylor cleared his throat, took out his pack of cigarettes, set it on the table, picked up his champagne, put it down again, and started to rub his eyes before stopping himself.

"Forgive me, Mr. Prime Minister. I've not had much chance to sleep lately."

"Nor have I, Mr. Taylor. You'll find no sympathy here."

Taylor cleared his throat again. "Right," he said. "The situation is as follows. Several months ago we found a unique opportunity, over at Twenty"—Twenty, to those in the know, referred to Operation Double Cross, sometimes represented by the shorthand XX—"in the person of a German spy named Schroeder. Schroeder had parachuted into Canterbury with the assignment of getting himself to Whitehall, finding employment, and tracking down a dissatisfied Intelligence man who might be able to give Uncle Adolf some clues as to the invasion."

"I seem to recall hearing of it," Churchill said.

"Yes, Mr. Prime Minister; I briefed you at the time. To make a long story short—if at all possible—I called on an old chum of mine to come into the game. His politics have been rather publicly inclined toward Chamberlain, which made him seem an apt candidate for turning. But he had lost his wife in the invasion of Poland, and so I felt that he must have abandoned his sympathy for the Nazis. He agreed to play the role of the disenchanted agent and, if possible, to penetrate the *Abwehr*."

Taylor picked up his cigarettes again, tapped one out, and lit it.

"At which point we as an agency became rather roundly distracted by the Heinrich affair," he said.

Churchill nodded, sipping his champagne.

"The Heinrich woman slipped through our fingers," Taylor said, "and it seemed as if we might lose her—until this man, Winterbotham, presented me with an idea. He suggested that if he were allowed to proceed and schedule his meeting with the *Abwehr*, the Heinrich woman would likely be instructed to honor the same rendezvous."

"Yes."

"I agreed—at which point I informed him that his mission was suspended, Mr. Prime Minister, until we had the woman safely in custody."

"Mm."

"And so it seems that he took it upon himself, Mr. Prime Minister, to deceive us about the true location of the meeting."

Churchill closed his eyes. He held up a hand and remained motionless for the better part of a minute. Then he opened his eyes, puffed on his cigar, and said calmly, "His wife is alive?"

"She is. We believe that he plans to trade intelligence to the Germans in exchange for her return."

"What intelligence will he be able to offer?"

"Nothing concerning the invasion, Mr. Prime Minister. But unfortunately, he has been made aware of many details concerning Twenty. It was necessary."

Churchill pursed his lips and chewed on them for a moment. "The Heinrich woman?" he said.

"We don't believe she ever reached the scene of the rendezvous, Mr. Prime Minister. But if she did, she's slipped through our grasp again."

"Forgive me, Mr. Taylor. I seem to have missed the *good* news in this rather disturbing tale."

"If I may," Robertson spoke up. "There is a bit more to it."

"Don't keep it a secret, Major."

Robertson looked at Kendall. "Go on, son," he urged.

Kendall sat as straight as he could as Churchill turned his gaze on him. He felt himself flushing but managed to proceed, despite his nervousness, without a stammer.

"I was the last to see Professor Winterbotham, Mr. Prime Minister, before he went over to the Nazis. I tried to intercept him on the beach, which is how I got this nasty scrape on my nose, here—"

"Just tell him what happened," Robertson said.

"Yes, sir. What happened," Kendall said, "is that the professor bent over me, after he gave me this smack, Mr. Prime Minister, and said that he was going to see his mission through—to infiltrate the *Abwehr*. He apologized for having manipulated Mr. Taylor and the rest, sir, but he said he had thought it necessary."

Taylor snorted.

"He said that in case the Germans were dissatisfied with his information and refused to let him return to England, sir, that he was prepared to escape. He repeated to me, several times, coordinates in the Baltic Sea, so that I was forced to memorize them. He said that we should have a seaplane waiting at five in the morning on the fourth of August, sir, if we wish to hear what intelligence he's gathered, sir."

"After misleading his superiors, risking the secret of the atomic bomb, and disobeying direct orders, he wants to be picked up."

"Seemingly, yes, Mr. Prime Minister."

Churchill shook his head. "Mr. Taylor," he said, "in your estimation, is this man a danger to Operation Double Cross?"

"He's no Nazi sympathizer, Mr. Prime Minister, if that's what you mean. But he will do whatever is required to secure the safety of his wife."

"Major?"

"It is high treason, Mr. Prime Minister. No doubt about it."

Churchill stood up. "Thank you, gentlemen," he said. "It is time for my bath. Please keep me apprised of any developments. In the meantime, lay your hands on a seaplane and prepare to meet Winterbotham at the coordinates mentioned. I assume your pursuit of the woman continues?"

"Of course, Mr. Prime Minister."

"Keep me apprised of that also."

"If I may," Taylor said. "There is another option, Mr. Prime Minister, with regard to Winterbotham."

"Mm?"

"We can minimize the risk of damage to Twenty, sir, by informing the Germans that Winterbotham is still in our employ—that it would be in their best interests to execute him immediately."

"And how shall we inform them?"

"By posing as the Heinrich woman, Mr. Prime Minister, and sending them a warning. Except for a single message, the Nazis haven't heard from her for ten years. And the man most likely to recognize her Morse style—her mentor—was killed at Flamborough Head. We'll claim that she met Winterbotham during the *treff* and discovered that he is a double agent. She managed to escape and send the warning. The deception should work."

"Then the Nazis will execute him," Churchill said. "And we'll never get the chance to hear what he may have learned about the *Abwehr*."

"But there will be no risk of him betraying Twenty, Mr. Prime Minister. It is the safest route to follow."

Churchill considered. "Very good, Mr. Taylor. Send your warning to the Nazis."

He turned and walked into the Cabinet Room, leaving the men around the table staring after him in the mellow morning sunshine.

CHAPTER TWENTY

POTSDAM, GERMANY
JULY 1943

They were entering Potsdam, several miles southeast of Berlin.

It was ten o'clock at night but the sun was still up, giving Winterbotham a fine view of the sleepy town outside his window—the majestic brick houses set back from tree-lined streets, the lush gardens, and the azure waters of Lake Griebnitz, visible in snatches between plots of land.

Potsdam, it seemed, had not suffered at all from the war. Winterbotham could not find evidence of even a single Allied bomb. He reminded himself that this superficial well-being was probably the very reason they had brought him there; it seemed fair to assume that the rest of Germany was in slightly worse shape. Still, he found the pristine surroundings . . . unsettling.

After looking out his window for a time, he turned to look at the young German beside him. Beck also was watching the houses go past, a slight smile on his lips. Beck was a few years above twenty, Winterbotham judged, and a model Aryan—so perfectly Aryan that next to him, Rudolf Schroeder seemed almost earthy. He had a strong chiseled jaw, razor-sharp cheekbones, close-cropped blond hair, and icy-clear light-blue eyes. His physique was lean but muscular, wide across the shoulders and narrow at the waist. His English was crisp and impeccable.

"*Herr* Beck," Winterbotham said.

Beck turned away from his window, still smiling.

"I do not wish to seem ungracious," Winterbotham said. "I appreciate the effort to which you have gone to make this meeting possible. But I am anxious to see my wife."

"Take my word, Professor, as soon as she reaches Potsdam, she will be brought to you."

"Where is she now?"

"In transit," Beck said. "Now, if I may take the liberty, Professor, I will encourage you to notice the palace coming up on our left."

The palace coming up on their left was a mammoth, discursive building done in a confusion of styles: stucco walls, stone portals, Oriental-looking chimneys studding a Tudor façade. A spacious, well-manicured lawn sloped down to the banks of Lake Griebnitz.

As they turned into the drive, Beck said, "She is Cecilienhof. There are one hundred and seventy-six rooms in the palace, Professor, which was constructed in 1917, just before the end of the Great War. I assume the history interests you? I know of your academic background."

Winterbotham said nothing.

"You will be our guest in one of her magnificent bedrooms," Beck continued, "and we shall hold our discussions in her main conference room. It is a sign of how important the High Command considers you,

Professor, that such a magnificent palace has been placed at our disposal. Only you and I shall meet, to begin with, although it is possible that we may have other visitors as well. Perhaps Admiral Canaris; perhaps even the *Führer* himself. In any case, Cecilienhof will be your home during your stay in Germany."

"How long do you suppose my stay may last?" Winterbotham asked.

Beck chuckled.

"It depends, of course, on what you have to tell us. Not less than one week, I should expect. Not more than two, or possibly three."

"Then my wife and I will be returned to England?"

"We must discuss the particulars. It seems that a return to England may cause problems—for yourself, Professor, more than for us. Perhaps a more neutral destination, at least for a time?"

"But we will be allowed to leave," Winterbotham said.

"Of course. You are a guest here. You are free to leave whenever you like."

The car rolled to a stop by the front porch.

"We will have refreshments," Beck said. "I know it is late, Professor, but I would very much like to begin our discussions tonight, if that is agreeable with you."

They sat at a round oak table in the main conference room. Windows facing onto the lawn had been cast open, and Winterbotham could hear the lake, a thousand yards distant, stirring in a night breeze. The dim, cavernous room around him was paneled in dark wood; the table was encircled by four tremendous chairs, each with lions' heads carved into the armrests.

It was minutes past midnight when Beck lit a thin cigarette, put his pen to paper, then looked up at Winterbotham expectantly.

"Well," he said. "Where shall we begin?"

The mosquitoes arrived with dawn.

They came off the lake, plump and brazen, just as Winterbotham and Beck were standing. Winterbotham finished the tot of brandy he'd been drinking; Beck slapped at a mosquito that had landed on his neck, inspected the carcass briefly, and then wiped his hand nonchalantly on his trousers.

"A good night's work," he said. "We shall rest now. The mosquitoes, you understand; we cannot keep them out except by closing the windows, and then the room becomes stifling. This afternoon, perhaps, we will pick up where we have left off."

"Will my wife arrive today?" Winterbotham asked.

Beck gave him a bland smile. "Perhaps this evening. Perhaps tomorrow."

Winterbotham followed Beck up a grand staircase to his room—a large, airy chamber with French windows looking out over the lake. As far as he could see, no guards had been posted outside. A small bookshelf near the bed was well-stocked; he eyed it for a moment. Then he circled the room several times before pausing near the window, staring out into the morning sun.

"Will you require anything else?" Beck asked. "A breakfast? Another brandy?"

Winterbotham shook his head. "I'll sleep well just as I am, thank you."

"It has been a pleasure meeting you, Professor, and I sincerely look forward to continuing our work together."

The young German left the room, closing the door behind himself softly.

Winterbotham looked after him for a moment. Then he drew a breath, held it, and heaved it back out as a sigh. Evasion, he had discovered, was exhausting work. He had been dodging questions for eight uninterrupted hours.

He moved to the canopied bed and collapsed onto it heavily. Sunlight streamed through the French windows, pricking at his eyes; he considered getting up to pull the curtains. Perhaps in a moment, he decided. He let his eyes drift closed instead. Before they resumed the interrogation—if one could call such conversational ballet an interrogation—he would ask for a bath, a shave, a change of clothes. Or would that be a mistake? Every amenity he accepted put him, however subtly, in the Nazis' debt. Perhaps it would be better to wait until these things had been offered—

"Forgive me, Professor," Beck said, "but I require clarification on a point."

Winterbotham opened his eyes. Somehow Beck had come back into the room, silently, and was sitting in a chair by the bed, consulting his pad.

"You have told me," Beck said, "that the British are aware that we use a three-rotor encryption device, correct? Yes. But, you insist, the British have not actually broken our codes. So I find a discrepancy, Professor. How is it that the RAF avoided being lured south on Alder Tag, if our codes had not been compromised?"

Winterbotham knuckled at his eyes before answering.

"You stopped bombing the quays," he said.

"Ah," Beck said. "And so you anticipated the invasion."

"Yes."

"And therefore anticipated our tactic of luring the RAF south."

"Precisely."

"Many thanks," Beck said, and smiled. "Now I shall be able to sleep. Good night, Professor."

He stood, bowed, and left the room again. After a moment Winterbotham returned his head to the pillow.

Five minutes passed. He was just slipping into unconsciousness when the door to the chamber burst open and Beck swept in, wearing a fresh uniform, looking rested.

"Professor!" he crowed. "How did you sleep?"

Winterbotham propped himself up on one elbow. He considered informing Beck that he had, in fact, not slept, and decided against it. Beck, of course, already knew.

"Very well, thank you," he said.

"Do you feel up to continuing?"

"Of course," Winterbotham said. He rubbed at his eyes again, then nodded, stood, and gave Beck a sardonic grin.

"Repeat, please," Beck said.

Winterbotham sighed. "Plugboard connections," he repeated. "Starting positions. The order of the rotors."

"Thank you. Proceed."

Winterbotham talked on. Beck let him speak, without interrupting, for nearly twenty minutes. Outside, the sun began to set; the mosquitoes turned slow and torpid.

"I think that is enough for today," Beck said then, smiling, always smiling. "Shall we take a walk before supper, Professor? A bit of exercise is good for the blood."

"If you like," Winterbotham said.

They walked around the lake. Winterbotham found himself staring at the scummy algae floating on the water—his eyes were too tired to pull themselves away. He watched the flitting nonsense of the mosquitoes and the water-skimmers and the dragonflies. Beck, beside him, kept his thoughts to himself.

After they had walked for ten minutes, Winterbotham said, "Any word on my wife?"

"Yes, as a matter of fact," Beck said. "She has been delayed. But she is safe."

"When do you expect her?"

"Difficult to say. Tomorrow or the next day."

They walked.

"You must love your wife very much," Beck said. "You have been married for many years?"

"Many years," Winterbotham agreed.

"And how did you meet her, Professor? If you don't mind my asking. She was a student of yours?"

"No. Her brother was a friend of mine, once upon a time."

"I see. He is not your friend any longer?"

"He's dead."

"Ah," Beck said. "My condolences."

He lit a cigarette and offered one to Winterbotham, who shook it off, took out his pipe, and began to tamp down his tobacco as they walked.

"You strike me as a reasonable man," Beck said. "It is a shame that others in England are not as reasonable as you. Germany has no quarrel with England. Germany only wants what is hers. And at the risk of betraying my cynicism, Professor, there is a mutual enemy whom we both face. England and Germany should be allies. Cynicism? Let us call it pragmatism."

"I see the wisdom in your words, *Herr* Beck."

Beck glanced at him in the twilight. "I believe that you do," he said. "I believe that you are here because you follow a higher moral calling, Professor, than the majority of your countrymen. You appreciate the value of peace."

Winterbotham lit his pipe, and held his tongue.

"Let us return to Cecilienhof," Beck said generously. "Another good night's rest will surely do us both good."

This time, Winterbotham had actually fallen asleep before they woke him.

He was shown into a different room, smaller than the one he had shared with Beck. He was presented with a different man, introduced as *Herr* Dietrich. Beck, he thought sourly, probably needed his sleep.

Dietrich asked about things that Winterbotham did not know. This, Winterbotham understood, was a standard interrogation technique. After Dietrich had quizzed him for hours about aviation tactics and Soviet offenses and gun placements and other subjects that were completely alien to him, he would (in theory) feel extremely eager to be asked a question he could answer. Then the topic would swing back around to code breaking or invasion, and he would stumble all over himself in an effort to gain his host's approval with correct replies.

"Our airplanes in Africa suffer one-and-a-half-inch holes in their armor," Dietrich said. "But always a single hole. Why is this?"

Winterbotham shook his head. "I don't know," he said.

"What weapon is producing the one-and-a-half-inch holes in our airplanes?"

"I don't know."

"We believe that the wing cannons on your Hurricanes are not equipped with reloading equipment. Is this accurate?"

"I don't know."

"What type of radio is used by the Piper Cub?"

"I don't know."

"We believe it is the S.C.R. Six Hundred, correct?"

"I don't know."

"I appreciate that this is not your area of expertise," Dietrich said. "But I would expect that any military man who pays attention to his surroundings would have, at the very least, an impression concerning these questions."

Winterbotham shrugged. "Perhaps I don't pay enough attention," he said.

"Perhaps not," Dietrich said. "Perhaps an easier question?"

Winterbotham shrugged again, lit his pipe.

"Ah, here is an easy one. Surely you can help me with this one, Professor. One would think that the transference of a battle-tested division from the Mediterranean theater to Great Britain would imply preparations for an invasion of France. And yet you told *Herr* Beck that you believed it was merely a precaution against a German invasion. However, you also told *Herr* Beck that fears of a German invasion have, as of late, dropped to nearly nothing. These statements are at odds, are they not?"

"Are they?" Winterbotham said.

"They are."

"I can only tell you what I know," Winterbotham said. "It's up to you to put the pieces together."

A blue vein pulsed in Dietrich's temple.

"I see," he said. "In any case, Professor, to return to the question of the one-and-a-half-inch holes in the armor of our aircraft . . ."

That night they allowed him two hours' sleep.

The next day he was interrogated from sunrise to sunset.

Finally, Beck leaned back in his chair, stretching languidly.

"It has been a long day," he said, "eh, Professor?"

Winterbotham was looking out the windows of the conference room at the tendrils of sunset reflected in the lake. He found himself beginning to agree with Beck—yes, he would say, I'm glad you understand, it *has* been a long day indeed—but quickly caught himself.

"Fatiguing," Beck pressed, "eh?"

Winterbotham nodded shortly.

"Are you hungry, Professor? Come, let us visit the dining room. Then we can retire early. Tomorrow is another full day, after all."

"*Herr* Beck," Winterbotham said, "if I may . . ."

"Yes, Professor?"

"You said initially that in order to avoid the mosquitoes, we would work only at night."

"Did I say that?" Beck asked, standing.

"You did," Winterbotham said. "Yet now we work at all hours. One would almost suspect, *Herr* Beck, that you are hoping to disorient me."

Beck, gathering his papers, smiled slightly.

"We change our routine time and time again," Winterbotham said. "You tell me one thing and then do another. You deny me sleep—"

"Deny you sleep!"

"Food is presented in abundance or in paucity. I am not allowed to bathe or change my clothes. I have not yet been allowed to see my wife—"

"I should apologize," Beck said. "We must have been working too hard, to give rise to such feelings of paranoia. Your constitution is suffering."

"I admit that your clumsy duplicity is tiring, *Herr* Beck. Now, tell me: Will I be allowed to see my wife, or will I not?"

"My dear Professor," Beck said, "after dinner you will have a bath. A razor, fresh clothing, whatever else you desire. Do not hesitate to ask me for anything."

"You've avoided my question, *Herr* Beck."

"I can only tell you so many times about the circumstances and the delays—"

"When might she arrive, do you think?"

"Tomorrow," Beck said. "At the very latest, the day after."

Beck walked Winterbotham to his room that evening, bade him a tart good night, and then retraced his steps down the hallway, down the majestic staircase, to the front porch of the mansion.

Here he smoked a cigarette, waiting for Admiral Canaris to arrive. He finished the cigarette, checked his wristwatch, and lit another. He was just finishing the second when he saw the staff Mercedes turn into the drive. A porter carrying a machine gun appeared from Cecilienhof and stood unobtrusively on one corner of the porch.

Admiral Wilhelm Canaris emerged from the backseat of the Mercedes without waiting for his door to be opened. He wore an unseasonable overcoat, brown, with a black suit underneath. As Canaris stepped out of the car, Beck caught a glimpse of a dog curled up at the base of the leather seats—brown on black, matching the overcoat and the suit—looking wistfully after its master.

Beck saluted.

"*Herr* Admiral," he said, "welcome to Cecilienhof. We are honored to receive you."

Canaris looked at him with undisguised distaste. "Seppl is hungry," he said after a moment.

"I will have the cook bring some beefsteak, *Herr* Admiral. To your room . . . ?"

"Of course," Canaris said. He whistled sharply; the dog slipped nimbly from the backseat and came to stand beside him.

They walked into Cecilienhof, Beck in the lead, Canaris and the dog slightly behind.

"How goes the interrogation?" Canaris asked. He was opening a vial of pills as they walked.

"I am afraid it goes poorly, *Herr* Admiral."

"In what way?"

"Winterbotham tells us little that we do not already know."

"Is he withholding information, do you believe?"

"*Herr* Admiral, he is most definitely withholding information."

Canaris thumbed two pills into his mouth. He dry-swallowed them, closed the vial, and returned it to his pocket. "Then coercion is called for," he said.

"Unfortunately, he seems to be aware of standard interrogation methods, *Herr* Admiral. He took the liberty of enumerating them for me earlier this evening."

"The *Führer* has taken a personal interest in this case," Canaris said. "He is anxious for information on the invasion—sooner rather than later."

"I understand, *Herr* Admiral, and await your guidance."

"The man's wife is here?"

"She is."

"We may be forced to use her earlier than we had wished," Canaris said. "I had hoped to save the woman as a last resort, but we must have an answer of some kind for the *Führer* within the next few days."

"I believe that conventional methods may still be effective, *Herr* Admiral. But since he is aware of them, they will take longer than usual."

"That is time that we do not have. Until now, *Herr* Beck, you have maintained the illusion of civility?"

"Yes, sir."

"And yet you are certain that the man is withholding information."

"Quite certain, *Herr* Admiral."

"I will consider the matter and suggest a course of action in the morning."

The *burr* of a motorcycle caught Beck's ear. He turned his head in time to see the vehicle pass a hall window in the settling dusk. After a moment, he heard the mansion's front door open, and then the pounding of footsteps down the corridor behind them.

"*Herr* Admiral!" a man called.

The messenger reached them and saluted, breathing hard. He opened a pouch under his arm and withdrew an envelope.

Canaris accepted the envelope without a word. He and Beck began to walk again as he jimmied open the flap and removed a single sheet of paper.

"Our agent in England has managed to send us a warning," he said after a moment. "Professor Winterbotham is still in the employ of the British."

Beck nodded.

"She suggests an immediate execution," Canaris said.

"I am not surprised, *Herr* Admiral. As I said, he has been less than cooperative."

"A shame. The *Führer* was hoping for results with this one."

"Perhaps the man can still be of use, Admiral. If we plan to execute him in any case, our hands are not tied during the interrogation. Give me permission to use my own methods and I guarantee you, *Herr* Admiral, that I will secure every bit of information the man possesses—within whatever time schedule you allow."

Canaris looked up. "You enjoy your work," he said after a moment, "do you not, *Herr* Beck?"

"I do," Beck answered.

"I am sure that you are skilled in your own fashion. But this man will not give in to the threat of pain. If he were that simple, the British would never have sent him."

"What do you suggest, *Herr* Admiral?"

Canaris looked at the letter in his hand again. He sighed. "The wife, of course," he said. "I suggest the wife."

CHAPTER TWENTY-ONE

RASTENBURG, GERMANY

The *Wolfsschanze*, set in a gloomy, thickly wooded corner of East Prussia, did not present an inviting façade.

Three concentric rings of minefields, pillboxes, and electrified barbed-wire fencing surrounded a dun-colored cluster of reinforced barracks. On this particular evening at the end of July, the sky and the forest had attained matching shades of gray.

Reichsleiter Heinrich Himmler passed through the multiple perimeters, passed through three separate security checks, left his car, and was escorted down a damp concrete staircase to the steel-banded door of an underground bunker. He surrendered his firearm, listened as he was announced, and walked through the door.

"Mein Führer," he said. "*Heil* Hitler!"

Adolf Hitler looked up from one end of a black marble table, where he had been bent over a map. He straightened, gesturing that Himmler should enter.

"My friend," he said. "Come in. I have news."

Himmler selected a chair at the end of the table, near Hitler. Both men sat. The *Führer*, Himmler thought, looked fatigued. His skin was pale, nearly translucent, and tinted a strange shade of yellow. His eyes were murky and half-lidded above dark smudges of exhaustion.

He smiled wearily. "Il Duce has resigned," he said. "Badoglio, our most bitter enemy, has taken over the government."

Himmler stared at him.

"I cannot believe it," he said after a moment.

"No?"

"It is not possible."

"No? I could not believe it myself. And yet it is true."

They sat in silence, then, as Himmler absorbed what he had been told. Mussolini had been forced from power; and so Italy would soon throw its lot in with the Allies. Militarily, of course, the significance would be negligible. The Italians were cowards and incompetents, and if they helped the Allies as much as they had helped the Germans, there would be no cause for concern. But politically—psychologically—if the Italians could lose patience with fascism, if their citizens could rise up and depose their leader and demand an end to the war, then could not the Germans do the same? Might this not presage a collapse of the Third Reich from within, even as its every flank was besieged from without?

Hitler, following his own dark line of thought, stared down at the glistening black marble before him. At length, he stirred and said: "It is not as bad as it may seem."

"No," Himmler agreed eagerly, and waited to be told why.

"Tomorrow I will send a man with orders for the commander of the Third Panzergrenadier Division. I will instruct him to drive into

Rome with a special detail. We will arrest the entire government. We will pave the way for another coup. Italy is not lost yet."

Himmler nodded.

"We must secure the Alpine passes," Hitler said. "We cannot allow the Allies to have access to Germany's southern flank."

"Yes, *mein Führer.*"

"We cannot shirk our duty," Hitler said, a bit shrilly. "Not now. The task cannot be left to another generation. The voice of history beckons us, my friend. We must rise to the challenge."

"We will be victorious," Himmler said.

Inside, however, he felt less confident. There had been a time, mere months before—was it really possible?—when Germany had seemed poised to conquer the entire world. Europe had fallen; the British had been on the verge of capitulating; the Russians had been ripe for a stab in the back. And now, within the space of a few short months, it all had gone sour. Before the disaster of Stalingrad, Germany had been engaged in a devastating, three-year offensive. Now, no matter how she tried, she could not recapture the initiative. At the start of July, five hundred thousand troops with seventeen panzer divisions had pushed against the Soviets in a last desperate effort, only to be thoroughly routed.

Hitler, rubbing at his eyes, looked as if he bore the entire weight of his military's failure on his own shoulders.

"I am faced with bad news from other quarters as well," he said after a moment. "Agent V Thirteen Fifty-three, whom your organization seems to consider of such value, failed to honor her *treff.* And the British traitor, even now at Cecilienhof, is offering considerably less assistance than I had hoped. He is almost certainly a double agent."

"Canaris is in charge of the interrogation?" Himmler asked.

"He is. And that is the other reason I have asked you here today, *Herr Reichsleiter.* Your man Hagen, representing the SS in this matter, was killed in the line of duty, correct?"

"Unfortunately, yes. He was a valued soldier of the Reich."

"I do not trust the good admiral to handle this matter alone."

"I think it likely, *mein Führer*, that I shall soon have the evidence we require to depose the admiral. My agents are working on the matter even as we speak."

Hitler nodded. "I cannot worry too much about Canaris right now; my attention is required elsewhere. The invasion, of course, is coming. But the invasion will be repelled. We will throw them back into the sea."

"I have no doubt of it, *mein Führer*."

"*Then* what will the Italians say?" Hitler demanded. "Will they abandon us *then?* I think not! And what will Canaris say, I wonder, when he sees that we shall be victorious after all?"

"He will be speechless," Himmler predicted.

"After we have thrown them into the sea," Hitler said, "we will attack, *Herr Reichsleiter*. We will smite them a blow without parallel in history. We will batter them without mercy—nothing so civilized as an invasion! We will throw death at them from across the ocean! We will have rockets! We will have bombs that split the atom! We are on the cusp, *Herr Reichsleiter*, on the *very cusp* of achieving these technologies! We will yet have victory! We will snatch it from the very jaws of defeat!"

"It will be glorious," Himmler said.

"I welcome the invasion," Hitler announced, and stood with such sudden force that his chair toppled behind him. "I welcome it," he said, stalking around the table. "But we must know *where*. We must know *when*. The British traitor must be forced to talk."

"I understand."

"I charge you to go to Cecilienhof yourself, *Herr Reichsleiter*, and take control of the interrogation. The admiral does not possess sufficient mettle, nor sufficient loyalty, to conduct this type of operation."

"Yes, *mein Führer*."

"Whatever the man knows, you will find out and report directly to me."

"Yes, *mein Führer.*"

"I trust you, my friend, to see this most important matter to a satisfactory conclusion. I put my faith, and the future of noble Germany herself, in your hands."

Himmler stood and saluted, his eyes shining.

"I shall not fail you, *mein Führer,*" he promised.

POTSDAM

Winterbotham was surprised to see that the vaunted Wilhelm Canaris—the head of Hitler's *Abwehr*, one of the most senior officers in the Nazi organization, and the archenemy of Taylor and his superiors at Operation Double Cross—stood a mere five foot five inches tall.

His hair was gray and thinning, his face sallow, his posture stooped. He wore a dark business suit that emphasized his weak, rounded shoulders. His eyes, which may once have been sharp, now possessed the haze that comes with too much dependence on chemicals, or alcohol, or both. And he smelled, rather strongly, of dog.

But Beck leapt to his feet when the little admiral entered the conference room, and saluted energetically.

"*Herr* Admiral Canaris!" he cried. "*Heil* Hitler!"

The Admiral seemed momentarily taken aback. Then he nodded, and waved Beck back into his chair. He came more fully into the room. Two guards, carbines in hand, entered behind him. One immediately slapped at a mosquito on his neck.

Winterbotham, sitting beside Beck at the conference table, half stood when Canaris had entered the room. Now he sat again, without waiting for permission.

"Professor Winterbotham," Canaris said. His English, although good, was far less polished than Beck's. "It is an honor to make your acquaintance."

Winterbotham, looking at him evenly, said nothing.

Canaris frowned. After a moment, he approached the conference table and sat, somewhat prissily. He removed a pair of spectacles from his breast pocket, polished them on his sleeve, and set them on the bridge of his nose.

"You are distressed, no doubt, by the continuing failure of your wife to arrive," Canaris said. "I cannot blame you for that. But I have the pleasure of informing you, sir, that she is now at Cecilienhof."

"My wife is here?"

"She arrived today."

"I demand to see her immediately."

"Yes, so I expected," Canaris said. "Yes . . ."

Beck pushed a thin sheaf of papers across the table. Canaris reached for his breast pocket again before realizing that he was already wearing his spectacles. He began to flip through the file, his eyebrows climbing higher on his forehead as he read.

"Hm," he said. "Yes. Hm."

Winterbotham watched, waiting.

"It seems to me," Canaris said presently, closing the file, "that you have not been entirely honest with us, Professor."

"On the contrary. I have been perfectly honest."

"No, I would not say so. You have not lied, and yet you have not told the entire truth, yes? A lie of omission, I would call it."

"I've told you all I know. I've satisfied my end of our bargain. And now I demand to see my wife."

"As soon as you are *truly* honest with us, Professor, you shall see your wife."

He removed his glasses, polished them again on his sleeve, and replaced them. "This humidity," he said.

Beck started to speak, but Canaris silenced him with a raised hand.

"Professor," Canaris said, "allow me to be frank. You are a man of letters. Yes?"

Winterbotham nodded.

"I am no scholar, Professor. But perhaps I can recall, if I concentrate . . ." Canaris made a great show of concentrating. " 'Learn how not to be good,' " he quoted. " 'Learn how to use this knowledge and not to use it, according to the necessity of the case. It is well to *seem* merciful, faithful, humane, sincere, religious, and also to be so; but you must have the mind so disposed that, when it is needful to be otherwise, you may be able to change to the opposite qualities.' "

"Machiavelli," Winterbotham said.

"Yes. Machiavelli."

"Your point?"

"My point," Canaris said. "I am willing, Professor, to change to the opposite qualities, according to the necessity of the case."

He stood.

"You will not see your wife tonight," he decided. "But if you continue to deny me my answers, Professor, you *will* see her—in a way you will not appreciate. Do you understand?"

Winterbotham gazed up at him frostily. "Threats, *Herr* Admiral?" he said. "I should have expected it."

"The guilt will rest on your shoulders, Professor."

"The Americans are right. You're mere gangsters—the lot of you."

"Consider your options, Professor. Cooperate, and leave here with your wife; or continue to withhold, and suffer her blood on your conscience. Ideals are worthless, sir, if they are all that one possesses."

"It is not ideals that keep me from speaking, Admiral. But if it were I would answer thus: 'Not all of me is dust. Within my song, safe from the worm, my spirit will survive.' "

Canaris frowned. "Baudelaire?" he asked after a moment.

Winterbotham shook his head.

"Coleridge?"

"I'm afraid not."

"Who?"

"Look it up," Winterbotham said, "if *Herr* Goebbels hasn't burned the book yet."

Canaris looked at him for another moment. He licked his lips, then turned sharply on his heel and led his guards from the room.

Once in the hallway, Canaris smiled to himself.

It was exactly as he had hoped. The man was no traitor. He was loyal to the British . . . and he would have their confidence.

He tried to wipe the smirk off his face as he moved down the hall in front of his smart-stepping guards. Himmler and his men were closing in; they were everywhere. They may have been watching him at that very moment. Beck himself may even have been in their employ. It would not do to betray himself in front of the Gestapo's spies.

But the smile lingered on his lips for the better part of a minute, nevertheless.

CHAPTER TWENTY-TWO

POTSDAM
AUGUST 1943

Winterbotham couldn't help but wonder, as he listened at the door of his room, if Kendall had come through for him.

Wondering did little good, but he had to wonder anyway. If Kendall had failed, after all, then he also would be doomed to failure. Even if he made it out of this room, even if he found Ruth and escaped Cecilienhof and found transportation and made it safely to the sea and stole a boat and reached the coordinates; and even if he did all of these things before the fourth of August, which, he assumed, must be rapidly approaching (he could not know for sure; he did not trust the clock in his room and was no longer willing to depend on his own sense of time);

even if all of these things happened, it all would be for naught if Kendall had not convinced the War Office to meet him at the coordinates he had chosen in the Baltic Sea.

He heard a tiny, slithery sound. He leaned inches away from the door, changed the angle of his head, and then pressed his ear against the wood again.

There were no guards at Cecilienhof—or so they would have him think. In fact, Winterbotham had seen three kinds of guards during his stay in the palace. There was the staff—the maids and the cooks and the porters and the valets—who carried firearms as they went about their daily business. Then there were the men with machine guns who lurked in shadows and around corners, not quite hidden from him but taking pains not to advertise their presence. It was one of these men, he assumed, who had just made the slithery sound; all the regular staff would be in bed at this hour.

Or perhaps it had been one of the SS. This third type of guard only recently had started to appear at Cecilienhof, as if the mansion were secreting them, like sap, as the summer wore on. The SS guards, in black, did not try to conceal their presence. They stood, looking intimidating, where halls converged, in plain sight, walking circuits around the lake, at the entrance to the dining room, in the conference room, in the front hall. They favored the staff and the slithery guards with nearly as many malicious glances as they gave Winterbotham himself.

Somebody, it seemed, did not trust Canaris. Somebody was encroaching upon his territory. In a matter of short time, Winterbotham was afraid, this somebody would make his presence known more forcefully; and then he would not be able to depend on even the pretense of civility which had, until now, kept him safe.

But matters were even worse than that. It was possible that Canaris would move ahead and carry out his threats against Ruth, Winterbotham knew, if he were to delay his escape much longer.

He swallowed, tasting the sour rust of fear.

Lunacy, he thought, *what you're about to do.*

He truly hoped that Kendall had come through for him.

The door to his room was unlocked.

He had discovered this on his third day at Cecilienhof. After making the discovery, he had spent a full hour searching his room, looking for hidden peepholes. But if they were watching him, he was unable to discover how. More likely, he thought, they were confident that his situation, his location, and the odds against him would keep him in line.

By any sane standard, they were right. Any man with half a brain in his head would never attempt what he was attempting now. He could step out of the room; but they would apprehend him within a stone's throw of his door.

He kept his ear pressed against the wood, after hearing the slithery sound, for nearly five minutes. Then he eased the door open and stepped softly into the hallway. The carpet, rich and expensive, muffled his footsteps. A strip of moonlight lay across the hall, illuminating a porcelain bust. Winterbotham put his back to the wall and moved past both moonlight and bust, holding his breath.

After achieving ten feet, he paused again, listening.

A rustle of wind. The lapping of the lake.

He kept moving.

After another five cautious minutes, he approached the grand staircase. His plan was to descend, cross to the west wing, and then try to find a door with guards posted outside. It stood to reason, he thought, that Ruth would be guarded. She would be looking for any chance to escape, unlike Winterbotham himself, who understood, in theory, that his only hope of leaving this place would be through the generosity of his hosts.

But his plan—if it could be called that—was filled with holes. What if guards were not posted outside of Ruth's room? Then he would never find her. And how was he to disable the guards once he had found them? He had no weapon, and in any case he could not risk making noise. Perhaps Ruth was not at Cecilienhof at all; perhaps it all had been a ruse. To reach the west wing he would need to cross through the mansion's spacious foyer, where his chances of being spotted by a guard were—

Stop thinking, for God's sake, and move.

He crept another ten feet toward the staircase and then paused again, listening.

The scuff of boots on carpet.

He drew a breath and controlled himself. He began to back up, moving past rows of doors, wondering if the shadows in the hallway were deep enough to hide him. A choice needed to be made, and now. Return to his room and wait for the guard to pass; but that would be as much as admitting defeat, because he would never find Ruth if he turned tail every time he faced a guard. Hide in the shadows, then; but if the man glanced his direction, he would be lost.

There was a third choice. Open one of these doors, which he was backpedaling past, and hide in a room until the guard moved on.

And pray that whoever was in the room did not awake.

The footsteps were drawing closer. Winterbotham tried the handle of the door he was passing.

It was unlocked.

Silently, he opened the door and slipped inside.

The room's window faced away from the moon.

Winterbotham stood stock-still and took in his surroundings. A single form lay in a canopied bed, covered from head to foot with a sheet, although the air was humid and hot. He could hear thick, slightly labored breathing. He put his ear against the door, trying to tune out the sounds of the sleeper. After a moment he caught the same quiet slithering as before—the guard dragging his heels on the thick carpet. He listened until he heard the heels slither past.

There would be little room for error. When the guard reached the end of the hall, he would turn around and return past this door.

Winterbotham counted to five, held his breath, opened the door, and stepped back into the hallway.

He moved quickly to the landing that overlooked the mansion's foyer. He paused, letting his eyes wander. The grand staircase before him swept down in a graceful curve, swept across a vast marble floor, and flowed into another staircase heading up, west, amid rococo columns, climbing putti and scrollwork, and minutely detailed coats of arms. Moonlight trickling in through high arched windows showed baroque ceiling reliefs, elaborately carved sculpture, and decorative delftware.

He would need to descend the close flight of stairs, cross the empty chamber—in plain view—and ascend to the western wing.

He went.

He reached the bottom of the staircase, hesitated for a fraction of an instant, and then struck out across the empty stretch of floor. His terror was thin and acrid. What fate lay in store if he was caught? Nothing worse, surely, than the fate that lay in store anyway.

He stepped onto an Oriental carpet, moved across a scatter of light-blue faïence tiles; then he had reached the far staircase.

That much closer to Ruth.

He began to climb.

There was a guard at the top of the staircase—SS. Winterbotham could see the lugubrious tip of one coal-black boot peeking out from behind the wood paneling. He put a hand on the banister to steady himself; kept climbing. What were his chances of reaching the top of the stairs without being seen?

He reached the top of the stairs.

The man was standing inches away, just around the corner.

Winterbotham reached for him.

He put one hand over the man's mouth and his other arm around the man's throat. He lifted, almost gently, and bent the man's back over his knee. He pushed, pulled, applied pressure in every way imaginable, willing the man's neck to break, or . . .

The man was struggling. Breathing hard, whistling through his nose.

Winterbotham covered the man's nose as well as his mouth.

The man kept struggling.

Winterbotham kept pressing.

The man kicked. He kicked again. Hit Winterbotham's shin; it stung. He tried to elbow Winterbotham in the gut, and Winterbotham let him, absorbing it.

Now he was struggling more weakly.

Winterbotham kept on.

When it was finished, he set the man down on the top riser.

He peered around the corner, down the hall.

One guard at the far end, lighting a cigarette, feathering smoke out of his nostrils.

Two more halfway down the corridor, standing outside a door.

His heart trip-hammered in his chest.

Ruth, he thought.

He bent down and frisked the man at his feet, found a gun, thumbed off the safety, and stepped into the hallway. He began to stride forward, keeping the gun held slightly behind his back.

One of the guards turned to look at him.

"Wor ist—"

Winterbotham gunned him down.

Put the gun on the second guard.

Gunned him down.

He fired at the third; the man ducked, vanished.

He covered the remaining distance between himself and the door with three large steps. He put his foot against the door, just below the handle, and the wood splintered. He put his foot against it again, and then the door was no longer there.

He stepped into the room.

Another guard, inside, firing—hitting him this time, somewhere in the thick part of his leg—he returned fire—missed—dark in here—he fired again—a window blew out—Winterbotham reached forward, found the man's head, and slammed it into a wall.

A noise from the corridor.

He turned, aimed at the wall to the right of the door, pulled the trigger twice. A suspended moment; then he heard a body fall.

Winterbotham turned around again, dropping the empty gun.

Shot, he thought. *Shot in the leg.*

In the corner, on a bed, huddled, quaking—

"Ruth?"

"Oh, my God." She sobbed. *"Harry?"*

He went to her.

She was too thin, much too thin—all ribs, each rib standing out in sharp relief, her vertebrae like pebbles wrapped in cloth—but he squeezed with all his strength anyway, conscious that he must be hurting her, unable to stop himself. She squeezed back, pressing her face into the hollow of his throat, heaving but not actually crying, her tear ducts dead, dry, dead, digging her fingernails into his back . . .

Ruth. Ruth.

He turned her face up with his hands.

Kissed her.

Weeping himself now, and still kissing her; she was so parched, so thin, so angular, half starved; and now her tears were coming, finally. Ruth, in his arms, Ruth . . .

"Oh, my God," she said again. "Oh, my God, Harry. Oh, my—"

He kissed her again.

They were forced apart by rough hands.

At first, Winterbotham tried to ignore the hands. Then one of them punched him in the temple; another closed around his throat, pushing him to the floor.

He heard the sound of a bolt being drawn back. A momentary reflection, near his temple, as the gun came around.

A jackboot flashed, connected with his ribs, cracking them.

Then they were all around him, a half dozen men. Kicking, grunting, breathing jerkily. Every time he tried to raise his head it was beaten down again.

He lost a tooth. He spat. A string of bloody sputum connected his mouth to the floor. Somebody was laughing, hoarse and harsh. Something hard crashed on the base of his skull, and he lost consciousness. Regained it, curled on his side, trying not to breathe because breathing hurt.

Another kick. A steel-tipped boot stabbed his kidney. The pain was bright and clear.

"Enough," somebody said.

He was dragged to his feet. Blinking, unable to see. Pushed out into the hall, supported between two SS men. Lights had been turned on. There was a man there, short, effulgent in black. Winterbotham was held in front of the man until his vision began to clear.

He blinked.

The man was Heinrich Himmler.

Himmler looked at him for a moment with disdain.

"Downstairs," he said. "The wife, too."

Winterbotham went for him. But four steely hands closed around his biceps, pulling him back.

Then he was being dragged down the hallway, trying to walk, unable to keep his feet beneath himself. He looked left and then right, feeling as if he were in a dream. The man on his left was Beck. Beck looked less dapper than usual; his blond forelock was hanging in sweaty disarray. A smudge of blood was near one corner of his pretty mouth.

He turned his head slowly, underwater, to look at the man on his right. He recognized this one also. Dietrich, who had quizzed him about Hurricanes and Piper Cubs. Dietrich also had blood on him—smeared on his tunic in the shape of a semicolon.

They moved down the corridor, half dragging, until they reached the staircase. Blinding lights had been turned on all through the mansion. Two SS men stood by the top of the stairs. They snapped salutes.

"Sieg Heil!"

"Sieg Heil!"

Now they were pulling him down the stairs. Winterbotham moaned. A rib was broken and it was poking around inside, hurting. Bullet still in his leg. Now they were coming off the stairs, Dietrich moving toward the front of the mansion, Beck deeper into the bowels. For an instant, Winterbotham was tugged between them like a wishbone.

"This way," Beck said. "*Herr Reichsleiter* wants him downstairs."

"Bring him outside," Dietrich said. "We are transferring him."

"Are you deaf? *Herr Reichsleiter* said . . ."

Dietrich let go of Winterbotham's arm, drew his Luger, and aimed it at Beck's face.

He fired.

A Mercedes was waiting by the front porch.

Winterbotham was pushed into the backseat, not gently. Dietrich bent down, folded Winterbotham's legs into the car, straightened, looked behind himself. He pounded on the window with one fist.

"Go!" he said.

As they pulled away, Winterbotham saw two black-suited SS emerging from the mansion onto the porch. He saw Dietrich turn to face them.

"Professor," somebody was saying.

Winterbotham, blinking, tore his eyes away from Cecilienhof. He looked around the interior of the car, trying to find the source of the voice. The Mercedes was sinking into the night; he could hardly see a thing.

They turned onto the main road with squealing tires, then accelerated.

"Professor."

In the front seat, he realized. Beside the driver. A man, craning around to face him.

Canaris.

"Can you hear me?" Canaris asked.

Winterbotham nodded.

"We are putting you on a plane. You will be in England by sunrise."

"My . . . wife."

"She will meet us at the airport. I anticipated that you would not leave Potsdam without her. Now, listen carefully—"

"They're following us," the driver said.

Winterbotham looked through the rear window again. He saw pursuit—two distant eyes of light. One car, or motorcycles?

As he watched, one eye winked out.

Canaris was talking.

"Hitler's time is finished. We will remove him ourselves if the prime minister agrees to our terms. Are you listening, Professor?"

"Yes . . . yes."

"We are prepared to remove Hitler in exchange for an immediate armistice, an immediate suspension of Allied bombing. But we do not offer unconditional surrender. We shall withdraw in the West. In the East, our countries shall fight together. Germany will hold a line between the mouth of the Danube, the Carpathian Mountains, the River Vistula, and Memel. Understand?"

"Yes."

"We require Churchill's personal guarantee before we can take further action. Tell him that the resistance is strong: myself, Rommel, Beck, Goerdeler, Lauschner. Impress upon him that Germany is not guilty. *Hitler* is guilty. Germany is not Hitler. We have a common enemy: the Bolsheviks."

Winterbotham looked behind them again. The second eye had vanished.

"If Churchill agrees with our terms," Canaris said, "he must notify us before the tenth of August. He will notify us by having the BBC play the same song twice in a row on any midnight between today and the tenth. The absence of such a broadcast will be taken as a rejection. Understand?"

"Yes."

"We have taken a considerable risk to deliver this message to him, Professor. If he does not agree with our terms, we cannot promise further negotiation. The war will continue; many more lives will be lost. On both sides. You must impress upon him—"

"I'll try."

"Convince him," Canaris said.

When they turned into the airport, Winterbotham saw, in the harsh artificial light, bodies sprawled on the outskirts of the runway. Standing over the corpses were three soldiers, machine guns in hand. The plane itself, a tiny Focke-Wulf, was idling on the tarmac.

Winterbotham got out carefully, helped by a hand on his elbow.

"Go aboard," Canaris said.

"Not until my wife arrives."

Their eyes locked.

From somewhere very far away came a muffled explosion. Canaris reached into his overcoat, removed a vial of pills, and put two in his mouth.

They waited.

The hum of an engine? No, still the wind. Winterbotham swallowed. He leaned against the plane to support himself, woozily.

"It is possible that they did not make it," Canaris said. "I beg you, Professor, go aboard."

Winterbotham shook his head.

The hum grew louder. A car, after all, coming down the road, invisible in the black night. The three soldiers raised their guns, setting their jaws.

A Mercedes pulled onto the airfield, rolled across the tarmac, drifted to a stop. Winterbotham pushed himself off the fuselage, which had been supporting him. He stepped forward, reaching out as the door opened.

Ruth came out of the car.

He took her in his arms.

"For God's sake," Canaris said. "Hurry."

Winterbotham and his wife climbed into the plane, arm in arm.

CHAPTER TWENTY-THREE

THE WAR OFFICE, WHITEHALL
AUGUST 1943

Once again, Taylor was on the phone when Winterbotham was shown into his office.

"He's just arrived," Taylor said. He waved at the chair in front of his desk. "No, Mr. Prime Minister, I'll have to get back to you. Yes, sir." He glanced up at Winterbotham, who still hadn't taken the chair. "Yes," he said, and waved again. "Yes, Mr. Prime Minister. Of course. Thank you."

He hung up, then looked at Winterbotham pointedly.

Winterbotham sat, favoring his good leg. He took out his pipe.

The window in the office was open; through it came the sounds of children playing in the park. Winterbotham prepared his pipe and lit it. His eyes followed the smoke as it drifted out the window.

"Happen to listen to your radio last night?" Taylor asked. "Around midnight?"

Winterbotham looked at him. "As a matter of fact," he said, "yes."

"They played 'Chattanooga Choo-Choo' twice in a row."

"I noticed."

"One of my favorites," Taylor said.

He opened his desk drawer, removed a folder, set it on the desktop, and pushed it to Winterbotham.

Winterbotham reached forward, picked up the folder, and opened it. Inside was a letter from the office of Andrew Taylor to Prime Minister Winston Churchill. It recommended that leniency be shown in the case of Professor Harris Winterbotham. By forsaking the right to prosecute, the letter suggested, England showed her appreciation for Winterbotham's successful penetration of the Nazi intelligence organization, the *Abwehr*.

Winterbotham closed the folder.

"Churchill has already agreed," Taylor said. "You're off the hook, Harry."

"It would seem so."

"Aren't you going to thank me?"

Winterbotham took a drag from his pipe. "Why?" he asked.

"Because I've saved your—"

"I mean, why did you do it?"

"Because you've rendered a service to England, old chap, whether you meant to or not. Now we wait and see if the admiral is able to hold up his end of the bargain. Besides, if this works out and they get rid of Hitler for us . . . and then it slips out that we hanged the agent who made the deal possible . . . Well, you can imagine."

Winterbotham smoked thoughtfully.

"Also," Taylor said, "it makes us even."

"Even?"

"When you were in Germany, we sent a message telling the Nazis that you were a double agent." He paused. "We recommended your immediate execution."

Winterbotham pursed his lips.

"To minimize the risk to Double Cross, you understand."

"Yes."

"We had no way of knowing whether you planned to—"

"I understand, Andrew."

"So, we're even."

Winterbotham said nothing. Taylor lit a cigarette.

"That's all?" Winterbotham asked.

"Assuming you've told us everything you have to say about your time spent behind enemy lines—"

"I have."

"How is Ruth, Harry?"

Winterbotham hesitated for a moment before answering.

"Alive," he said.

"And?"

"Grateful to be out of there."

"Of course."

"But she won't talk about it. Or even, I believe, think about it. She's pretending it never happened."

Taylor nodded. "I like the sound of that—pretending nothing ever happened."

"Do you?"

"All's well that ends well, Harry. You've got Ruth; I've got intelligence about the Gestapo and the *Abwehr*; and Churchill's got Canaris. And, I'm glad to say, we don't believe that Katarina Heinrich was able to deliver her intelligence to Berlin."

"Why do you say that?"

"If she'd tried to wire it, we would have caught the signal—there's far too much data for her to send quickly. If she tries to send it in a letter, well, now that the censors know what to look out for . . ."

"And if she brings it there in person?"

Taylor smiled crookedly. "A young lady named Jane Moore was found on Jermyn Street, Harry, two days ago. Her face was bludgeoned beyond recognition. But her mother was able to identify a mole—"

"Yes?"

"The strange part of it," Taylor said, "is that fifteen days ago a Jane Moore booked passage on the *S.S. Europa*. She arrived in New York City yesterday."

"America?"

Taylor nodded.

"Why would she return to America?"

"We were hoping you could shed some light on that. Having seen her face-to-face."

Winterbotham shook his head. "I wouldn't know."

"Perhaps she sickened of the game again—just as she did ten years ago. Perhaps she wants to vanish, return to a normal life, hm?"

"I wouldn't know, Andrew."

He stood up. Taylor promptly stood up opposite him and offered his hand across the desk.

"Harry," he said, "let's put it behind ourselves. What do you say?"

Winterbotham looked at the hand for a moment. He reached out and shook it.

"Let's seal it with a drink," Taylor said. "Say, tonight at the Savoy? We'll have a game, drink a bottle of Dom, and discuss—"

"Sorry, Andrew. I've got plans."

"Of course," Taylor said. "Perhaps later in the week? Or—"

"I'll let you know," Winterbotham said.

NEW YORK CITY
AUGUST 1945

Katarina heard the news as she was dressing for her date.

Her date was a young man named Ted Ridgeway, a veteran of D-Day, missing two fingers on his left hand, who now laid pipe in Brooklyn. They had met when he had come into the restaurant and ordered a sandwich with a cup of coffee. Tonight would be their fourth date—and, although Ted didn't know it yet, their last. She had met another young man at the restaurant, one who had all his fingers and beautiful eyes to boot.

She was applying the finishing touches to her lipstick, listening with half an ear to the song on the radio, when the announcer burst in.

"We interrupt this broadcast for a special announcement from Washington. President Truman has issued the following statement: 'At seven-fifteen P.M., Washington time, a bomb was dropped on the city of Hiroshima. It is an atomic bomb. It is a harnessing of the basic power of the universe. The force from which the sun draws its power has been loosed against those who brought war to the Far East. It was to spare the Japanese from utter destruction that the ultimatum of—' "

Katarina ran to the bathroom, sick.

Afterward she lay with her head resting on the rim of the bowl, listening.

"An area of four square miles, approximately sixty percent of the city, has been destroyed. Casualties are unknown, but one witness's estimate places them at between seventy and eighty thousand. President Truman is demanding unconditional—"

She vomited again.

Then she rinsed her mouth, spat, went into the living room of her tiny apartment, and turned off the radio.

She stood, looking out the sooty window at the city, thinking, rubbing absently at her shoulder.

She thought for about five minutes.

Finally she went back to the mirror. Her lipstick was ruined. She blotted it off and began to apply it again.

The bomb had worked.

The bomb had worked, and they had dropped it on the Japanese.

If she ever grew tired of waitressing, she thought, the Russians might pay a very pretty price for the secrets in her head.

In the meantime, she had a date.

She finished her makeup, put a dab of perfume behind each ear, and looked at herself in the mirror again. What she saw there pleased her: an ordinary woman, pretty enough, dressed well.

Simple. Honest.

And boring, of course. Boring, most of all.

Boredom, she had discovered, had its advantages.

But for certain types of people—and Katarina knew herself well enough, now, to know that she was this type of person—boredom could remain appealing for only so long. There would come a time, surely, when security would lose its luster.

For the time being, however, it sounded just about perfect.